Who's Been Sleeping in My Bed?

Who's Been Sleeping in My Bed?

GEMMA BRUCE

BRAVA

KENSINGTON PUBLISHING CORP.
http://www.kensingtonbooks.com

BRAVA BOOKS are published by

Kensington Publishing Corp.
850 Third Avenue
New York, NY 10022

ISBN 0-7582-1141-4

First Kensington Trade Paperback Printing: July 2005
10 9 8 7 6 5 4 3 2 1

Printed in the United States of America

Contents

WICKED WIDOW

Chapter One

The trouble with giving up casual sex, thought Nan, frowning at her fingers splayed open on the steering wheel of her Jeep Liberty, was that she hadn't had any sex at all. Not for six months, maybe more.

She added a last stroke of polish to her pinkie and dropped the brush back into the bottle. This didn't speak well of her mores or her desirability. And with stakeouts five out of seven days a week, the chance of meeting a potential long-term relationship was looking bleak.

She was parked in the woods outside Rupert Sims's Long Island estate, the Jeep's windows shut against the mosquitoes, the air conditioner barely functioning.

But she knew better than to turn on the engine. She wasn't alone. Another car was parked several hundred feet to her left. She could just see the passenger window through the trees. His engine was purring away. He was keeping cool, but that little mistake had alerted Nan to his presence. She wasn't so stupid.

Her cell phone wheezed out the theme from *Dragnet*. She reached for it without thinking. The bottle of nail polish toppled over; Vamporina Red oozed onto the console.

By the time she uprighted it, she'd missed the call—caller unknown—her phone was sticky red, and every nail of her right hand was completely ruined.

Nan sighed and started to remove the wrecked polish.

She should be getting hazard pay. How was she supposed to be at the Sims's yacht, dressed like the society bitch that she wasn't—anymore—when she couldn't even go home to get ready.

It wasn't like she had accomplished anything in the last two weeks, except follow Rupert Sims from one posh restaurant to another, one posh office building to another, and one health club, where she waited two hours every day for Sims to come out, no sweatier than he had gone in. The only thing she had to show for her work was two bug bites on her backside that she got while squatting behind a tree to take a pee.

Men had it so easy. The guy in the other car could piss in a beer bottle without ever having to leave his air-conditioning.

Who was he? And why was he watching Rupert Sims? It was unlikely that Rupert's wife, Mathilde, had hired them both, so who hired him?

Not the Feds. Much too handsome for the CIA, too well dressed for the FBI. And she'd never seen an ATF agent in a Maserati. She blew on her nails, then picked up her binoculars. The sun was behind her now, so she could risk a peek without giving herself away.

And what a peek. The guy was a knockout. Heathcliff in a James Bond car. Dark hair with just a hint of curl, much too long for a government employee. Cheekbones that could give you a paper cut, a jawline that made her salivate. She adjusted the focus. "And where did you get those big eyes, Grandma?"

Too bad she could only get a look at his torso. Maybe he would get out of the car. Maybe she should follow him home—just to check out his credentials.

Or maybe, she'd just get a closer look at his license plate and run the numbers through the computer. A name would be nice. Then she'd know what to call him when she fantasized about him at home in bed alone.

She reached over the seat and grabbed a roll of toilet paper, just in case she was wrong, and he had made her. If he thought she was out taking a pee, he'd relax his guard, and she could get close enough to see the numbers. She opened the door just enough not to let the cool air out or the mosquitoes in and took off through the trees. She made a show of the toilet paper roll and hoped that it distracted him from seeing the binoculars hidden under her T-shirt.

Damon Connelly reached for his field glasses the minute the Jeep's door opened. The sun was in his eyes, but he'd have to risk a quick look and hope the light didn't catch the glass and give him away. Red-blonde hair pulled back in a ponytail and piled on the top of her head. Tiny pink T-shirt. Hadn't anyone told her about keeping a low profile? Jeans so tight that she couldn't chase a perp if her life depended on it; and designer running shoes, that didn't look like they had jogged into the nearest Bloomingdale's.

Damon chuckled to himself. Hannah Harrington-Scott, Debutante Detective.

He liked her name. Certainly better than the one on her business card. Nan Scott. It was too harsh for her. She deserved three names. Hannah Harrington-Scott rolled off your tongue like melted butter.

He had run her plates three days ago, as soon as he'd taken this gig. She was employed by Women-Tek, a detective agency that catered mostly to women, though not exclusively, and that's what made it hard to figure out who had hired them. He hadn't been able to hack into their client list. Somebody had set them up a safe system. A boyfriend probably. Damon hoped he was getting paid well for his services, unless he belonged to Hannah. He didn't like the idea of that at all.

He'd been watching her at close range for three days and had a perpetual hard-on to prove it. Just knowing that she was parked in the trees nearby made him so hot that his windshield was fogging up. He cranked up the air conditioner and aimed the blowers at his crotch.

He reached for the dossier lying on the passenger seat beside him. It was two inches thick, though most of the information came from the society pages of several Long Island weeklies.

There were lots of pictures: Hannah at the country club in a ball gown, at the yacht club in tiny little shorts with some guy's arm around her waist. The announcement of her engagement to Anthony Grant Taylor, accompanied by a picture of the happy couple. Only Hannah didn't look happy even on newsprint.

A girl after his own heart. Rich kid. Wild child. Nothing soft about Hannah, except maybe her lips. He wouldn't know for sure until he tested them for himself. And he meant to do just that.

Damon flipped past the pictures to the sealed police records of juvenile court. Shoplifting, breaking and entering. Hotwiring a Jag—her stepfather's.

The old man swore out a complaint against her, then packed her off to some tough love camp in the Adirondacks. And that was where she met her partners at Women-Tek, Geena Cole and Delia Petrocelli, two other bad girl debutantes shipped off to be coerced back into high society.

What did they do, make you drop and give them twenty if you used the wrong fork?

Damon snorted. Life had to be easier at Camp Wilderness than at the juvenile facilities where he had spent most of his summers surrounded by barbed wire.

But they both had had pretty much the same success. The Cole woman was involved in a murder investigation and dropped off the society pages of the *Manhasset Press*. Hannah left her stock trading fiancé at the altar and went back to her wild ways. Delia seemed to be the only one who took—until a few months ago when she filed for divorce from her plastic surgeon husband and joined Women-Tek.

As for himself; nobody had even tried to mainstream him back into society. Which is why he— But he'd rather think about Hannah Harrington-Scott. Actually, he couldn't help but think of her. The woman was gorgeous. And if he believed the background check, smart and . . . disappearing into the woods.

He leaned forward and adjusted the binoculars. A roll of toilet paper came into focus. He shook his head sympathetically. Some jobs were just made for men.

He dropped the binoculars and leaned back against the seat. He could relax while she was in the woods taking a piss. Then he imagined her leaning over and pulling down those tight jeans, hanging her bare butt—damn, the air conditioner wasn't working.

He squeezed his eyes shut and tried to think about the many ways of being tortured that didn't include beautiful women wiggling bare asses at him.

Nan turned her T-shirt inside out and pulled the camouflage side over her head. The undergrowth was thick, but a girl couldn't be too careful. She'd learned that the first week at Camp Wilderness when she'd discovered two bear cubs and had been chased up a tree by their angry mother.

She'd torn her favorite jeans and broken three nails in the scramble. She was scared past pissing. It was horrible, but exhilarating. She'd quickly realized that being chased by bears and stalking deer was infinitely more interesting than balancing on four-inch heels, flapping eyelashes at stockbrokers and investment bankers at the yacht club.

She crept silently through the bushes until she was close enough to train her binoculars on the front of the Maserati. A quick glimpse and the numbers were stored in her brain.

She risked a sweep across the front windshield. The guy

was asleep. The lazy son of a bitch. He couldn't have gotten that fancy car from detecting, not if he made a habit of sleeping on the job. She let the glasses linger on his face, then slowly scan down his neck to his T-shirt, tight enough to outline some pretty impressive pecs. Back up to his shoulders and down his arms. They were nice, too. And not too hairy. Just the way she liked it.

Damn. She had to pull herself together. Obviously, being celibate wasn't a viable alternative to fuck 'em and leave 'em. But after her near miss with Anthony Taylor, she refused to invest any more than twenty minutes a pop.

Reluctantly, she lowered the binoculars and stuck them back into the waistband of her jeans. She retraced her way through the woods, stopping to change her T-shirt back to pink and pick up the roll of toilet paper, before she sauntered back to the Jeep.

As soon as she climbed inside, she put in a call to the office. "Hey, there's some joker in a black Maserati staking my stake. Run a check on the license plate, will you, and get back to me ASAP."

"Shouldn't you be getting ready for the ball, Cinderella?" Geena's voice was a husky drawl, a device she developed to cover up her Swiss boarding school accent.

Nan checked out the state of her nail polish. "I am, boss. And hurry, will you. I have to be at the Sims's yacht in half an hour and I don't want him to get away before I get a chance to nail him." She flipped the cell closed and threw it on the seat.

She'd like to nail him, all right, in more ways than one. *No casual sex*, she reminded herself. And no dangerous sex. He could be a paid assassin for all she knew. And even if he weren't, she knew that he would definitely be dangerous.

Forget it. Not worth it. No way. Bad idea. Anyway, she had a party to get ready for.

She reached up and pulled the elastic out of her hair.

* * *

Okay, that did it. He was standing at high noon, ready to shoot at anything that moved. And she was moving. He watched her delicate arms lift over her head, long fingers pull the band from her ponytail. She shook her head and a golden-red cloud of hair spilled across her shoulders. He thought he might explode. Then she started brushing it in slow, sensual strokes that he imagined running over his chest and belly, down his thighs and at last coming to encircle him in exquisite torture. He almost came just thinking about it.

She unbuckled her seat belt. Getting out again? No. She was standing on her knees in the front seat. She pulled the T-shirt over her head. Damon gripped the binoculars and tried not to drool.

His better self was telling him to put the glasses away. Voyeurism was not his thing. But the thing that counted was telling him not to blink.

She was petite and she wasn't wearing a bra. The field glasses clunked against the window, Damon jerked back and rubbed his forehead. Steady, boy. Steady.

He shifted in his seat; things were pretty uncomfortable south of his border. His jeans seemed two sizes too small. Maybe if he just undid the top button. Okay, two. That relieved the ache a bit until she reached over the back of the seat and the line of her small, firm breasts were outlined against the black upholstery.

Jesus, somebody just kill him now.

Damon licked his lips. They were dry, his Adam's apple was cutting off his air supply. *Don't stop*, he thought as she stretched all the way over the seat back, butt up, and came back with . . . something.

Damon readjusted the focus. A black stretchy dress. She pulled it over her head, then wriggled it down to her waist in a come hither dance that drove him wild.

It must be the new vitamins, or the fact that he had given up cheap sex for meaningful relationships. Which was stupid, now that he thought about it. He never stayed in one place long enough to have a meaningful relationship. An occupational hazard, but, shit, he was getting old.

At thirty-three, he was beginning to think about things like matching bedroom furniture and backyards with swing sets. It was probably some kind of reaction to trauma. Or midlife crisis. Men like him didn't get to settle down. Wouldn't know how to even if given the chance.

Okay, how about a short-term meaningful relationship. Right now, before she finished. Then he wouldn't have to jerk off in the shower in order to fit into his tux trousers.

There. She was done, and he could leave to change for the party at the yacht. Oh no, not yet. And he knew what she was doing. He got a flash of flesh as she wriggled out of her jeans and pulled the dress down over her ass.

Was she wearing underwear? God, he really needed to know.

His cell phone started to vibrate. Join the club. He picked it up. "What."

"It's Ernie. How much longer are you going to be? I need the Maz back. It's booked for eight tonight. You sound like you been running. Is the case breaking?"

"No. Just sitting here."

"Then how come you're out of breath?"

"Thinking about running. I'll have it back at seven-thirty, but I'll need another set of wheels."

"I got a nice BMW. Class act for the valets at the marina."

Nan's cell phone rang. She sat down and answered it, while she untied her shoes and pushed her jeans onto the floor.

"Okay," said Geena. "The car comes from a rental place; all private clients trying to look richer than they are."

"Did you get a name?"

"No. I said *private*. No phone number. No website. No computer files. Nothing. I've sent Delia down to see what she can find out. Stand by. And watch your back tonight. I don't like this at all."

Chapter Two

Nan scanned the deck of the Sims's ninety foot catamaran, the *Chardonnay Lady*, trying to get a fix on the guests. Wondering if one of them would go berserk, pull out an Uzi, and riddle the crowd. Unlikely. They'd all passed through a very high-tech metal detector posing as a grape arbor when they came aboard.

The whole yacht was decked out in grapevines, wicker furniture, and red and white checked table clothes. Bottles of pinot noir and blanc de blanc, grown and bottled by Rupert's Long Island winery, adorned every table, were served from the bar. It might be Mathilde's charity event, but Sims Cellars was getting a lot of free advertising.

Nan's gaze came to rest on Rupert Sims. He was standing on the deck one level up, his arm around a curvaceous, platinum blonde whose lips and tits had *Made by Goodyear* written all over them.

Nan shivered. Rupert reminded her of a glassy-eyed vulture. Tall and rotund, with a large head that jutted forward from stooped shoulders, and a curving beak of a nose that overpowered the rest of his face. He was squinting down at the deck below, like he might swoop down any minute and snare one of his guests.

And she had no doubt that if he got his talons in you, you were dead meat—literally.

The Similioni family had started out in the meat packing industry on the West Side of Manhattan, expanded into Jersey garbage where their real fortune was made, before moving on to more genteel ventures like wine making and horse breeding.

On Rupert's other side, standing almost as close to him as the blonde, his ever-present body guard, Barney, fidgeted with his bow tie. He moved with the disjointed jerks of a praying mantis. His eyes bugged out of a nearly cadaverous face. She wondered if they could move independently of each other. She had no desire to find out.

Nan smiled at herself. A bird, an insect. Must have come from sitting in the woods all afternoon. She tried to come up with an animal analogy for the blonde and failed.

Though to tell the truth, sitting in the woods in a Jeep didn't hold a candle to being out among the trees tracking a worthy adversary. And spying on a schlump asleep in his car or balancing a glass of seltzer and a rusk of pâté while trying to keep the gold chain of her purse from slipping off her shoulder, didn't quite measure up to the feeling that zinged through your arm, then your whole body, as you released the arrow and it soared through the sky. Actually, the only thing that came close to that feeling was good sex.

And she wasn't seeing any of that, either.

Life had been pretty tame since Camp Wilderness. Knowing that she could fend for herself with only a handmade spear or a bow and arrow had given her a certain cachet. And she missed it.

When Geena started Women-Tek, she'd eagerly agreed to join the firm. She was at a low point in her life. Only to be expected after failing to show up at her own wedding, leaving five hundred guests and two sets of unbelieving parents to make the best of it. The catering bill alone had cost over twenty thousand dollars and no one had stayed to eat.

When she finally called home, her stepfather told her she

was an embarrassment to the family. Ha. It wasn't even his family. But her mother was too distraught to talk to her. She hadn't called again.

She jumped at the chance to help women break out of the mold, rid themselves of backgrounds that were stifling them. So far, they had dealt mainly with women trying to put the screws to their philandering husbands. A good cause in the scheme of things, but not exactly exciting.

But there was always another case around the corner and a chance to prove her worth besides on a tennis court or at Sunday brunch. This case might be the one she was waiting for.

She caught sight of Mathilde Sims, who toodled her fingers at her from across the way. It was easy to pick her out in a crowd, she was very tall, very well-dressed and very maintenance heavy. Nan toodled her fingers back at her.

Mathilde had shown up at the office one afternoon, a hysterical mess. Someone was trying to kill her husband and she wanted it stopped. That alone was enough to make them sit up and listen. Most of their clients would be ecstatic if someone would kill their husbands.

But Mathilde was made of stronger stuff. She was younger than Rupert, expensive to keep. Not that Rupert would notice, with his billions. She obviously knew a good thing when she had it, and she seemed to genuinely love Rupert. But mainly, she was afraid she might get caught in the crossfire.

They took the case, just for a chance to see some action.

Probably not tonight, though. There was security everywhere; the waiters, the bartenders, several cute cabin boys who looked too young to pack police specials. But that didn't fool Nan. It wasn't baby fat that made their jackets bulge under the armpits.

Nan sighed. She'd see more action if she were carrying a tray of wineglasses.

Mathilde smiled as Carl Sims, Rupert's nephew and heir

apparent, sidled up to her. She turned to say something to him, which brought his mouth to the same level of her rocket launch nipples.

Chacun à son goût, thought Nan. To each his own. Mathilde could have tucked him under her arm and scored a touchdown with him. He seemed very popular with all the women. And it was obvious that Mathilde and he were very close. Maybe his extra inches were where they couldn't be seen.

None of her business, except that it ratcheted Carl up another point on the suspect scale.

The back of her neck gave a warning tingle. Someone was watching her. Slowly she placed her glass on a table and glanced up. The Man in the Maserati was leaning against the rail not ten feet away, his eyes fixed on her, his expression— she could only call it predatory.

After a moment of recognition and disbelief, Nan wrenched her eyes away and leaned over to peruse the selection of delicacies on the buffet table.

This was getting weird. Mathilde had issued Nan an invitation to the gala so she could get a look at potential suspects. But who had invited Mr. Maserati?

And why did he look so damn tasty in a tuxedo. And *why* did he have that canary-eating smile on his face?

Heat rose to her cheeks. Surely, he hadn't seen her changing clothes in the Jeep. He was asleep two hundred feet away, separated by trees and bushes. She glanced up over the tray of crudités.

He waved. The smile stretched into a grin. Nan felt annoyance spark in her gut. So what if he had seen a bit. Big deal. She gave him a bored look and picked out a cherry tomato, which she popped in her mouth.

She felt someone come up behind her. A large hand squeezed her butt. She nearly inhaled the cherry tomato. She eased to the right, but the hand held on. Great. She was stuck between the crab cakes and a dirty old man. She spit the tomato into her hand, pushed it underneath the lip of the platter, and reached for a celery stick—Lethal Weapon III.

Damon rested on his elbows against the rail and watched Hannah lean over the buffet table. He had a straight shot. The neckline of her dress was just loose enough that if he had his field glasses, he would be able to see right down to her navel. He had to get closer.

Hannah looked up, her expression comical. Then he saw the reason why. Some sleazebag had his hand on her ass.

Damon pulled his jacket over the weathervane in his pants and strode over to the table. He stretched across her and snagged a celery stick from her long, supple fingers. The light scent of her cologne tickled his nose. He paused to inhale more deeply, then ground his heel into the sleazebag's foot as he turned to leave.

The man's hand dropped as an "Oh" of pain curled his lips. "Bitch," he said to the back of Hannah's head and limped away.

Damon smiled. If anyone was going to fondle that ass, it was going to be him.

Meaningful relationship, he reminded himself.

So why couldn't he have a meaningful relationship with hard-hearted Hannah? She looked like she contained a lot of meaning—except she was leaving the party. He quickly scanned the deck. Rupert was still there with his goon and the bimbette. So where was Hannah going?

He jolted after her, right into the path of a redhead in a bugle-beaded miniskirt.

Nan risked a peek over her shoulder to make sure No-name wasn't following her—just in time to see a redheaded vamp slink up to him and stick her hands down his pants. Nan couldn't keep back a shiver of vicarious thrill. Rich people sure knew how to give parties. Not all rich people, she reminded herself. Her parents were rich and their parties were dull as dishwater.

At least the redhead should keep him busy long enough for her to find his car and search for clues to his identity. She passed one of the busboys, another bodyguard or she was Miss Manners, and walked down the gangplank, swaying on her spike heels. Just another drunken society broad.

Actually, it was pretty hard to walk down a gangplank in four-inch heels.

She sashayed across the wooden pier, beneath more lighted grape arbors, and crossed the street. Once on the tarmac of the parking lot, she gave a quick look around, then stepped into the shadows.

She kicked off her shoes and crouch-walked her way toward the parked cars. She waited until the attendant leaned over to light his cigarette and dove behind a Lincoln Town Car. She heard a high-pitched groan, the sounds of scuffling. She froze, ears alert. It was coming from the inside of the Lincoln. A mugging? She poised on her haunches, ready to act.

Then a muffled, "Baby, oh baby," and Nan relaxed. At least someone was seeing action tonight.

She left them to it and, keeping low to the ground, she began to search up and down the rows of cars. Geena said that tonight he was driving a silver BMW. Only about twenty parked here. With New York plates starting with JG. She found it on the fifth click of her penlight.

Now for a little breaking and entering, a trick she had learned not at Camp Wilderness or cotillion classes, but from Bennie the Welch several cases back.

She fiddled her nail file into the lock, heard it click open. She reached for the door handle and was thrown hard against the side of the car.

"Spread," said a low, gruff voice. Not the parking attendant, too tall and slim. "Now." His body pressed hers against the car. She had just enough time to push the nail file into her cleavage.

"Is that a pistol in your pocket—" The rest of the rejoinder was cut off by a large hand covering her mouth. Her attacker was breathing hard, but she didn't panic. She recognized his brand of soap from when he had passed her at the buffet table.

"Don't scream."

She shook her head as much as she could with his hand holding her in place. He was strong and she was definitely at a disadvantage, but she wasn't afraid of him. Not at all. Strange.

"Make one sound and I'll snap that pretty neck in two."

His body moved away. The boner that had been sticking into the small of her back disappeared. A shoe pushed her bare feet apart. He released his hands, then shoved one into her back, while the other frisked her. She couldn't keep back a shudder when his fingers brushed her breast.

His free hand trailed down her right thigh, leaving burn marks every place they touched. Down the other leg.

Where are you going to look next, Sherlock?

He was thorough; she had to hand him that. Right up her ankle, to her calf, to her inside thigh. Then it slowed and his fingers came to rest on the thin fabric of her thong. Lingered there.

"Find what you were looking for?" she whispered, her voice hoarse.

"Shut up." He meant it as a hiss, she knew he did, but it was more like the purr of a really big kitty cat.

Finally his hand moved away and played down the inside of her other thigh.

Nan's senses slowly returned to normal, almost. Her mind refocused on the job at hand. Turnaround was fair play and now it was her turn. She swept her foot back and hooked it behind his ankle. He went down, hard. Sometimes men were so easy.

She rolled him onto his stomach on the pavement, straddled his butt, and had the tip of the nail file pricking the side of his neck, before he knew what hit him.

"Ouch," he said and tried to buck her off. "Get off me before you get hurt. I know you're only packing a nail file."

"Yeah, but it's aimed right at your carotid artery. Care to test my accuracy?"

"Shit. I thought you just got lucky. How did you know that."

"Learned it gutting deer."

No-name snorted.

"After I killed it with a bow and arrow." She pressed her hips into his. "Do you always get hard-ons for people you're tailing, or was it the redhead?"

He grunted. "Not the redhead, and I might never get another one if you don't ease up."

"Sorry." She lifted her hips slightly.

He rolled over and suddenly she was the one on the bottom, and he was straddling her. She could feel everything he had. And it felt like a pretty nice package.

"That was a dirty trick. And you're wrecking my dress."

He smiled. A slow, sultry smile that made her want to tear his clothes off. He had somehow lifted her nail file in the flip, and he traced circular patterns with it on the soft skin above her low cut dress. She couldn't keep her legs from spreading.

There was a sudden commotion nearby, the sound of people getting nearer. He yanked her up and pushed her against the car again. Only this time he was kissing her. Deep and hot with his pelvis matching every circle and thrust of his tongue.

The group passed by them. Someone snickered, "Hey, my turn." His companions pulled him back and they continued across the parking lot.

Maserati Man didn't stop kissing her. Maybe he thought there was going to be a parade. And she didn't really mind being kissed in a dark parking lot by a drop-dead gorgeous alpha male. Actually, she couldn't think of a thing she'd rather be doing.

Shit, she was on assignment. And besides, she wasn't having casual sex anymore. At least not without knowing what to call him.

Nan pushed at his shoulders. He broke the kiss but didn't move away. He looked down at her with eyes heavy enough to suffocate her.

"Cut it out. I saw that movie, too. When you need cover, kiss the girl. Now how about sharing some information?"

"Later."

Damon moved his hand from her neck; his fingertips trailed down her bare skin to the neckline of her dress; dipped beneath the fabric. He felt her shiver.

His fingers found the valley between the two firm peaks of her breasts. He pressed his erection into her stomach and used his free hand to stretch one strap of her dress off her shoulder. Hell, it wasn't enough, but he couldn't bring himself to move his other hand from the warmth of her skin. He wrapped his arm around her back and pulled at the other strap, then tugged the bodice down to her waist.

Her breasts sprang free, taut and hard nippled, each begging for his touch, his mouth, his tongue. He circled the outer curves of flesh with his fingers and she . . . oh, God, her hands were moving inside his jacket, down his sides.

Don't stop, he pleaded, and cupped a firm breast in each palm. Her hands roamed down his hips to his thighs. He released her just enough so she could fit her hands between them. She was moving slow, too slow.

He pinched the bud of her erect nipple. She gasped and her hands slid to where he wanted them. He could feel himself pulsing against her fingers. It wasn't close enough. He needed flesh on flesh, not flesh separated by a metal zipper and silk boxers.

But she was doing a damn good job. He could feel the sweat roll down his temple.

He let his hands slip away and lowered his head to lick the tip of a nipple, first one, then the other. He found the hem of her dress and eased it slowly upward until his palms squeezed her ass, skin against skin. The thin silk string of her thong rolled beneath his fingers, an aphrodisiac so powerful to his hyped-up senses that a guttural exclamation escaped him before he could stop it.

He rested his head on her shoulder, ran his cheek along her neck, slick with sweat. His sweat. He was struggling to hang on. Technique deserted him. He sucked in his breath.

Her fingers were playing him like a flute and he thought he might explode before he could take another breath. He had to fight the urge to release her long enough to open his trousers for her. And then gloriously he felt her fingers slide beneath his cummerbund; his fingers slipped beneath her thong. She unbuttoned his waistband.

He slid her thong down over her cheeks as she slowly pulled his zipper down. It was exquisite torture. Climax by metal teeth.

He stopped moving, stopped breathing, as her hand found him and her fingers closed around him. He wasn't going to make it. He gritted his teeth as she slowly marked the outline of his erection—sexual frisking. Her fingers slipped beneath his boxers and freed the tip of his penis. One finger ran across the cleft and the bead of moisture straining for release.

He knew he was getting behind, but he couldn't seem to move. His mouth was attached to her nipple, his hands were frozen halfway to her waiting folds. And he couldn't move.

If he could, he would pull off the dress that was bunched around her waist; he'd tear off his jacket and shirt and pants. And they would make love naked—on the asphalt.

Shit, they were in a parking lot.

"Your turn," she whispered.

He forgot the parking lot. Forgot everything but the woman

touching him. His fingers splayed through the triangle of hair between her legs. His hand cupped her, and he thought he would die. His mouth moved from her breast . . . found her mouth. He thrust his tongue between her lips while his fingers slid through the moisture of the lips below. Her hand tightened convulsively around him. And he felt the first waves of his climax.

No, he ordered himself. Begged himself. Pleaded with his dick to just hold on for another second.

Then suddenly her hand was gone, leaving only air on his flaming erection. She pushed his hand from between her legs and shoved him away.

He became vaguely aware of laughter, getting louder. Of Nan efficiently pulling her dress up—and down—while he stood there with his dick sticking out between the tails of his dress shirt.

"The party's breaking up," she hissed at him.

He shook his head to clear it.

"Move it."

Easy for her to say. She didn't have to push a boner back into tuxedo pants. They had come to rest around his thighs. He reached for them. Mechanically began to pull them up.

"Jesus." She yanked his pants up to his waist, buttoned them, and reached for his zipper.

He managed to bat her hands away. This was a delicate operation and she was impatient—and she was gone. Just like that. Disappeared.

He looked around, peering into the shadows as he stuffed his shirttail into his pants and sucked in his belly long enough to ease the zipper closed.

Where the hell was she?

Voices were all around him, guests headed toward their cars. It was too late to get out of sight. He braced his hand on the hood of the car and pretended to open the door until they passed. Then he heard Rupert's voice calling out from the yacht to someone getting into a nearby car.

Damon turned around, dragging his senses back to the immediate situation.

Rupert stood at the top of the gangplank, the platinum porn star on one side, his bug-eyed bodyguard on the other. His wife stood a few feet farther along the rail, looking daggers.

But there was no sign of Hannah Harrington-Scott.

Chapter Three

Nan barely had time to snag her shoes before the parking lot was inundated with people. The party was breaking up earlier than she expected. It was a good thing she had planned an overlap in her and Delia's watches. She skulked to the far end of the parking lot and put her shoes on before stepping out onto the sidewalk.

She began walking away from the marina to where she had left the Liberty several blocks away. She kept to the shadows not wanting to draw attention to herself, from the departing guests or from Mr. Big Eyes and bigger—whew. It had been a close one.

She hadn't felt this drawn to a stranger since Anthony Grant Taylor had picked her up at the Winter Ball. And look how that turned out. She had tried to be what everyone expected, but she couldn't live up to her good intentions. So she ran. And tonight her good intentions had been put to the test again. Another failure. But oh, what a failure.

She could see Delia's Lexus up ahead, parked equidistant between two streetlights, making it impossible to see if the car was occupied.

Nan shook herself, reached in her purse and pressed Delia's code on her cell phone. The passenger door opened a bare crack; the interior light was turned off. Good, Delia was learning fast.

She headed toward the Lexus and slipped into the front seat. She and Delia peered at each other until their eyes adjusted to the darkness. Then Delia let out an exclamation.

"What have you been up to? Wild party?"

Nan smoothed back disheveled hair. Noticed that her dress wasn't in great shape, either.

"Playing roll and tussle in the parking lot."

"Are you okay? You should have beeped me. I would have come running."

"Thanks, but I had it under control, and I managed to lift his wallet while he was down." She pulled a thin, black billfold from her cleavage and clicked on her penlight.

They both peered at the driver's license.

"Damon Connelly," read Nan.

"Sounds like a name from one of those exorcism movies."

Nan looked up. "You're right." Then she noticed the fine sprinkling of white that dusted Delia's black sweater and slacks.

"Delia."

Delia looked down and quickly brushed away the evidence.

"I know. I know. But it's my anniversary—or should be—and I was passing by the donut shop and . . . . Well, I just had a moment of weakness." She snatched a white paper bag off the dashboard. "You take the rest." She thrust the bag at Nan.

"Too late, and anyway, you'll need sustenance for the night watch."

Delia sighed. "I already had three. And I'm not trusting my willpower."

Nan took the bag and stuck it between her seat and the door.

Nan knew about backsliding. She'd been guilty of it herself just a few minutes ago. At least you didn't wear sex on your hips the next morning. And Delia had been doing so well in the two months she'd been with Women-Tek.

Nan and Geena had stared openmouthed when Delia first

walked into the office and hovered timidly in the doorway. It took a few seconds before they recognized her.

Her hair was cut in an unflattering shag, which hung flat to her face and nearly covered what had been her best feature, wide, startling blue eyes. She was wearing a knit pants suit, which though obviously expensive, did nothing to hide the lumpy hips or the paunch of her stomach. Delia had never been thin, and she had gained a good forty pounds in the ten years since Camp Wilderness.

Definitely a case of the cobbler's children, or in Delia's case, the plastic surgeon's wife. While her husband was at the office, making women beautiful, she stayed home, getting fat, dowdy, and insecure.

Geena was the first to recover.

"Delia," she squealed. Geena never squealed. It jerked Nan back to reality.

"Delia," she mimicked and followed Geena to the door, where they all hugged and chattered until Delia burst into tears.

She was not their first case of philandering husband syndrome, but it was definitely the one that struck closest to home. And they pursued it with a vengeance. As soon as the divorce was final, and Delia was awarded a hefty settlement, they offered her a job.

She gratefully accepted it, and her makeover began in earnest. She'd already lost twenty pounds—until tonight, anyway.

Nan ruthlessly pushed the donut bag out of sight. "Got your laptop with you?"

"Of course. Thought I'd work on our website while I'm keeping an eye on Rupert, which reminds me. I'd better get going. He's still at the yacht, I presume, or you wouldn't be sitting here."

"He was when I left, and he has to drive this way back to the main road. He'll either be in the Jag or the Mercedes, most likely with Sherry, the blonde."

Delia sighed again.

"Think of it as on-the-job training. I used to have to do the night stakeouts. Once you get your chops honed, we'll share. In the meantime, can you run Damon Connelly through the computer while you're keeping an eye on loverboy and see what you come up with?"

"No problem." Delia pulled her laptop from beneath Nan's feet and flipped it open. She copied the specifics of Damon Connelly's license, then handed it back to Nan.

Nan shuffled through several hundred dollar bills and a couple of credit cards. She read off the numbers while Delia typed them in.

"What are you going to do with the wallet? That's stealing."

Nan turned the wallet over in her hand.

"You could drop it in the parking lot and he'll think it fell out of his pocket during the struggle," said Delia, enthusiastically.

"Good idea," said Nan. Actually, it was a good idea. She had already considered it as an option. But where was the fun in that? Keeping the wallet would give her an excuse to see Damon again. And when she did, she'd be armed with more information and that would give her the edge she needed.

She opened the car door. "Call me as soon as you get anything."

"I should at least be able to verify the address and get a credit rating, and maybe an employer in the next hour or so. And if Rupert took his Viagra tonight, I'll probably have a lot more by morning."

"Lucky you. Well, I'm going home. I'm beat." All that extra-curricular activity in the parking lot had worn her out. Her stamina sure wasn't what it used to be.

She said good night, surreptitiously taking the donut bag with her, and walked a half block to where her Liberty was parked on the street. She checked for unwanted visitors before she quickly jumped inside and drove away.

The porch light looked welcoming as she turned the Jeep into her driveway and pulled to a stop beside the nineteen-thirties bungalow. Now, if there were only someone waiting for her inside. She edited that. Someone she *wanted* waiting inside. The idea of grappling with an intruder while wearing stiletto heels was definitely not something to look forward to.

But her neighborhood was safe and if not exactly up to the standard of her last incarnation, it was comfortable and only two blocks from the beach.

She locked the Jeep, set the alarm, and went up the front steps. Her key was in the door when she heard the porch swing creak. She whirled around and took an aggressive stance. Which probably looked ridiculous in the outfit she was wearing.

Damon Connelly was sitting on the swing, pushing himself back and forth with one foot. He cradled a wine bottle in his lap. A plastic grocery bag sat on the seat beside him.

Nan gritted her teeth. How did he know where she lived? She'd left *her* driver's license in the Jeep when she went to the party.

She stood glaring at him, while he smiled nonchalantly back at her, his deep brown eyes twinkling with self-satisfaction.

He shifted his weight, then stood up. She held her ground, but he merely picked up the grocery bag and walked past her to the door.

"Thought you might be hungry." He turned the key and pushed the door open.

She watched his back. She was hungry, all right, but not for whatever was in the bag.

"Shouldn't you be watching Rupert Sims? Or whoever you're hired to watch?" she asked.

She thought that would rattle him, but he didn't even hesitate as he made his way down the hall. She had no choice but to follow him.

"I figured since your friend Delia is on the job, I might as well save myself the boredom. Rupert was ushering the bimbette into his car when I left. I figure they'll still be at it when we're washing the dishes."

He did dishes? This looked promising. Even if he were a hit man, which was looking very unlikely. He must have had plenty of opportunity to snuff Rupert by now. So who and what was Damon Connelly?

"What are you doing here?" she asked as she followed him into the kitchen.

He shrugged and put the wine and bag on the counter. "Dinner?" He tossed a smile over his shoulder. "Dessert?"

"Who hired you? And for what?"

Damon shook his head as he pulled out a carton of eggs from the bag. "Client confidentiality."

"Fair enough. What about professional courtesy? Want to share what you've found out so far?"

"Hmm." Damon opened a cabinet and rummaged around until he found a sauté pan. He placed it on the stove, opened another cabinet and brought out a bowl.

Nan began to get nervous. He didn't even have to guess which cabinets to look in.

"I know that you're Hannah Harrington-Scott. You work for Women-Tek. I know you ran out on your Wall Street fiancé minutes before the wedding."

Hannah stared at him. How did he know all this, when all she had was a name and two rental cars? Okay. It was all public record stuff, but still . . .

Damon walked over to the refrigerator. He was acting like he owned the place and she was the guest.

"So, hard-hearted Hannah. Why did you jilt Anthony Taylor?"

A frisson of unease skittered over her. There was no way he could know about the hard-hearted Hannah part. Anthony's best man had called her that. She'd never told anyone about it. It was too humiliating and it wasn't true.

Damon paused with his hand on the refrigerator handle and looked at her, eyebrows raised.

Nan swallowed. "Tulle gives me a rash."

He grinned, then opened the refrigerator and looked inside. He shut it with a bang and shuddered. "Ugh. Don't you cook?"

"I know how to open a yogurt carton, I can use a toaster, and I have ten restaurants that deliver on my speed dial." She was letting him sidetrack her. This was not going the way she planned.

"We won't need a toaster tonight." He tossed a baguette at her. "I won't ask if you can use a knife."

She put the bread on the kitchen table.

"What do you want?" She paused, then added, "Damon."

It didn't phase him.

"I thought you must have been the one who lifted my wallet. Pretty clever. Learn that at Camp Wilderness?"

Shit, the man was uncanny. And scary. And beautiful. And too damn cocky for his own good. He was facing her now, an egg cradled in each hand, and her thoughts immediately conjured his hands on her breasts barely an hour ago. Now, he was in her kitchen about to cook dinner.

He'd ditched his jacket, cummerbund, and bow tie. His pleated shirt was open at the neck, revealing the soft indention at the juncture of his collar bones. Her eyes strayed over him, then downward, and there it was, standing at attention. Begging her hands to reach out and touch him.

She felt uncomfortably warm and knew she was blushing. "Seems like Rupert isn't the only one on Viagra around here." Her words weren't as steady as she intended; neither were her knees.

He glanced down, then looked at her sheepishly. Definitely not the look of a hired hit man. Right?

"I think it's you." He carefully placed the eggs back in the carton. "Maybe we should start with dessert."

Chapter Four

Nan's heart skittered to a stop, seized up for a moment, then banged back to life, hammering at her rib cage. Okay, just one little backslide, just one night. She deserved it. And besides, Delia had eaten three donuts.

It didn't have to be a backslide. Damon Connelly might be the kind of man who liked to talk after sex. She could find out a lot of information that way.

Who was she kidding? She was rationalizing. She knew it and she wanted to ignore it, but she made a last-ditch effort to control herself.

"I'm not having casual sex these days."

Damon's eyebrows twitched. It was such a turn-on. "It won't be casual. I promise."

He stepped toward her. She stepped back against the table. His hands slipped around her waist. He lifted her up and sat her down on the top.

Nan reached back to steady herself. Her hand squashed into the baguette, but she was beyond caring.

He eased a hip bone between her thighs, then stepped between them. Pulled her forward until she was straddling him. Her skirt rolled up her thighs. She locked her ankles behind him and pulled him even closer.

He groaned as body parts came together in a teasing dance. Then his mouth covered hers so violently that she fell backwards. He grabbed her around the shoulders and held on, assaulting her mouth with thrusts of his tongue. Mashing his lips against hers, driving her teeth against her lip, drawing blood.

He eased up and ran his tongue along her teeth and lips, licking the blood away. "Sorry," he mumbled and went in for a second offensive.

This time he was gentler. It was even better, knowing that he was holding himself back. It gave her a chance to reciprocate.

She was vaguely aware of her cell phone ringing; a faint echo from inside her purse that she'd hung over a chair back. She briefly considered reaching for it, but couldn't let go of Damon.

His hair was soft and just the right length for wrapping around her fingers. She did and pulled. He groaned again and deepened the kiss. This time she fell backwards onto the tabletop, taking Damon with her.

The French bread went down for the count. Neither of them noticed. Damon's hands were everywhere, roaming at will, his touch hitting every spot but the one that needed it most.

"Not a table, either," he said against her ear. And suddenly she was lifted up. And being carried across the room, her legs still locked around his waist.

He shouldered the door open and stepped into the hall.

"Bedroom," he said.

"Yes," she answered. Didn't understand why he laughed.

He started down the hall with her clinging to him. Paused and threw the first door open. It was the closet. A muffled expletive and he started up again. The bathroom.

"And behind door number three . . ." she said breathlessly.

"Aha," said Damon as he opened the door to the bedroom.

Anticipation rushed through her. Just one little backslide, she promised. He'd be gone in twenty minutes—forty, max. But until then . . . Shit. He'd stopped just inside the door. Why was he just standing there?

"Hmm?" she asked.

Damon jerked. "Just looking." Then he moved again, across the room, and they fell on the bed together. He loomed over her, expression stark, eyes glittering with something scary.

A part of her brain, the part that was still trying to think rationally, was clamoring for her attention. She didn't know anything about Damon Connelly. She was nuts to let this man into her house, much less into her bed. And then the part of her that was responsible for her being sent to Camp Wilderness spoke up. *You'll get information this way. And have a hell of a ride along the way.*

She consigned her rational self as well as her good intentions to the bottom of Long Island Sound and reached for the buttons of Damon's shirt. It made the tussle in the parking lot look like an amateur sting. This was a fight to the finish. They groped for each other, getting in each other's way, but neither yielding ground.

Finally, Damon pushed her to her feet. His shirt hung by one arm. His trousers were halfway unzipped. Her dress was up by her waist. He steadied her on her heels, then pulled the dress over her head in one smooth movement. She stood before him in nothing but four-inch heels and a beige silk thong.

A sharp crack of sound, somewhere between a laugh and a cry, escaped from deep in his throat. He was breathing hard and taking her in.

He yanked the sleeve over his wrist and tossed his shirt past her. She started to reach for him.

"No," he said. "Stay right there. Just like that." His eyes were feasting on her. Scrutinizing every inch of her. While her insides were tugging with desire, with impatience, and with shear physical need. Her thong was wet with anticipation.

Damon shucked off his trousers, boxers, shoes and socks. Then he stood before her.

She licked dry lips and his cock jumped in response. What a sense of power. So why didn't he come to her or draw her toward him.

They stood facing each other, not more than four feet

away, discovering everything they could by sight, but Nan was eager to get to the touch and taste part. And so was Damon if she knew the signs. And she knew the signs.

Then he moved and she was in his arms, their bodies pressed together, sharing heat, exchanging desire. He didn't kiss her this time or suckle her, but scooped her off the ground and laid her gently across the bed. He lifted her leg, slipped off her shoe, and held her bare foot in his hand.

His tongue flicked across her toes. Nan wriggled. Jesus. The man even made feet erotic. He nibbled each toe, then slid his tongue up her instep leaving a heated wet trail to her ankle.

Oh, boy. She didn't think she could wait for him to make his way all the way up her leg. She reached for him again, but he pushed her hand away. Continued to lick and nibble his way up her calf and thigh. Exquisite torture. It was time to reel this baby in.

"Damon," she whispered.

"Soon." He nuzzled the crease at her hip, just inches from where he needed to go. She wondered if he needed a road map. She shifted under him, trying to give him a clue. His breath puffed out over her belly, making her shudder. He was teasing her.

Nan's whole body clenched in anticipation. Okay, she was going to die without ever getting to the really good part.

Finally, his tongue slipped beneath the tie of her thong. He followed the string to the triangle of fabric. She felt the rasp of his tongue on her skin, now just centimeters to the left of home.

"Damon."

He kept moving, bypassing where she needed him, then coming back a little closer and skirting off to the side again. She was squirming beneath him. Out of control, helpless to make him hurry.

Then his tongue slipped out of her thong and he moved away. Nan felt a wash of disappointment.

But he moved back to her, his mouth inches above the fabric. His head dipped, his teeth closed over the silk triangle, soaked from both their body fluids. He jerked his head. The fabric ripped as the thong came away in his mouth.

He tossed it to the side and dove to his final destination.

Nan whimpered. She never whimpered, simpered, or whined. But she felt like doing all three. She fell into a vortex of pleasure. The movements of his tongue, the nip of his teeth diffused waves of heat through the rest of her body; drove an acute tightening deep inside her.

She was caught up in the moment, yo-yoing between trying to guess what he would do next, and not caring at all as long as he kept going. She was turned on by the unpredictability of it all, and totally helpless to reciprocate. Finally giving up, she succumbed to the escalating rhythm of his tongue and her response to it.

She grabbed his hair, pulling him into her. He urged her toward the brink, winding her tighter and tighter, until the spring uncoiled and she rocketed through space. Damon hung on all the way, riding her until the last contraction subsided.

He followed his tongue up the center of her body.

"Can't wait," he said and thrust into her, before she could even say "condom." He pumped hard and fast, his muscles tight, his breath coming out in gasps.

She expected his climax every second, but he held on. He rolled with her until he was on his back. He grabbed her hips and pushed her against the thrust of his hips. The mattress rebounded as their thrusts increased in speed and strength. They rolled again until they made it to the other side of the bed.

They were slick with each other's sweat, bodies sliding against each other while the friction of each thrust grew wilder.

She was just going over again, when Damon joined her, crying out in a sound that was wrenched from him. She added her voice to his; like a couple of alley cats. It was earthy, lusty, and it sure was sweet.

Neither of them moved for a long time after that. Nan,

pressed beneath the weight of Damon's body, felt their hearts beating in tandem, a pounding staccato, then slowing together, and coming to rest in a counterpoint of rhythm, until at last, a satisfying lethargy overcame them.

Well, hell. Damon was right. Nothing casual about that.

He lifted his weight and moved off to the side. They both groaned when he slipped out of her. He pulled her close and draped his arm across her waist, comfortable—and possessive, she thought.

"I have a condom somewhere," he said.

"The horse is out of the barn," Nan murmured. Then the implications began to sink in. "I hope you always have safe sex."

"Yeah. Until tonight." Sex was the only safe thing in his life. "You?"

"Always."

"Good. Birth control?"

"Yep. A girl can't be too careful."

"No, they can't." He circled her navel with a gentle finger. "You really shouldn't allow strangers in your bed."

She smiled lazily at him. "It's okay. There's a .38 police special under my pillow."

Damon jerked away from her, jumped off the bed, and looked down at her, full frontal.

What a view.

"Loaded?"

You sure are. "Of course. So don't try any funny business."

Damon gingerly sat back on the bed. Looked at her with a half frown on his face. "Will you give me a warning before I do something to make you shoot me?"

"One." She pulled him back down and kissed him.

Damon awoke in the night, his brain clouded, his body sated. Then he became aware of the woman asleep beside him. The moonlight coming through the window turned her skin to an opalescent white. Hannah. He pulled her close, fitted his body to her back, and drifted into sleep.

When he awoke again, it was light outside. He was alone.

He pushed himself up on his elbows. Looked around. He'd been right last night in spite of the distraction. The furniture matched. The bed, the side tables, the bureau were all dark oak. Mission style or Arts and Crafts or something.

Gradually his brain focused on another fact. He had stayed the entire night. He never did that. Never fell asleep after sex. Never let his guard down. He had done all three with Hannah.

Stupid. And stupid to have let her get his wallet. It was sloppy work, and sloppy work got people killed. And when Hannah found out the particulars of his identity, it would kill any chance he had with her.

He pushed the sheet away, threw his legs over the side of the bed, and sat up. Ran his fingers through sleep-mussed hair. Tried to think.

She was probably already running a check on him. He dreaded knowing what she would find. And she would find it. There was no doubt about that. Damon Connelly—armed robber, rapist, murderer, and popular hit man.

And that would be the end of him and Hannah Harrington-Scott. At least he would have last night to remember. A small and unsatisfying consolation. He wanted more. He wanted all of her. All of the time.

He stood up and looked back at the bed, already feeling the memory of making love to Hannah slipping away. The sheets were crumpled and twisted. The bed a war zone. A king-size bed. Comfortable. How many men had preceded him in that bed, he wondered.

Stupid to feel that rush of jealousy. He had no right to be jealous and besides, he was never jealous. Never stuck around long enough to know or care. But this was different. He knew it from the start, and he knew it now at the finish. Better to leave before she found out. There was no way to explain Damon Connelly's past. No way he could, at any rate.

He leaned over and hauled the spread back onto the mattress, then reached for his clothes. Had to get down on all fours to fish his shoes out from under the bed. Lifted out the thong that had come to rest inside one of them. He crumpled the little piece of silk in his hand, reached for his trousers and slipped it in the pocket. A memento. Reached back under the bed for his other shoe.

"Nice view."

Damon jerked up and banged his head on the bed frame. He backed out and sat down cross-legged on the floor to rub his head.

Hannah stood in the doorway dressed in jeans and another skimpy T-shirt. She looked good enough to eat.

"Come here." Damon stretched out his hand.

Hannah stayed where she was and shook her head. Her ponytail swung across the back of her shoulders. He felt himself getting hard.

She smiled, slow and enticing. He hit full erection.

"I'd really like to stay and play, but I have a job."

So she didn't know yet. He hurriedly got to his feet. She danced away from him, but let herself be caught.

"I really have to go. A meeting."

Damon shook his head and held on. That meeting would probably be his downfall. And this would be the last time he would ever hold Hannah Harrington-Scott in his arms.

He kissed her, hard, demanding. She pulled away. Tilted her head a little, a gesture that he was learning to recognize. She was thinking. He didn't want her to think. He just wanted her here and now. Forever.

Stupid. He let go. They stood looking at each other for a long moment, then Hannah feathered a kiss across his cheek. "Gotta go. Your wallet's on the kitchen table."

Damon tried for a smile. He was never any good at smiling, not genuine smiling, and this attempt hurt.

She flashed a megawatt smile back at him. And then she was gone. Again.

Chapter Five

Nan sat in the parking lot in back of the two-story frame house where Women-Tek had their offices. Geena's Honda was in the lot and so was Delia's Lexus.

She took a deep breath; tried to wipe off the postcoital glow she knew she was wearing. Nothing like a little—a lot—of wild, abandoned sex to make a girl happy.

But she wasn't paid to be happy. She was paid to find information. And she hadn't. She'd spent eight hours with the man and still didn't know anything more than she knew at the outset—his name. And every inch of his hard, sculpted body. And that she was feeling way too fond of a man who might be a hired killer.

She wondered if Delia had been more successful. In a way, she hoped she hadn't, and that was wrong. *You're on a case*, she reminded herself. *No more randy thoughts. Mind on the job.*

She gave herself a pep talk all the way across the parking lot and up the back steps to Women-Tek. She paused outside the office door, feeling only a little nervous. Maybe he was just another hardworking detective. She remembered him asleep in his car, asleep in her arms, and shivered. She crossed her fingers, steeled her expression, and stepped into the office.

"Morning all," she said brightly. She tossed her briefcase and knapsack on the sofa by the door.

Geena looked up from her desk. Her eyes narrowed. "Morning."

Delia's head poked out of the door to the second office. "Hi."

"How was your night with Rupert and Sherry?"

Delia stepped all the way out. "I just got back. The miracle of modern drugs, they kept it up, literally, all night. When they left the love nest this morning, poor Sherry was staggering toward her car. What the woman endures for love . . ." Delia shuddered.

"For money," Nan corrected.

"I guess. Anyway, they were there the whole time. Though Bug-eyed Barney did sneak out around three. I didn't follow him, but he was only gone ten minutes and came back with a Burger King bag." Delia screwed up her face. "Poor guy. What do you think he does while they're at it? Sits in a chair, eating French fries, and watches?"

"A gruesome thought," said Nan. She turned to Geena who'd been watching her intently from the moment she came through the door.

Nan began to get a prickly feeling. "Well, boss?"

A frown played across Geena's face, and some other emotion.

Nan bit her lip. "What?"

"Please, please say you didn't fuck him."

"Barney?"

"Damon Connelly."

"Oh." It was Nan's turn to frown. "All right. I didn't fuck him."

"But did you?" asked Delia, coming to stand on Geena's side of the desk and looking unhappy.

"What is this, the Inquisition?"

"Did you?" asked Geena.

Nan shrugged. "Yep. Made him and laid him." She fought to keep a reminiscent smile from popping out at the image of Damon's bare butt sticking out from under her bed. Her eyes slid guiltily away from Geena's intent ones. "So okay, I know

I said I wasn't having any more casual sex. I did a little back-sliding. I couldn't help myself. And it wasn't exactly casual. It was more . . ." She threw herself into the nearest client chair. "I've got it bad, girls."

"God damn it," said Geena through clenched teeth. "You don't know anything about this man."

"I know that he's had his appendix out."

Geena groaned.

Delia looked like she might cry.

"What?" asked Nan, sitting up. This wasn't about her breaking a resolution. It was about— "What did you find out?"

Geena pushed a manila folder across the desk to her. Nan picked it up with fingers that were suddenly stiff. She leaned back in the chair, crossed her legs and opened the folder.

There were several pages and none of it was good.

It became difficult to breathe as Nan read the dossier on Damon Connelly. She shook her head minutely as she read things that she couldn't wrap her mind around. He didn't look forty. She'd guess more like thirty or thirty-five, max. And his hair was dark, not light brown. He could have dyed it. The height was about right. The weight was wrong. But weight fluctuated.

She turned the page. Juvenile detention camps from age twelve. Adult arrest for armed robbery. Murder. She sucked breath into tight lungs. Scanned down the page. Rape. Rape? No. It wasn't possible. Not Damon. He was passionate, but not violent. She wouldn't believe it. She stared at the word until it went out of focus, then forced herself to keep reading. Suspected hit man. Six convictions. Two overturned on loop-holes, one on improper procedure, the other three overturned by a higher court. *A judge on the take.*

The list of his crimes and prison sentences read like a cal-endar until three weeks before, then nothing. Until now.

"Good work, Delia." Nan tried for enthusiasm, but her tone wasn't quite up to the mark.

Delia's lips trembled. "It was a long night."

"What about the last three weeks?" Nan had to force the words out, struggle to make them sound unconcerned. She failed miserably. She could tell by the way her two friends were watching her.

Delia flinched. Cleared her throat. "Dropped off the radar. Probably went to ground. Or out of the country." She shrugged. "On vacation?"

"Are you sure this is the right Damon Connelly?"

Delia lowered her head. "There aren't that many, and none of the others came close to a match," she said abjectly.

Nan closed the folder and carefully placed it on Geena's desk.

"I'm sorry." Delia's chin quivered as her eyes met Nan's then slid away.

"Now, don't cry," said Nan. "You don't see me crying, do you? At least I'm alive to tell the tale, right?" She pushed herself out of the chair. Prayed that her legs would hold her up. "Just let me pee before I give you my report. Extra-large deli coffee. Back in a sec."

She made it down the hall to the bathroom before being violently sick. Tears stung her eyes. Fuck. Fuck. Fuck. It couldn't be true. She'd slept with a rapist? A murderer? A hit man? She couldn't have. There had to be a mistake.

She rinsed out her mouth. Splashed cool water on her cheeks and tried to limit the damage to her makeup. Damon, a rapist. Her mind stuck on that one thing. Murder she could handle, maybe, but not the other. What was she thinking, she couldn't love a murderer. Love? Who the hell said anything about love. She pressed her forehead against the mirror above the sink. Christ. What had she done?

And now she would have to nail him for real. Put him behind bars. Forever. A sob escaped her; she crammed her fist to her mouth. Well, it was her job. And she'd do it. And she wouldn't look back. Wouldn't remember. Any of it.

She blew her nose and made the long walk down the hall back to Women-Tek. She'd put a good face on it. Geena and Delia wouldn't be fooled, but they would pretend to be. And the three of them would get on with their lives and their work.

She opened the door. Geena and Delia, heads bowed together over the desk, jumped apart, looking guilty and concerned.

"Okay," said Nan. "We'd better use the conference room. I have reams of things to report."

They followed her into the next room, carrying files and looking glum. It took an hour to go over the latest research: Rupert's movements of the last week, Carl's gambling habits, Sherry's other significant other. Rupert's alleged links to organized crime.

"I'm sure of it now," said Geena. "I've had Johnny Acres on it. Mathilde guessed right. After years of clean living, Rupert has done some major backsliding—uh—I mean, taken up with his old buddies, gambling, extortion, you name it."

"So why would they take out a hit on him? Has he pissed somebody off?" Nan asked distractedly. She couldn't get her mind off Damon as a rapist.

"I don't know. But if it is a hit, it's too big for us. I shouldn't have accepted the case. We're not equipped to deal with murder."

"Sure we are," Nan snapped back. "We can't spend the rest of our careers spying on shithead husbands. This could catapult us into the big time."

She glanced up. Her heroic effort was obviously not working. Now, Geena looked like she was about to cry. Nan was the only one in control, and she knew it wouldn't last much longer.

"So what are we saying," asked Delia, waving a file at the other two. "Is the nephew off the hook?"

"No," said Geena, pulling herself back to a professional demeanor. "Carl's in debt with a capital D. Rupert has paid his creditors before, but maybe this time . . ."

"He appears to have the hots for Rupert's wife," said Nan. "That could definitely put an end to Rupert's generosity."

Delia frowned. "If there's a contract on Rupert, all Carl has to do is sit around and wait."

"*If* there's a contract," said Nan, making a last-ditch effort to save Damon's reputation and her heart.

Geena shook her head. "Johnny A. said the word is out on the street that there's going to be a hit and that Damon Connelly is the man."

"So if they know this, why don't they do something about it?" asked Nan. "And why would Mathilde come to us? She has to be savvy enough to know we couldn't stop it."

"Maybe she isn't up on the habits of the mob," said Geena.

"Oh, please," said Nan. "Mathilde is no dummy. And tell me this. If this is a hit, what are they waiting for? Connelly has been here, how long, four days that we know of, maybe more. And he's had plenty of opportunities to kill Rupert and nada, zip, nothing."

"Yeah," said Delia. "Usually with a hit, the guy flies in, does the deed, collects the cash and flies out again."

Nan and Geena both looked at her.

"At least on television."

Nan shook her head. "Well, I don't buy it. And it has nothing to do with the fact that I slept with Damon Connelly." *Not much*, she thought. Besides everything. "Somebody might be using the rumor as a chance to get rid of Rupert and blame it on his business associates."

"And who would you suggest?" asked Geena.

"Carl is the heir to a huge fortune. Sherry could be tired of getting pounded by the vulture, or her boyfriend might be pressuring her. What about the boyfriend? Have we even checked him out?"

"I'll get on it," said Delia, but Nan could tell she was only humoring her.

"And what about Bug-eyed Barney?"

"I checked him out. He's been with Rupert for fifteen years. He may have broken bones up and down the East

Coast, but as far as we know, he's completely committed to his boss, and has never once stepped out of line with him."

"It could still be the blonde."

Delia nodded her head enthusiastically. "Ye-e-e-ah, she spends every other night with him. Talk about opportunity."

"But everybody knows she's with him," said Geena. "Which leaves her with no alibi. You were watching them all night."

Delia sighed. "Yeah, and besides, if Rupert kicks it, she'll lose all those great perks, the jewelry, the fancy car, the . . ."

Geena closed the file she was holding and smacked it down on the desk. "At this point, it doesn't matter who is out to kill Rupert. I'm calling Mathilde Sims. I'll apprise her of our findings so far, then I'm returning her retainer. Regardless of who is out to get Rupert, she needs more firepower than we have, if she's going to save her husband."

"No, not yet," said Nan, standing up abruptly. "First we deal with Damon Connelly, then we can pull out if you still want to." She gathered up her files and shoved them into her briefcase. "Delia. You keep looking at the last three weeks. I want to know what he's been up to. Everything: where he's been, who he's met with, everything."

"Wait a minute," said Geena, standing up so quickly that her chair rolled backwards. "Who's the boss here?"

"You are," said Nan, snatching her briefcase off the table. "But you gave me a job, and I'm going to do it." She grabbed her knapsack and headed for the door.

"Where are you going?"

"I have a stakeout to get to. See you later."

"You're off the case," said Geena. "I'm calling it quits for all of us."

Nan didn't stop to respond. She marched out the door and down the hall to the parking lot. Her eyes were blinded by tears by the time she climbed into the Jeep. She dashed them away and screeched out of the parking lot.

She headed straight back to the bungalow. She didn't expect to find Damon still there, but she needed something from the house. And she would take her chances.

She was right. He was gone. Didn't leave a note or any sign that he'd been there, except that the kitchen was clean, the wine bottle corked, the two glasses washed and resting upside down on the counter. The eggs were gone, probably to the trash since they'd never got around to eating them or putting them in the fridge. The baguette was also missing. Nan found both in the trash beneath the sink.

Stealing herself, she went into the bedroom. Stopped. The bed was made. Her clothes were folded neatly on the dresser. There were no signs of their wild lovemaking but a slight musky scent that lingered in the air.

Nan's lip trembled, but she held back her tears. Time for crying was over, or would come later, but now she had a job to do.

She marched determinedly to the bed, pulled back the bedspread and reached under the pillow for her .38. Her hand touched paper as well as the pistol. She tossed the pillow aside and picked up the note that lay on top of her gun.

Three words. *Trust me, Damon.*

She crumpled the note and threw it to the floor, then carried the .38 to the closet and reached up to the top shelf for the box of shells. She found her hunting knife instead. She pulled it down and let her fingers close around the familiar shape and weight of the heft. It fit perfectly in her fingers.

She only had a premise license for the pistol, not a license to carry. She wasn't that great of a shot with a handgun anyway. But with a hunting knife . . . She pulled it out of the leather sheath and gingerly ran her fingers down the blade. Nice and sharp. And she was dynamite with a hunting knife. As long as her quarry was already dead or only two feet away.

She returned the .38 beneath her pillow, snapped the knife onto her belt and left the bungalow without a backward look.

Chapter Six

He should have just told her. Compromised his assignment and himself. He should have balked at the whole idea when it was first presented to him and let them find someone else to deal with Rupert Sims.

Damon smacked the steering wheel of the MG he'd picked up from Ernie earlier that morning. A totally unsatisfying gesture since the steering wheel was practically in his lap.

Whoever heard of a stakeout in an MG? Sure, it was a small target, but it was also damn uncomfortable. Even with the seat pushed back as far as it would go, you had to be a contortionist to fit behind the wheel.

He was parked conspicuously in the trees, in full view of the entrance gate to the estate. He didn't have time to wait for things to take their course. He wanted Rupert to know he was there, waiting for him. It was bound to have hit the crime hotline that there was a contract on him. It was time to jack up the heat, force Rupert to action, hopefully into the arms of Damon's superiors. Then Damon could deal with more important things. Things like trying to explain to Hannah . . .

He shifted in the bucket seat. Scanned the woods for the hundredth time for her Liberty. Maybe Women-Tek had already pulled her off the case. That's what he would have done. If they had made his ID, they would know they were in way over their heads. For the wrong reasons, but true, nonetheless.

Fuck. He hated this. It had sounded so simple. Just frighten Sims into making a move. Then he was handed the background check on Hannah Harrington-Scott and nothing had worked out the way it was supposed to since then. If only it had been somebody else, if he hadn't seen her change clothes in her front seat, if he hadn't touched her, kissed her, gone to her house . . .

He pulled his mind away from that. He'd been blindsided. And he was caught, hook, line, and sinker. He knew it the minute he'd opened his eyes in Hannah's bedroom that morning. Hannah was the woman he had been waiting for, the one he wanted for that elusive long-term relationship, hell, forever. Which would have been fine a month ago. Even a week ago. Of all the goddamn bad luck.

Who was he kidding. It would never work out anyway, so what was he bitching about. There was nothing long term about him, not his job, not his name, not even his attention span. What made him think this would be any different.

A few days or weeks at the most. Hell, a few weeks would be a record for him, but he wasn't even going to have that. One night. Just another goddamn one-night stand. Because once Hannah knew who he was, she'd be more inclined to slit his throat than take him to bed.

Did she know now? Did Delia, the computer whiz, have his rap sheet laid out on the table for Hannah to read? Was she horrified? Disgusted? Afraid?

God. He hated Damon Connelly. More than he hated him back in juvie detention. If that was possible. Even though— uh oh. Something was happening.

Damon reached for his field glasses and trained them on the figure that ran down the front steps of the mansion and jumped into a parked Jaguar. Mathilde Sims.

Tires squealed as she backed the Jag up, then sped forward, flying down the driveway and grazing the entry gates as they began to open. The car fishtailed as she made the turn toward town.

Damon started the MG and pulled out of the woods. Keeping a discreet distance, he followed the wildly veering Jag. What now, Mathilde?

Nan sped west on Route 27A. She felt numb and sick and she dreaded seeing Damon sitting in the woods, yards away, worlds away, and soon prison walls away.

She shuddered; part of her was still fighting the truth. How could she have fallen so hard for him if he was all the things his dossier said he was. What did that say about her? That she couldn't hack the idea of being married to the moneyed elite, so she had chosen a killer, a rapist, a hit man to love?

She blinked tears away. She'd total the Jeep if she didn't pull herself together. And she needed to keep her wits if she were going to confront Damon with what she had just learned. She had to hear the truth from him. That's the only thing that would make her believe it was true. Of course, he probably would lie—

Her cell phone rang for the third time since she'd left Women-Tek. She checked the caller ID. Geena. She let her voice mail pick it up. It rang again. This time she recognized Mathilde Sims's cell number.

She pressed the talk button on her headset.

"You have to help me. Please."

"Mathilde? Mathilde, what's happened? Where are you?"

No answer, just the sound of Mathilde sobbing.

"Calm down. Take a deep breath and tell me where you are and what happened."

"They shot at me. Someone shot at me," Mathilde wailed.

"Where?"

"At the estate. In my own home."

"Are you there now? Did you call 911?" Nan knew the answer before Mathilde had a chance to speak. She could hear highway noises in the background of Mathilde's phone.

"I'm going to the yacht. I'll be safe there. Please help me. Meet me there."

Nan pushed away a ripple of dread. If someone was trying to kill Mathilde, she'd be a sitting duck on the yacht. She might not even make it that far.

"Mathilde, listen to me. You have to stay calm. Is anyone following you?"

"Yes. I saw his car," Mathilde whimpered.

Damon? Or someone else. "Drive to the nearest police station. I'll meet you there. What's your location?"

"What?"

"Where are you?"

"Oh. I jus-just turned onto—I don't know. I'm close to the marina. I'm going there."

"Not a good idea. Go to the police." But Nan was talking to empty air. Mathilde had hung up.

Silently cursing, she pressed recall. No answer. All she needed was a panic-stricken woman on her hands. She wasn't a bodyguard. She considered calling the office for backup, but Geena would waste valuable time trying to convince her to back off the case. And if she called the police, they would want her identification, would ask for specifics, if they believed her at all. And by that time, it might be too late to help Mathilde.

There was nothing for it but to meet Mathilde and convince her to go to the police. She made a U-turn in the middle of the street, turned at the first major intersection and headed toward the marina. She drove straight to the pier and parked in the loading zone. There was no sign of Mathilde or her car. Talk about sitting ducks.

Nan disconnected her cell and dropped it into her knapsack. Then, she slipped out of the Jeep. Using the door as a shield, she scanned the area.

Everything seemed normal enough. Two docks over, several women were stretched out in deck chairs, soaking up the sun and enjoying a midmorning cocktail hour. In the same slip across from the *Lady Chardonnay*, a crew was washing down a blue and white two-master.

The parking lot across the street was fairly empty. Nan swallowed the tightness in her throat, as the image of Damon rose to her mind. Pressing her against the BMW, his body hard against hers . . . She thrust the scene away and concentrated on a trio of businessmen who were going into the Marina Restaurant for an early lunch. They looked innocent enough.

She heard Mathilde's car before she saw it. A Jaguar squealed around the corner and came to a stop inches behind the Liberty. Mathilde jumped out and raced toward her.

"He got stopped at the railroad crossing," she gasped. "But he'll find me. I know he will. Hurry." She grabbed Nan's arm and pulled her down the dock toward the *Lady Chardonnay*.

Nan knew Mathilde was too crazed to listen to reason, so she went with her, keeping an eye out for another car in hot pursuit. She didn't ask Mathilde to describe the car. It didn't matter, since Damon was probably driving something totally different from the day before.

They reached the yacht's gangway just as something whined past Nan's head. At first she thought it was an insect, until she saw the wood of the dock explode into splinters.

Mathilde screamed. Nan hustled her up the gangway, then pushed her onto the deck floor. Another bullet whizzed past.

"Is the crew aboard?" Nan asked in an urgent whisper.

Mathilde shook her head spasmodically.

Damn. "Can you steer this thing?"

"Yes." Mathilde didn't move from where she was crouched, staring blankly at Nan.

Nan shook her. "Then do it."

They crawled across the deck and up the steps to the pilothouse. Mathilde fell into the captain's chair. "The lines."

Nan gave her a thumbs-up. She'd been on yachts often enough in her former life to remember how to cast off. She just hoped she could get the job done before their stalker could get off another round of shots. She crept back on deck. Peeked over the rail for a quick look around, then dashed down the gangway to the dock.

The lines were heavy, but the hooks were well oiled and the first one came away fairly easily. She let it fall against the hull; she'd worry about winching it in later. She headed aft to release the other one.

She heard the yacht's engine catch, the water bubble as the throttle was let out. She managed to release the second line before the chain was yanked from her hand. The yacht lurched forward. Nan raced back to the gangway, careless of her vulnerability. She scrambled up the incline. The *Lady Chardonnay* swung away from the pier just as she reached the top. She jumped to the deck as the gangway tore away from the dock in a screech of splinters and twisted metal.

Nan was thrown to her knees. She grasped the rail and used it to pull herself to her feet and peered over to see if anyone was running after them. No one shot at her, but she heard the squeal of tires. That stopped her for a split second. If Damon was driving, who was shooting at them? Did he have an accomplice?

The yacht lurched away from its berth. Nan fell backwards and rolled along the deck until she was stopped by the giant steel winch. They'd crash into the other pier if Mathilde didn't settle down. She stumbled across the deck and up the stairs to the pilothouse.

"Steady," she commanded as she came up beside Mathilde. "Straighten her out."

Mathilde turned the wheel, overcompensating. They careered toward the blue sailboat. The crew waved frantically to get their attention.

Nan grabbed the wheel and straightened the yacht out.

Sweat was dripping in her eyes. She wiped it away. This was totally nuts. Two women without a crew or a captain trying to maneuver a ninety-foot pleasure boat. But it was too late to worry about that now. She concentrated on getting them through the narrow passage of the marina and out to the bay where, hopefully, they would be out of range of speeding bullets.

It seemed to take an eternity before they cleared the buoys of the marina. Nan steered the *Chardonnay* into the bay and cut the throttle before handing the controls back to Mathilde.

"Hold her here. We're out of range of most firearms, but keep below sight lines just in case. If you see any approaching vessels besides the harbor police, take her farther out. I'm going to check to make sure we don't have any company on board."

She waited until she was back on deck before pulling out her knife. It couldn't stop bullets, but it could do some serious damage to flesh at close range.

Chapter Seven

Nan took a minute to scan the horizon and the entrance to the marina. No craft followed them. She slid open the door to the salon, flipped on the lights, and peered into the room before she stepped inside. She carefully made her way aft, opening cabinets, peering into the galley, looking for any cubby large enough to hold a man. Past the dining and sitting area and onto the lower deck. A quick look behind the bar. No one there. She hurried along the port side and checked the forward deck. Retraced her steps and climbed the spiral stairs to the upper level.

The sun was beating down on the white painted surfaces, the breeze whipped at her hair. She squinted into the glare and eased herself into full view. The deck appeared empty, but she took the time to look between the banquette and tables, then peered cautiously over the sides of the dinghy.

So far so good. She didn't relish having to search the sleeping berths. Everything was built in and enclosed. A hundred places for a villain to hide. She climbed back down to the salon and down again to the living quarters.

She stood outside the door, listening. Not that she would hear anything through the dense mahogany. She grasped the door pocket and slid it open. Stared into the darkness. Taking a breath, she slipped inside and felt along the wall until she

came to the light panel. Randomly pressed a switch. And
ducked.

Light suffused the tiny teak-paneled foyer. She crept along
the wall, opened the door to the first head. Closed it. Looked
into the first guest stateroom, pulled out the captain's drawers beneath the bed. Far-fetched, but she couldn't be too careful. Did the same with the second stateroom; found nothing.
Recrossed the foyer and opened the door to the master suite.

Again she felt for the light panel. Slowly pressed the dim-
mer switch upward. Light grew from darkness to gray, then
to light. Nan drew a sharp breath as the room came into
focus. It wasn't what she expected to find. And for a minute
she refused to understand what she saw. Then adrenaline
kicked in. She crossed the short space of carpet to the king-
size bed and the body that lay against the pillow. A very neat
hole bore through the center of Rupert's forehead. The car-
nage on the pillows behind him was . . . Nan tried not to
look at it.

There was no point in touching the body to feel for a
pulse. Rupert Sims was dead as a doorpost. She fought the
wave of nausea that rolled through her gut, even as she
stepped to the side of the bed to get a closer look.

She forced herself to touch his hand. Cool to the touch.
And the blood and other stuff on the pillow had turned dark
as it dried. He had been killed right here on the yacht. He
hadn't been dead long. A few hours maybe. She pulled her
hand away. Another wave of nausea attacked her. She swallowed it back.

She hadn't witnessed a bloody carcass in a long time and
never a human being. She tried to think of him as game, just
so she could turn her back on him long enough to check the
closet and head.

She was getting a bad feeling. A worse one than she was
already feeling. Delia had only tailed the Mercedes until they
dropped Sherry off at her apartment. Had Rupert and Barney
come straight to the yacht after that? And where was Barney?

Had he finally snapped? Was he skulking along the shadows of the yacht waiting for a chance to kill them? Or making his escape?

It didn't make sense, even as she thought it. But she was willing to consign Barney or anyone else to hell, if it kept Damon from being the murderer.

She turned from the bed. Her toe clunked against something hard. She looked down, even though she already knew what it would be. And she was right. The murder weapon. A handgun, a .38 that looked a lot like hers.

Her hands were shaking when she pulled open the closet door. Nothing but clothes and shoes. She moved to the master bath. Opened the door.

And found Barney. Not waiting to shoot her, but sitting on the toilet, wide-eyed as always, pants around his ankles, a perfectly round black hole in his forehead, the magazine he had been reading open on the floor and splattered with blood.

Her stomach heaved and she slammed the door shut, just as an ear-piercing scream rent the air behind her. Nan whirled around.

Mathilde stood in the doorway, mouth frozen open, fingers clutched to her throat. She was staring at the bed.

Nan sheathed her knife and hurried toward her, trying to block her view of Rupert's body. "Get back on deck. Now."

"Rupert," she screamed and pushed Nan back into the room.

Nan grabbed her by the shoulders. "Mathilde! Somebody has to man the controls. Please. Come on. I'll call the police."

"No!" whimpered Mathilde and wrenched away. She stared down at the body, shaking her head.

Nan came up beside her and they both stood looking down at Rupert's lifeless body.

"Ladies."

Nan recognized that voice. A shroud of disappointment fell over her. Slowly she turned to confront him.

Damon stepped into the stateroom. The pistol he held was aimed at Nan, but his attention was riveted on Rupert's body.

She stared at him openmouthed. How did he get on board if he was following Mathilde? And why was he here? It seemed like a lot of running around. Follow Rupert and Barney to the yacht, kill them, then go to the house to finish off Mathilde, then follow her here. Why not just shoot her as she left the house?

But he had shot at her. And missed. The image of those perfectly round holes sprang to her mind. Damon would not miss.

Mathilde broke and ran at Damon.

"No," cried Nan. She was surprised when there was no explosion or flash from the pistol he held. It just wobbled as Mathilde threw herself into his free arm.

"John, John, thank God you're here." Mathilde clawed at his shirt; a pathetic little gesture that looked ridiculous coming from Mathilde. He tried to push her away to no avail. She stuck to him like a barnacle.

Nan should have reacted. Tried to overpower him in the momentary confusion, but she stood rooted to the floor, thinking, *John*?

"She killed Rupert. Don't let her kill me," Mathilde begged between sobs.

Nan managed to recover enough to say, "Don't be a fool, Mathilde. You know I didn't kill Rupert. I don't know who you think *John* is, but his name is Damon Connelly and he's a hired hit man."

Mathilde shook her head and continued to cling to Damon.

Then Nan saw Damon's expression and it hit her so hard and so low, that she staggered back against the bed.

Damon Connelly was a hit man. John whoever-he-was was not. And he wasn't a detective. He was just a common ordinary murderer. And a nasty suspicion seeped into her numbed mind.

She'd been set up. Damon and Mathilde were in this together. Mathilde hadn't hired her to protect Rupert, but to take the fall for his murder. The murder that the two of them must have planned together.

She'd walked right into their trap, like an innocent doe. Love? She had been thinking love? An involuntary cry escaped her. What a fool she had been.

"No wonder you wouldn't tell me who hired you. I thought it was organized crime, but it was Mathilde, wasn't it? And she hired me to watch Rupert, so I'd be on the scene when he was killed. Clever. Very clever."

Damon's head jerked toward Mathilde. "Mathilde hired you?"

"Oh, please." Nan stared hard at Damon/John, blinking back tears of betrayal. She'd be damned if she'd let him see how much she cared.

His gaze flitted from Nan to Mathilde and back again. He tightened his hold on Mathilde, and Nan's sense of betrayal deepened. All the time, he had been working for Mathilde. All last night—How could he? How could she—she pushed the memory away. She wouldn't go without a fight.

If she could somehow reach the hunting knife that was only inches from her fingers. She took a step toward the side of the bed. Thinking furiously. There was no escape. She'd never get past Damon. But she might be able to drop behind the bed long enough to draw her knife. Would a mattress stop bullets fired this close? And could she get close enough to stab him before she died?

"Don't move," Damon ordered. His voice was tight and harsh. "Shit."

Her heel hit metal. The pistol. She had forgotten about it. The odds suddenly got better.

"Or what?" Nan managed. She nudged the gun barrel with her toe until the handle was facing her. "You'll shoot? Say you caught me red-handed and I tried to kill you, too." Her voice cracked; she couldn't stop it.

It was now or never. Just drop, aim, and fire. She had no choice.

Damon looked back at Mathilde. "I think we need a few questions answered before we proceed."

"Proceed to what?" Nan's tone was sarcastic, she hoped. The pistol was lying there at her feet. Why didn't she just do it? What was she waiting for? "The part where you tell me who you really are? Did you kill Rupert or did Mathilde?"

"Don't be a fool. I didn't kill Rupert, I'm—"

"A thief, a murderer, a hit man, and what else? Mathilde's accomplice and lover? How many names do you go by?" She wouldn't be able to shoot him. Not even knowing what he was and how he'd used her.

"You've got it wrong, you little hellion. Now, I want some answers—from both of you." He tried to ease Mathilde away, but she clung to him, whimpering and grasping at his shirt.

In the momentary distraction, Nan dropped to the ground, grabbed the pistol and crouched, aiming it at Damon. Damon hadn't even tried to stop her.

"Now you don't move, either of you."

Mathilde froze.

Damon's eyes flickered with intensity. "Hannah."

Nan slowly stood up, keeping the pistol trained on the two of them. "Don't call me that. Drop your gun."

"Nan."

"Don't call me that, either. Don't call me anything. Just drop the gun and move away from the door. And take lady-bird with you."

"Okay, stay calm. Just let me put the safety back on." He didn't wait for her okay, but flicked the safety catch. The gun dropped quietly to the carpet.

Nan's mouth opened. She shut it. It was actually working. Hooray for Hollywood. She began to edge toward the door. She could feel the pistol trembling in her grasp and just hoped that Damon/John didn't see. She felt sick, not triumphant.

She paused at the door and took one last look at the man she had fallen in love with.

"Oh," she said, her voice steeled with sarcasm. "Nice fuck, by the way." She backed out the door as her tears finally brimmed over.

She turned and bolted up the stairway to the main deck. She'd never get to the ship to shore radio to mayday the harbor patrol. She could already hear Damon's footsteps behind her. She leapt onto the rail and without another thought dove overboard.

Chapter Eight

The pistol flew from her hand when she hit the water. Part of her mind registered that she had just lost the murder weapon, but the rest was concentrating on getting away from the yacht and out of pistol range.

She wouldn't have much of a chance once they spotted her.

She swam beneath the surface, fighting the buoyancy of the saltwater that kept pulling her back to the surface. It was a struggle, but she managed to stay under until her lungs couldn't hold air a second longer. She had to take a breath or drown.

She angled upward; her head broke the surface and her body was spit out of the sea. She gasped for one breath before forcing herself back into the water. It wasn't enough, but she didn't dare take longer.

This time she stayed closer to the surface. She didn't have the strength to fight the salt and still be able to distance herself from the yacht. She wasn't sure which direction she was headed and at the moment, didn't care.

She just kept swimming, hoping she was headed for land. She didn't relish drowning any more than she did being shot. When she surfaced again, she took enough time to look around, while she pushed off her sneakers to get rid of the extra weight.

She dove again. In the brief moment she was above water,

she had seen a strip of land. But it was really far away. Mathilde must have ignored her order to keep the boat steady. Nan had no idea how far they'd come or where she was.

But land was her only hope of survival. She headed for it. If she could reach it before they spotted her, she might be able to get help.

She was having to resurface more often now. She was getting tired. The next time she came up for air, she took the time to look for the yacht, treading water as she turned in all directions. Found it and her heart sank in disappointment. It seemed to be in the same position as before. Surely she had made some progress in outdistancing them.

The sound of the engine carried on the water. It was still idling. They would be on deck, searching for her; waiting for her to appear above the waves before coming after her. Well, they would have to come; if she had to dive again, she would drown.

Her arms and legs were burning from fatigue, but she turned to her stomach and began swimming for the dot of land. It was her only choice. She swam, hand over hand, until her shoulders ached and her kick died to a sputter. She was getting weaker. And it seemed that the land got no closer.

Finally, she turned to her back, spit out seawater and forced air into lungs that threatened to seize up. She floated, keeping her eyes on the yacht, willing strength back into her arms and legs, and waiting for the first shot.

A sailboat was tacking across the bay away from her. If only it would turn and come toward her, she might get help from the people on board. But it continued to move across the horizon until it was swallowed up by the glare of the sun. She closed her eyes and light dots danced on the inside of her lids. Then she heard it. A motor getting closer, but not the yacht. She opened her eyes to see a speedboat heading in her direction.

She waved feeble arms and realized that they couldn't see

her over the lifted bow. Soon it would plow right over her. She flipped to her stomach and began swimming like her life depended on it. It did.

The boat passed her in a deafening roar of engine. The wake rolled over her, swamping her efforts to escape and forcing water into her nose and mouth. But it also propelled her away from the boat's engine. She lost all sense of direction: forward, back, up or down as the waves swept her along. Her body banged into something hard. She grabbed for it as the water rolled by.

And she was still alive when the waves subsided and calm returned.

She was clutching one of the buoys that marked the water depth along the shoreline. Clinging to it, her head just above the water, she worked her way around until it shielded her from the yacht.

She rested long enough to get a second wind, then swam toward the nearest point of land.

It seemed an eternity before her feet reached down and found solid ground. Not exactly solid; the sand drifted away, her feet sank, and she pitched forward. She floundered against the drag of the water, stretched her legs downward until she found another foothold, and finally managed to drag herself onto a tiny beach of sand and pebbles.

She coughed and gagged, took in air, and coughed again. Slowly her head stopped spinning; her eyes began to focus. She pushed to her hands and knees and crawled across the sand to the curtain of sea grass that rose behind it, and collapsed, hidden among the prickly stalks.

She must have slept or passed out because the sun had passed its zenith when she at last sat up. She cautiously rose to her knees and looked over the tips of the beach grass. The bay lay before her; several boats dotted its surface. But none of them was the *Lady Chardonnay*.

She blinked several times, shook her head, and looked again just to make sure the yacht was really gone. Had they given up? It didn't make sense. How could they let her go, knowing what she knew?

She tried to orient her position to the sun. She must be on the south shore of some piece of land, but that was all she could manage. Her brain must be waterlogged. Where was she? And where were all the people? Not a soul on the beach, just a row of dunes that rose up behind her. Shit. She was on a beach in the most densely populated area on the East Coast. It was summer and there wasn't a lifeguard, sunbather, or concession stand in sight.

Maybe it was a private beach. Maybe she'd find a nice mansion on the other side of the dunes, complete with bottled water and a telephone.

She crept through the sea grass, ignoring the slash of the scaly stalks across her face and the chafing of the salt-encrusted jeans on her legs.

She found a path through the dunes, and a sign at the entrance. *No fires, no camping, no swimming, no hiking, no pets, no trespassing.* Well, that about covered it. No wonder nobody was here. No fun.

She reached the crest of the dunes and peered down the other side. A depression filled with beach heather. And beyond it, higher dunes with a forest of windswept scrub oaks and pine trees growing precariously on its slopes. She followed the path into the depression, then climbed through the forest to the top of the second row of dunes—and found just what she expected to find: marshes; crisscrossed by tidal streams, and probably filled with mosquitoes. Another expanse of water—the Sound?—and another strip of land that was barely visible in the distance.

She growled in frustration. It was too far to swim. And even if she could, chances were just as good that she'd land on the only other deserted strip of beach on the East Coast as they were of finding herself in the middle of downtown Newport.

She sighed and retraced her way down the sheltered side of

the dunes and into the heather. She paused to look out over a sea of downy shrubs, their tiny black berries just beginning to form.

It was beautiful and if she didn't have two murderers chasing her, she would enjoy spending time here.

But she did and she needed to get a plan.

She knew her way around wilderness and this certainly qualified. She could probably hold them off indefinitely. What she needed was a base of operation. And she found it a few minutes later, set back in the shrubs near another path that led down to the shore: a dried wooden platform with a primitive roof and a half wall that opened onto a pond. A duck blind. But not hunting season.

The pond was clear as a mirror, surrounded by grasses and banks of moss. So tempting. It would be too much to ask that it held fresh water.

She leaned over and dipped her hands in. The water was warm, almost hot. It must be fed by a thermal spring. She touched the tip of her finger to her lips. And no salt. Thank you, God. She was thirsty, but she knew better than to drink untested water. She'd have to boil it first.

Which meant building a fire—an illegal fire. And just hope the Coast Guard would arrest her before Damon/John and Mathilde found her and killed her. But in the meantime, she could wash the salt out of her clothes. She unsnapped the knife that had miraculously survived her swim. Then she stripped out of her clothes, threw them in the pool and waded in after them.

The water was only chest deep and it felt heavenly. The temperature was just right for a long soak. She lowered herself until only her head was above water. So much nicer than the frigid waves of the Sound. She let the warmth invade her body until relaxation set in, and she began to think how nice it would be to share this with . . . anyone but Damon Connelly. She stood up.

A breeze wafted through the trees and she shivered. She

rescued her clothes from the bottom of the pool and scrubbed them hard. Then she walked out of the pool, dressed in her wet underwear and T-shirt and left her jeans spread out on a shrub to dry.

She wandered off the trail, gathering pieces of wood dry enough to start a fire, while she kept an eye out for something to use as a container for the water.

She had just dumped an armload of kindling on the beach and was going back to retrieve her jeans when she saw something lying at the low tide mark. A message in a bottle? A genie with three wishes? A box of dry matches? Or just a useless piece of garbage. She went over to investigate.

It was Damon Connelly.

He was out cold. Or maybe dead. After a second of stunned disbelief, Nan dropped to her knees and laid her fingers on his neck, checking for a pulse. A larger hand grabbed her and pulled her down. She fell across him.

Damon's arms wrapped around her in a full nelson. He was pretty weak and the struggle was brief.

She pushed away from him and sat back on her heels. "Still alive, I see."

"Hannah?" he asked feebly.

"I told you not to call me that."

Damon tried to raise himself to his elbow, but fell back onto the sand.

Then she saw the trickle of blood and seawater that snaked down his temple and her anger evaporated. "Hold still." She leaned over him and separated hair that was matted with blood, salt, and sand. Probed his scalp. An inch long gash slashed diagonally toward his ear.

"How many fingers do I see?" asked Damon.

"You'll do. Have a falling out among murderers?"

"I didn't—" His sentence dropped off as she began frisking him.

"No weapon." His eyes closed and his lips curved into a faint smile as her hands passed over his legs. "Ummm."

Her hand swept over his pocket. Stopped when she felt something hard. Flinched, then realizing there really was something in his pocket, she slid her hand inside.

"Good. Really good."

"Stop it." She yanked her hand out, taking the contents of his pocket with her. "What's this?"

Damon blinked. "Radio part. Didn't want them calling for reinforcements."

Them? Was there more than the two of them in this? She stuffed the part back into his pocket and moved to the other side.

When she was satisfied that he was weapon-free, she stood up and turned to search the horizon. No *Lady Chardonnay*.

"Where's the yacht? What happened to Mathilde? What happened to you?"

"They panicked. Hit me over the head. Guess they tossed me overboard."

"They?"

"Yeah."

"Who? Why?"

Damon merely groaned.

Nan grabbed him by his shirt and hauled him to a sitting position. "Look, you lying, conniving, murdering son of—"

Damon lowered his head to his hands. "I'm going to throw up."

He did. With Nan holding his head. He tried to lie back down, but Nan held him upright.

"Better?" She gave him a little shake to get his attention. "Now start explaining."

Damon clutched his arms around his chest and started shivering. His teeth began sending out an erratic Morse code of dits and dots.

Nan tried not to look concerned. Tried not to care whether he lived or died. Tried to steel her heart against that woebegone look on his ashen face. She failed.

"Oh, shit. Can you walk if I help?"

She pulled him to his feet, threw an unresponsive arm over her shoulder, and supporting most of his weight, staggered across the beach toward the dunes. She dropped him unceremoniously on the sand and began digging out a pit for a fire.

She stacked the wood into a teepee at the bottom of the pit. She reached for her belt and the knife strapped there and touched bare butt. Shit. Her jeans were still drying on the bushes. She darted a quick look toward Damon.

His eyes closed quickly, but not quick enough. His mouth was curved in his signature predatory smile. Not quite up to its usual wattage, but predatory nonetheless.

Her heart thunked against her chest. Damn. She turned away before he saw the blush creep over her face and raced up the path spurting sand in a wake behind her.

When she returned a few minutes later, she was fully clothed and holding her case knife at the ready.

Damon was sitting up, looking like a rakish Robinson Crusoe.

She skirted around him and stood over him out of reach. "All right, start talking."

He looked up. "What's for dinner?"

"Your liver if you don't come up with some answers to my questions."

"What questions? I'm cold and hungry."

"Stop whining. Did you kill Rupert or did Mathilde?"

"Not me."

God, he acted more like a pouting two-year-old than a dangerous hit man.

"Why did she call you John?"

"That's my name."

"Are you Damon Connelly or John somebody? Because if you're not Damon Connelly you should really let me know."

He just shrugged and avoided her eyes.

This was getting her nowhere. Maybe she should tie him up and torture him until he talked. Umm. Now that had possibilities. *Shit.* She needed to keep focused or risk getting murdered. Forget torture and where that might lead, just secure him. She unbuckled her belt and pulled it off.

Damon perked up.

"Put your hands behind you," she ordered.

"Not now, Hannah, I have a headache." He touched his head and winced. "Maybe if we got something to eat. Can't you snare a rabbit or something?"

Nan found herself inexplicably on the verge of tears. She bit her lip, hard enough to draw blood. It didn't make her feel better, but it did steel her nerve.

"Are you Damon Connelly?"

"Didn't you get my note?"

Nan snorted. "Trust you. Right. You're a hired killer. Among other things. How could you. How could I—"

"Like this." He reached toward her. Her knife flashed as she swiped it across the air. He fell back, toppled over, and curled into a ball.

It was probably a trick. She'd missed him by a mile. "Get up." No reaction. She poked at him with her foot. Nothing. She sheathed her knife and dropped down beside him.

"Jesus. I'm freezing," he mumbled. His skin was cold and clammy. Hypothermia. He must have been in the water a long time. It was amazing he survived.

It shouldn't matter. It would be better if he were dead. She would be safer, and the world would be a better place. But she didn't really feel that way.

"What you need is a hot bath."

"F-f-funny."

"No really. It isn't the Ritz, but it's got hot water. But you'll have to walk."

"Can't." He curled tighter.

She flicked his butt with the tip of her knife.

"All right. All right." He struggled to his feet.

Chapter Nine

Damon fell back into the water with a splash. She hadn't even given him time to take off the one shoe he was still wearing. She just pushed him in, fully clothed, and walked away, hands on those tight little hips, looking back over her shoulder like she wanted to kill him.

"Aren't you coming in with me?" he called after her. "What if I pass out and drown?"

"If you pass out, it will be because all the blood went to your dick, and you deserve it." She stomped off, leaving him alone.

God, his head hurt. He unbuttoned his shirt and pulled it off. Let it float on the water while he threw his one shoe on the bank, then took off his jeans and boxers.

He eased down into the water, let his head fall back and the warmth reach his scalp. The cut on his head stung like crazy and he gingerly washed the salt and crud away. He found a soft spot of moss that grew down to the water's edge and lay back.

That was better. He might live after all.

Only it wouldn't really matter if he didn't explain things to Hannah. He'd blown the job, but he would be damned if he'd blow his chances with Hannah. Rupert Sims was dead. Somebody had beaten them to him and Damon knew who it was. Not that it made a hell of a lot of difference now. Rupert wouldn't be testifying against anybody ever again.

He might as well tell Hannah everything, not that she would like him any better as John Connors. But that was all he had to give. She'd have to take it or leave it. Take or leave him. And that's what frightened him. Actually the fact that he was thinking in those terms was pretty frightening.

Maybe he did have a concussion. He held up two fingers and looked at them. Two fingers. Okay, so maybe he was just losing his mind.

As soon as he felt halfway human again, he wrung out his clothes and laid them over the sides of what looked like a dilapidated duck blind. Duck would be good. With orange sauce.

Now that he was getting back to speed, he realized that they were in a predicament. Stuck on an island, obviously, or Hannah wouldn't still be here. Once Mathilde and whoever her accomplice was got their fear under control, they would be back looking for Hannah and him. His stomach clenched at the thought of her getting hurt.

He'd have to do something to protect her. They would probably be safe until morning. The sun was setting fast and even though Mathilde might remember their position when they went overboard, she wouldn't be able to do anything about it before light.

A rustle alerted him to Hannah's return. He slid back into the water and draped himself across the mossy bank, the lower half of him floating just below the surface of the water. He closed his eyes and tried not to get turned on by the thought of her.

He watched through half-closed lids until she came to stand beside the pool, feet spread apart. She was holding something bundled in leaves with one hand and a—he opened one eye wider to get a better look—a spear. Christ. Hannah the Amazon. A very petite but lip-smacking Amazon.

"Damon."

He held his breath, trying not to respond.

"Damon?" She stepped in the water, spit out an expletive and stepped out again, shaking the water off the cuffs of her jeans.

Come on, he thought. *Just come here.*

She scowled at him. "This had better not be one of your tricks." She hesitated, then unzipped her jeans, pushed them down her legs—God, she had incredible legs—and stepped out of them.

She waded toward him until the water covered her little patch of bikini underwear. Damon used every piece of willpower he possessed not to move. Then she was waist deep in the pool, the cotton of her T-shirt soaking up the water. She was driving him out of his mind. *Don't stop.*

He closed his eyes completely, not wanting to give himself away. But something else was going to do it for him. The closer she came, the harder he got. He eased his hips down in the water, hoping she had missed the evidence.

She must have. She splashed over to him. "Damon?" There was an edge of hysteria in her voice. Fear that he was dead? She must care a little. She leaned over him.

He pulled her into his arms and hung on while she fought like a wildcat to free herself.

"Stop it, I'm an injured man," he said when he finally managed to pin her to the carpet of moss. "I'm not going to hurt you. I—" He lost his train of thought.

She was moving beneath him, in a halfhearted attempt to free herself. But all she managed to do was to arouse them both.

He slid into the water, pulling her with him. "I'll explain everything. It's too late to matter."

She stopped fighting. Looked at him with that little tilt of her head. It made him want to kiss her. But that would have to wait.

"Okay, start talking." Her words were clipped, but her heart was beating fast and furious against his chest.

He pulled her closer until the silk between her legs caressed the tip of his erection. She tried to move away, but he kept her there. If he hurried with his explanation, maybe they'd . . .

"I'm not Damon Connelly. I just, uh, appropriated his name and profession for a particular job."

She stopped moving and he felt her weight settle against him. *Oh, yeah. Better hurry.*

"Then who are you? And why are you impersonating a hit man and a rapist?" She bit out the last word. That had really troubled her.

"Stop asking questions. I'll tell you what I can. And you'll have to trust me for the rest."

He expected another derisive snort at that, but she crossed her feet behind his back and settled in for the story. Settled herself on him.

Damon fought to keep his train of thought. "Rupert Sims contacted the, uh, people I work for. He'd gotten involved with some of his old business associates and couldn't uninvolve himself. He agreed to testify against them in exchange for protection, a new identity, the usual stuff."

"You work for the government?"

He placed two fingers over her lips to silence her. "But he got cold feet. Decided to take his chances. Then word reached him that a contract had been taken out on him. He was scared. We thought he'd turn pretty fast, but the man hired for the hit met with an untimely accident."

"Damon Connelly?"

He nodded. "And I took his place in order to keep up the pressure and to make sure no one else killed him before we got him."

"Oops."

"Oops is right. Now the whole thing is shot to shit and we, they, have to start all over with another stooge."

"I didn't kill Rupert."

Damon laughed softly. "I figured that out about the time

you lunged for the murder weapon and disappeared over the side."

"And you're really not Damon Connelly?"

"Nope. You can call me John. From now on." And that was as far as he got with his explanation until much, much later.

Hannah's arms tightened around his neck. She released her leg hold on his waist and slid down him until she was poised for entry. He pulled her panties aside and obliged, entering her with an uncontrolled thrust. She cried out, but before he could apologize, he realized that she was laughing—and crying. And he felt weak in the knees. He walked them over to the moss and leaned her against the bank. Her breasts arched toward him, the water lapped at her butt and legs.

He pulled out slowly until just the tip of him was enclosed in her warmth. Then he drove himself in again. And again. Each time he bore into her, she pushed back, and the water slapped against them and rippled away, heightening his response.

His body threatened to race out of control; he slowed down. He lifted his chest away and looked down at her, at them, attached like a mythical animal at the groin. The new box of condoms in the glove compartment of the MG flashed across his mind. Too little, too late. He and Hannah were completely naked, joined flesh to flesh in Shangri-la. This had to be a sign. Surely.

She was looking back at him, her gaze burning the air between them, and he pressed higher into her, slowly, claiming every bit of her as his.

Hannah's breath came out in a rush. He thrust into her again, faster, harder. Rushing toward oblivion. They shattered together. And lay panting; listening to each other's heartbeats, while the water stilled and settled around them calm and serene.

Damon looked down at her, bemused. Her eyes were closed. The red-gold of her hair spread across the velvety green of the bank. He slipped his arm under her waist, and keeping her pressed to him, slid her into the heat of the water.

She smiled lazily and sighed. He shifted onto his back until she was floating on top of him, the length of their bodies touching. Damon felt himself grow hard inside her. God, she was going to kill him, but what a way to go. He smiled. This time he'd take time for foreplay.

He moved inside her, just enough to get her attention.

"The fish," she murmured.

"Very romantic."

She sighed a laugh. "The fish I caught for dinner. They're on the ground. We should cook them . . ."

"Hang the fish." He slid his palms over her wet back, cupped his hands over her ass and circled her against him until he was rock hard and she was panting. He swam them backwards until they came to the opposite bank, slid his hands up her sides and lifted her arms until her hands touched the grass. Then he ducked under water, sliding out of her and along her body, slipping her bikinis down until his mouth was where his dick had been. His fingers spread her open and he blew bubbles until she began to squirm and he was out of breath.

He surfaced between her legs, facing her, his shoulders supporting her thighs. Held her when she tried to turn over. "Hold onto the bank."

Her hands groped at the grass and he lifted her up until his tongue could reach every place he wanted to be. He licked from front to back like she was his favorite ice cream. Only this one was hot and sweet.

She made a funny catching sound, high and soft. He licked again. She pushed forward against him. His erection throbbed below the water. He tried to touch all of her at once. She shuddered. Arched against him and pushed against his shoulders until she was kneeling on the ground. It was the most beautiful sight he had ever seen. But when he followed her, she turned over and held him still. She shifted to sit on her knees. Which brought her mouth so close.

Her breath caressed his dick, and he jerked so hard that he nearly fell back into the water.

Hannah chuckled and blew on him again. Chills played up and down his back. He pressed his hips forward and she responded with a flick of her tongue.

Damon groaned. Another flick of her tongue, then a slow, burning lick from base to tip while her hands slipped between his legs and cradled his balls.

They tightened in response; her tongue reached the tip of him. She squeezed him gently as her lips replaced her tongue and she sucked him in. His world constricted; her tongue swirled around him and he exploded into oblivion.

Chapter Ten

Nan knelt in the sand by the teepee of wood. She was once again wearing her bikinis and T-shirt. Her jeans and his jeans and shirt were spread out on the beach grass to finish drying in the last warm rays of the setting sun.

She finished adjusting the twigs and placed a handful of heather down in their midst. She snapped open the leather sheath of her hunting knife, then turned the sheath over and unsnapped a smaller back pocket.

Damon watched in awe as a length of solid flint slid out.

She placed the flint at an angle toward the down and struck knife to flint. "Not ideal. I should have some char cloth, and a piece of carbon steel, but this will have to do." She struck at the flint again and shrugged. "Haven't had to do this in a while."

She continued striking the knife against the flint, while Damon leaned forward to watch, his skepticism written plainly on his face.

Without warning a small piece began to smolder.

Nan dropped the knife and flint and blew lightly onto the tinder, sheltering the thin line of smoke with her body. It went out. She tried again and after several attempts a tiny flame curled up the mound of down and caught the finger-size pieces of tinder.

She continued to blow on the flames while she added

pieces of wood. When the fire was blazing, she ran the fish through with her makeshift spear and wedged the spear into the sand so the fish hovered above the flames.

She sat back and caught Damon watching her. His expression made her heart leap. She couldn't tell if his heightened color was a blush or the beginnings of sunburn.

He looked away and slapped his face. "Is this the part where we get devoured by mosquitoes?"

Nan shook her head. "Move closer to the fire. They don't like the smoke."

"Neither do I," he grumbled and scooted closer.

She smiled at him. "You wouldn't last an hour at Camp Wilderness."

"No. But I'm dynamite in back alleys." He pulled her back until she sat close to him, his arm encircling her. "And I'm better at stealing a car than you are."

Nan pulled back to look at him. "I only did that once."

"I know. Your stepfather's."

"How did you know that?"

He squeezed her shoulders. "All in a day's work."

"So how many cars did you steal?"

He shrugged. "Lost count."

"Did you ever get caught?"

"Lots of times."

"Then you've been in jail."

"Lots of time." He grinned but his voice became serious. "Only as a juvenile. I grew up and stopped—" He paused.

"Getting caught?" she finished for him.

He stared at the fire. "Look, Hannah, I'm not your average pristine citizen. I'm not even very nice. But what I do . . . what I do is, let's just say, it's condoned by certain authorities."

"You're some kind of agent?"

"Not exactly an agent."

"Then what?"

"I sort of freelance for the good guys."

Nan frowned at him. "Doing what?"

"Whatever."

"Killing? Not Rupert?"

He looked affronted. "No."

"What about Damon Connelly?"

"I didn't kill him, either, but I would have been glad to oblige. I met him at—well, one of those times I got caught. We sat next to each other at mess. Alphabetical. Connelly, Connors." He shrugged. "He was a mean son of a bitch even then. Had us all scared to shit. Killed a kid once with a knife made out of a soupspoon.

"Jimmy Lutz. Just a little runt of a thing with red hair and freckles. Not even a bad kid. Just a troubled kid from the suburbs, one of those who fell through the upwardly mobile cracks. No wilderness camp for him; they put him in there with us." He laughed, a bitter sound as he remembered, and Nan slipped her hand in his.

"And he didn't come out. He died for bullshit. Connelly was out two years later. Rehabilitated. God, I hated him."

They grew silent; watched the flames, Hannah occasionally turning the spit so the fish would cook evenly.

"I didn't kill him," he said into the darkness. "But I could have. I have killed. I guess you've probably figured that out."

Nan hadn't figured it out and she didn't want to know. She pulled the spit out of the sand and used her knife to push the fish onto leaves. She handed one to Dam—John.

Their eyes caught in the firelight. She turned back to the fire and checked the coffee can of water. They'd found it in the duck blind, filled with ashes and cigarette butts. But she'd scrubbed it with sand, then washed it in the pond before filling it with fresh water, while Damon watched, thinking that a part of them was in that water.

They ate in silence, appreciating the taste of fresh catch. And finished their meal with sips of hot water from the coffee can they passed back and forth between them.

"I'm not one of the good guys, Hannah. But I work for the good guys. Sometimes you have to . . . you know."

But she didn't.

She continued to feed the fire as the night grew dark around them. And Damon marveled at the dichotomy of her, debutante, wild child, woodswoman, wonder woman.

And he felt the loss of what might have been between them if things had been different. And he had no one to blame but himself.

They slept huddled by the fire, arms and legs entwined, their bodies molding out depressions in the sand. They didn't make love or talk. Just lay together, hearts beating, lost in their own thoughts, and waiting for morning and the return of the *Lady Chardonnay.*

Damon looked up at the stars and wondered why he'd come so close only to lose the woman in his arms. And he would lose her. It couldn't last. Not after the things he'd told her.

Nan held his arms tight around her, trying to put herself in his place, but couldn't manage it. She had killed deer, rabbits, squirrels, but never a human being.

But she couldn't judge him because he had. It was a necessary job, like being a policeman or a soldier. Someone had to do it, she was just glad it wasn't her. She leaned close to him and whispered in his ear. "It's all right. I do understand."

He heard her, but didn't quite believe her. He pulled her close and held on for dear life.

Dawn was just breaking when they heard the sound of an engine, growing closer. Without speaking, they hid in the grass and looked out to sea. Not the harbor police or the Coast Guard, but the *Lady Chardonnay.*

"Damn," muttered Damon.

"Damn," Nan agreed. "I can't believe no one came to make us put out the fire. I'm writing a letter to the Harbor Commission."

The yacht dropped anchor just outside of the buoys.

Nothing happened for a few minutes, then another sound replaced the purr of the engine.

"They're lowering the dinghy," said Nan.

"All right, this is how we play this. You'll—" Damon began.

"*We'll* stay put," said Nan, guessing what he was about to say, and giving him a sideways look. "If they spotted the fire, they'll beach the dinghy and start looking."

"And you'll—"

"*We'll* wait until we know their strategy and then decide."

"You think they'll have a strategy?"

Nan looked at him in consternation. "Well, if they don't, we'll—"

"Separate and separate them."

She nodded. He gave her a quick kiss and they settled in to wait for the dinghy to land.

Nan saw him first. Carl Sims, dwarfed by the automatic weapon he held crooked in his arm, stood in the prow of the dinghy as it slid onto the beach and came to a stop on the sand.

"Fuck." Damon grabbed Nan's elbow, "Stay—"

"No. Which one do you want?"

"Jesus, Nan. I can't let you."

"You don't have a choice." She met him stare for stare. John's eyes were hard as flint, then they surrendered.

"You go around to the other side of the boat. Try to catch Mathilde off guard."

"What are you going to do?"

"I'm going to distract Carl and run like hell until you can come and save me." He grinned at her.

She nodded and kissed him quick and hard. Then she moved away and crept through the sea grass toward the point of land at the end of the beach.

When she was at the edge of the dune she peered through the grasses. The dinghy was beached and Carl was running toward the spot where she had left Da—John. He held the artillery across his chest, ready to fire.

She fervently hoped he tripped and drilled himself full of holes. She should be the one eluding Carl, not D—John. She was the one with wilderness experience, she knew how to stalk quarry and she knew how to hide so that she wouldn't be seen, heard, or smelled.

She pulled her eyes and mind away. John could take care of himself.

Mathilde stood in the prow, her hand shielding her eyes as she watched Carl scramble into the grasses. Nan stepped into the water, silently, smoothly, not making any movement that would alert the wicked widow.

She circled the dinghy, going out far enough so that she could climb into the starboard side. There was nothing she could do about the sound of water dripping onto the deck as she pulled herself on board.

Mathilde turned just as she threw her legs over the side. For a moment she only stared at Nan, while Nan pushed to her feet, and stood up. Then she gabbed an oar and swung it at Nan's head.

Nan ducked as the oar fanned the air over her head. The action pulled Mathilde off balance. Nan threw herself forward.

Her head connected with Mathilde's stomach and her breath went out in a huge *whumf*. Mathilde hit the deck, flailing underneath the weight of Nan's body. She screeched and snarled, kicked and clawed the air and any part of Nan she could reach. Nan pinned her arms to the deck and sat on her.

The repeated rat-tat of gunfire split the air. God, Damon—John—shit. Nan released one of Mathilde's arms. Mathilde rose up, and Nan's fist connected with her surgery enhanced jaw. It landed with a crunch; Mathilde fell back and her head hit the deck with a thud.

Nan flipped her over. Another round of gunfire, farther

away. She pushed off Mathilde and flew to the tack box. Pulled her knife out and cut the nylon lead line to the anchor.

The dinghy wobbled as she ran back to Mathilde, tied her hands together, pulled her feet back until her knees were bent at a ninety degree angle and tied them, too. Mathilde was trussed like a deer on a car hood.

Nan didn't give her a second look but sheathed her knife and jumped over the side. She hit the beach at a full run. Another round of fire. At least he was still firing. It must mean that John was still alive and uncaptured.

She didn't slow down until she was at the top of the dune path. Carl was wading through the beach heather toward the stand of trees and shrubs that grew along the secondary dune. She searched the heather for a fallen body and breathed a sigh of relief. John must be hiding in the woods.

Her relief didn't last long. She heard the sound of someone crashing through the undergrowth. Saw the flattened top of the trees move as someone passed through. Carl saw it, too. And he followed it into the trees.

As soon as he disappeared beneath the branches, Nan began to run. The sand slowed her down; her calves were burning by the time she reached a path into the woods.

She entered the trees several hundred yards from where she had seen Carl disappear. She stopped to listen, heard them thrashing around downwind of her. But they were coming in her direction. Then she saw a flash of movement.

John was staying on the trail. Dangerous, but he would lead Carl straight to her. She whistled to alert him, a high bird call that was answered not by John, but another bird. Great. She hoped he didn't get confused. No. He was running down the path toward her. She turned and monkey-climbed up an oak whose misshapened limbs spanned the path. She shimmied along a branch hoping it would hold her weight. John passed beneath her, so close that she could have reached him with her toes. She pulled up her feet. Carl ran full tilt past her. She dropped. Carl went down.

She eased off him ready to knock him senseless, but Carl didn't move.

"That's my girl."

Nan looked up. John was leaning against a tree, his arms crossed like he was out for a stroll. He grinned at her, then wandered over and looked down at the recumbent Carl.

He shook his head. "You know, with your brawn and my brains, we'd make a perfect team."

Carl moaned. John scooped the rifle off the ground and training it on the fallen man, he hauled him to his feet. He quickly frisked him and relieved him of his cell phone. Then he motioned with the rifle for Carl to start moving.

Nan watched, her exhilaration of the chase aborted by his statement. Partners? What kind of partners? Was he serious, or was he just being his usual flippant self?

Silently, she followed him back into the sunlight.

John laughed when they reached the boat and he saw Mathilde trussed up like a hunting specimen. He flashed Nan an approving look.

He used the rest of the line to bind Carl's hands and feet, then used the confiscated cell phone to make two calls.

Two? One to the Coast Guard or harbor police and one to whom? His boss, apprising him of the death of Rupert Sims? He didn't say, merely snapped the phone shut and slipped it into his pocket.

"Won't be long," he said. "Thank God that's over."

Nan nodded shortly, while she pushed down the disappointment that had superceded her relief. It was over. Mathilde and Carl would be taken off to jail and John would go back to wherever he came from. To his next assignment. And she would go on to hers.

A sharp stab of disappointment pierced her heart. He was glad that it was over. Well, hell, what did she expect. Really, what *did* she expect? She wasn't ready to live happily ever after with anybody. Not even Da—John Connors. Hell, she couldn't even remember to call him by his real name. If it was real.

She kept her eyes trained on their two prisoners. John did the same.

It was fifteen minutes before two large police boats roared into view. One veered away toward the yacht; the other one headed for the beach. When they were twenty feet away the pilot cut the engine, the motor was pulled up and a young officer dressed in Bermuda shorts dropped a ladder over the side and climbed into the water to guide the prow onto the sand.

Two uniformed men jumped to the sand, relieved John of his weapon and hustled Mathilde and Carl toward the boat and into the cabin. Two duffel bags arched over the sides and hit the beach with a thud. Forensic beach toys.

A man in a light gray suit stood on board watching the procedure. As soon as the prisoners disappeared below, he climbed down the ladder and walked fastidiously across the sand toward Nan and John.

"Connors," he said.

So okay, maybe his name was real.

The two men walked off some distance and talked, heads bent together, John occasionally nodding or shaking his head. Nan felt like the proverbial third wheel. Didn't she get to be debriefed, too? But neither of them paid her the least attention. Finally they turned and walked back toward her. The man tipped his chin at her, but continued past her toward the waiting police boat.

Jeez. *And thank you very much, too,* she thought. John had lagged behind and was walking slowly toward her. If this was good-bye, she'd be damned if she'd hear it now, then have to sit next to him back to Long Island pretending like it didn't matter. He could just wait.

She turned and followed the suit back to the boat, where the men were busy preparing to cast off. The suit turned around and looking past her, called out. "I suppose you want a few days off."

"At least that long," John called back.

Was he planning to spend them with her? That would be nice, she supposed. The sex was good. But it would just prolong the inevitable.

She grasped the ladder and started to climb. Suddenly she was whisked backward and dumped unceremoniously on the sand.

"What the hell?" she asked as John asked, "What's the hurry?"

"Don't they have to question us?"

"Nope. None of this happened. They'll finagle a plea bargain out of Mathilde and Carl. Then they'll start life anew as Mr. and Mrs. Small Town Couple in Small Town, U.S.A. Not as good as Rupert, but hey." He lifted his hands in a futile gesture.

The boat cast off and the engine roared to life.

Nan jumped up and brushed sand off the seat of her jeans. "They're leaving."

"Looks like it."

"But they're coming back, right?"

"Tomorrow."

She blinked in confusion.

"In the meantime . . ." He opened one of the duffel bags and pulled out a bottle of champagne. Shrugged, a half smile playing across his lips.

Nan looked down at the duffel bag; saw the tent pack lying next to it.

"Thought we could get started on a long term, uncasual, meaningful relationship." It was a statement, but the tilt of John's eyebrows turned it into a question. A question whose answer he was unsure of.

"How long term," she asked suspiciously.

"Um."

Nan listened to the whir of the boat's engine recede in the distance.

"Forever?"

Forever? Nan looked at him incredulously.

He was looking down at his feet.

She shook her head, amused. "At least that long."

John's mouth curved in a smile. It was the first one she'd seen that had no ulterior motive behind it. And it was perfect.

He caught her watching him. He shrugged and tossed the champagne bottle toward her, then hoisted the duffel bags and tent and took off toward the dunes, whistling.

MAN WITH A PAST

Chapter One

"Come on, boss. We've got a table at Falconi's for seven-thirty."

Geena Cole looked up from her desk at Women-Tek. Her two partners, Nan Scott and Delia Petrocelli, were dressed for the elements, Nan in a distressed bomber jacket, Delia in a London Fog trench coat belted at the waist. Rambo and Mike Hammer go Long Island.

Geena smiled, even though she was feeling anything but happy. "You two go on. I want to finish up the report on the Hollander case and I have to get up early in the morning."

"You're not going rappelling in this weather, are you?" asked Delia.

Nan gave Geena a halfhearted smile. "Well, if you change your mind, you know where to find us."

Geena fiddled with her pen while she listened to their footsteps echo down the hall, then the outer door click shut. The office seemed suddenly lonely and isolated. Sort of like Geena felt.

Maybe she should have gone with them, but she knew she would be out of place, especially the way she felt tonight. Not because she was the "boss" of the detective agency, but because Nan and Delia were getting on with their lives and she was stuck in limbo. Nan had John, even though he had the uncomfortable habit of disappearing for weeks at a time and then showing up just as unexpectedly. He'd been gone three weeks this time and Nan hadn't heard a word from him. But she trusted him to return and if she was worried about his safety, she didn't let on.

Delia was on an upward swing. She'd divorced her philandering plastic surgeon husband six months ago, and had lost thirty pounds and three dress sizes since coming to work for Women-Tek. Her self-esteem was growing daily, and it was just a matter of time until—

Geena tossed her pen onto the desk blotter. What was wrong with her? She never got maudlin or weepy, and she certainly never felt envious of her friends.

It was only November, too early in the season for light deprivation. It must be the weather. It had been a gray nasty day. Now it was a dark, nasty night. Rain slashed against the windowpanes; the wind moaned a haunting dirge as it swept down the street.

Geena shivered, pushed her tortoiseshell glasses resolutely up her nose, and looked down at the report on her computer screen. The report was finished. There was no reason to stay at the office. It wasn't like she didn't have anywhere to go.

Right. To a huge, sterile condo that overlooked Long Island Sound. It was way too big for her, but she'd bought it to appease her mother.

She could hear her words, even now. "You're an heiress even if you insist on this little hobby of yours. You have a responsibility. I should never have let your father send you to that wilderness camp. I told him, I said, Herbert, how is learning to rub sticks together going to teach her how to be a lady? But he said . . ."

And that was the problem, wasn't it. Camp Wilderness was supposed to make her appreciate her responsibilities as a member of a rich and pampered society, but it had made her self-reliant, independent, strong, with no desire to return to the entitled existence she had always taken for granted.

Once back on the social register, she had rebelled again,

this time for good. It had the same effect on Nan and eventually, Delia. Well, at least Nan and Delia had left their old life behind. Geena was still tied to hers. Only by one thin strand, but it was a strong one, incapable of being cut. Because it tied her heart to the past.

Cabot Vandermeer the Third. Her childhood friend, her teenage love, lost to her forever. It was days like this, rainy and chill, that brought the memories back. It had been rainy that terrible day, too, when he walked out of her life, leaving her empty and frightened and without hope. Someday she would have to get over him. It had been ten years. It was time to move on.

She heard the outer door whoosh open and close again. Nan and Delia must be coming back. She'd go with them. Hell, it was time to stop moping. She'd have dinner, then drive up to Mohonk; have her equipment ready at dawn, even if it was still raining. Just another challenge to overcome.

She closed the Hollander file and stood up just as the office door opened. "All right. You win. I—" She looked up. Not Nan and Delia, but a tall, bulky man, dressed in a sailor's pea coat, work pants, and boots. A dark cap was pulled low over his forehead and a beard covered the lower part of his face.

Geena froze. She should have locked the door when the others left. It was too late for walk-in clients. This man didn't look like a client. He looked like he was up to no good.

She slipped her feet out of her sensible pumps and unconsciously flexed her fingers as she eyed her visitor.

"Can I help you?" She was glad to hear that her voice sounded calm, in spite of the adrenaline coursing through her.

The man didn't move or speak. Just stood blocking the door. The cap hid his eyes, but she didn't need to see them to feel the intensity of his gaze.

She could take him, but she might need a weapon. She glanced toward the lamp on the corner of the desk. Heavy enough—just grab, yank the cord free, and aim at his head.

* * *

Cab stared at the woman standing behind the desk. He'd waited in the rain all afternoon until the other two women left. He didn't recognize them, and since there was still a light coming from the office of Women-Tek, he thought Geena must still be inside.

But this woman couldn't be his Genie.

His Genie was tall, but that was all they had in common. His Genie was all angles, not willowy. And full of fun and passion, not serious and self-assured like this one, her hair pulled severely back from her face. Heavy framed glasses magnified her eyes. Geena had traded her glasses in for contacts.

The woman flexed her fingers. They were strong and capable. His Genie had magic fingers. He shivered, thinking of those fingers, soft and curious, exploring his body and driving him wild with teenage lust.

And he felt a stab of incredible disappointment.

Then she pushed the frame of her glasses up her nose and he knew. He knew. It was the same gesture he'd watched her make a thousand times as they grew up together. The recognition was almost as devastating as his initial disappointment had been.

She was so different. Maybe too different.

For years, the thought of Geena had been the only thing that had kept him going. A fugitive, living hand-to-mouth around Europe, assuming one alias after another. Working at any job that didn't ask too many questions. He'd liked the freedom of his life, but he didn't like always looking over his shoulder. So when he heard that his uncle Ronald was going to have him declared dead, he returned to the States.

He knew Geena would help him. She'd always helped him, from the first day his family had moved to Long Island into the penthouse across from the Coles, where he'd pulled the fire alarm just to see what would happen, to the day she'd helped him escape the police.

When his father died, and he was sent to spend holidays and summers with Max while his mother traveled to mask her grief, Geena stood by him. She was a constant visitor and sometimes his only friend. Shoring him up when he faltered, shooting him down when he got out of hand, and flirting shamelessly with Max to save him from punishment when he'd committed some outrageous prank. No matter what, Geena had always been there for him.

Over the years, she'd given him so much and he'd taken it as his due. Her loyalty, her friendship, her virginity, and on that last horrible day, every penny from her savings account.

Now he was doing it again, showing up out of the blue and expecting her to take care of him.

He could feel his palms beginning to sweat. Palms that were callused and rough. His skin was weather-beaten. His soul was hard. He was different, too. It had been madness to come here.

She was staring at him with distrust and . . . distaste. A common, scruffy, workingclass lout. That's what she was seeing and that's what he was. He'd been a fool to return.

He took a step backward. If he could just get out the door. Take away the last five minutes. Run again.

She hadn't recognized him. It would be better if she never saw him again. He'd get someone else to help him prove that he hadn't killed his uncle Max. Then he would return to his rightful place as heir and come to her, reclaimed, and ask her to forgive him.

He lowered his head, trying to hide his face. "Sorry," he mumbled, took another step back, and bumped into the edge of the door. He stumbled, caught his balance. But in that brief instant, his head lifted and he was staring into Geena's dark eyes.

Her expression changed from wary to disbelieving. She shook her head minutely as if to clear it. She frowned at him hard. Then slowly she began to edge around the desk toward him. He knew he should run, get the hell out of there before it was too late, but her eyes pinned him to the carpet.

Christ. What had he been thinking? She might be married with children by now. Might hate him for running off and never sending her a word. Might even turn him in. He had to get out.

He watched her lips form unspoken words, *Oh, my God,* as she moved closer, closer, until she was close enough to touch him. And still he didn't move. He couldn't.

She stopped, dipped her head to see under the cap. "Cab? Cab. Is that you? Is it really you?"

Cab managed a disjointed nod.

He staggered back when she threw herself at him and wrapped strong, sleek arms around him.

It was Cab. She knew it, even though his body was different. Not the lanky kid she had loved, but a man, strong and hard and . . . unresponsive. She gradually became aware that he was not returning her embrace. He just stood there as if he were a statue. Not just strong and hard, but cold and hard.

She pulled away, suddenly embarrassed and disappointed— and devastated. She had reacted without thinking. Something she never did. That was the first thing they taught you at Camp Wilderness and the first rule in detecting. Think before acting. She looked up at him. Saw the distance in his eyes. The rejection in his stance. And her heart constricted. He'd come for a reason, but not the one she had waited for all these years.

She was still clasping his arms; she let her hands drop and stepped back, her world icier than she had ever thought possible.

"I'm sorry," she mumbled and reached out to the desktop to steady herself. She gestured to a chair. "Won't you sit down?"

She backed around to the other side of the desk and lowered herself into her chair. Slipped her feet back into her shoes and felt a little more in control with the desk separating them.

He stood at the door, watching her, making no move to come in or leave.

"It was just a . . . a . . . I was just so surprised," she finished lamely.

"Your hair's different."

Geena blinked, touched the clasp that held her shoulder length hair at the nape of her neck.

"And your voice."

She nodded. She'd worked on losing the Swiss boarding school accent so that clients would find her more approachable. His voice was low and gruff, and ten years settled between them like an impassable chasm.

He pulled the cap from his head, and Geena's stomach flip-flopped. His hair was darker, but still held shots of lighter blond. Golden boy, they called him in high school. Everything he touched was made magic until that fatal day when his uncle was murdered and Cab became a wanted man.

She had never believed he killed his uncle. He wouldn't. Not for all the money on Long Island. She'd cleaned out her savings to help him escape. Had spent years poring over files, looking for clues to prove his innocence. And had gradually given up.

"Please, Cab. Sit down."

He glanced toward the open door. Then moved toward it. She had to grab the arms of her chair to keep from running after him. He was going to leave without ever telling her why he'd come.

But he closed the door and locked it.

Geena tried to calm her racing pulse. She kept silent while he unbuttoned his coat and hung it neatly over the back of his chair. He suddenly looked more like the old Cab, not as bulky as he'd appeared in the coat, but filled out and muscular. A man who lived rough, not like the pampered boy in the penthouse next door.

And she was no longer the flippant, entitled girl who sneaked out to wild parties, who drank and smoked and made love to Cab in his room when his parents were out of town, who spent hours with him under the eaves of the attic in Max's Long Island estate after his father died, making plans and exploring each other's minds and bodies.

A frisson of pleasurable memory drifted over her. She

clamped it down. That was over. This was something else. And she needed to find out what he wanted.

"What—"

"I—"

They both stopped as suddenly as they'd begun, looked at each other, then looked away.

"Is it safe for you to be here? Have you been cleared? Where have you been?" Once the questions started, Geena didn't seem to be able to stop them. "I'm sorry about your mother." She stopped. "Cab, you did know that your mother . . ."

"That she's dead. Yes. That's one of the reasons I came back."

And the other reason? she wanted to ask, but didn't dare.

"I know this is strange, and if you want, I'll walk out the door and never show my face again."

"No. Of course not. Only tell me—"

Cab let out his breath. His whole body seemed to soften and it was everything she could do not to rush to him, to take him in her arms and comfort him. But he didn't want that. He'd made that clear. She crossed her arms and hugged herself, trying to chase the chill away.

"I'll tell you everything, but—" He looked around the room. "Is there coffee or something? I've been standing in the rain all day, waiting for your colleagues to leave and—"

Geena jumped up. "I'll make a fresh pot. It's in the other room." She hurried toward the enclosed porch that they used as a canteen, half afraid that he would take the opportunity to flee.

She measured coffee into the filter and filled the carafe with water. She heard movement from the other room. *No. Please don't run. Not again.* She shoved the pot under the filter and jabbed the on button. She turned, meaning to race back into the office. To stop him. But ran into a hard, broad chest.

Cab's arms closed around her. "Genie. I've missed you so much."

Chapter Two

Cab reached blindly for her. He didn't care if she didn't want him. He needed to touch her once more. He couldn't stop himself. He tightened his arms around her. Her body was stiff, but she still made him feel warm and safe.

He had to tell her that he was still a wanted man. That she would be an accomplice if they caught him here. And he would tell her in a minute. But first he needed this just once more, to keep a part of her with him for the next ten years, as he had the last ten. Just a few more seconds and then he'd have coffee and leave. He couldn't put her in jeopardy; but for a moment, he let his need override his rationality. It felt so right.

And then she relaxed. All in one motion, the stiffness left her and she molded herself to him. And he wanted to cry out in relief, but there were things he needed to say, to explain, before he could allow himself to hope.

He rubbed his cheek along her hair. His beard caught at the fine strands and he wished that hiding his face hadn't been a necessity. His fingers fumbled with the clasp that confined her hair. It opened and fell to the floor. Her hair settled around her shoulders, shiny and soft. He splayed his fingers through the sleek strands, buried his face in them, drinking in the faint aroma of vanilla.

He brushed her ear with his lips and felt the first stirrings of his arousal. It had been a long time. He fought to keep his hands from running over her back, of grasping her ass and pulling her into him. To take each other without words like they had in younger, happier times, tearing off their clothes and falling onto the heap of pillows on the attic floor of Max's mansion.

She lifted her head and his lips found hers. They came together in an explosion of feelings. Feelings that had been pent up and ignored for too long. At least for him. God, he wanted her. And he had no right to her.

She pulled away. "We shouldn't be out here. Someone could see you."

"Oh," Cab said, his mind fuzzy. "Oh." He pulled away from her. "Are you married?"

She smiled, then walked him backwards until they were back in the office, away from the porch windows.

"No," she said and pulled his head down to continue the kiss.

Geena let herself revel in the heat of long suppressed passion. Exploring Cab's mouth, feeling the rasp of his beard on her face, the strength of him. They were no longer inexperienced teenagers. They were adults and nearly strangers. But the old feeling zinged through her, strong and deep.

His tongue invaded her mouth, his hands kneaded her back. And for the briefest moment, she allowed herself to believe that their love for each other hadn't died, only changed.

She knew as well that this moment was tenuous. That he might have to disappear again. And if he did, she would be even lonelier than before, now that she had tasted the adult Cab.

Well, at least they had the here and now. She began walking him backwards toward the sofa. He went willingly, as if he didn't even notice they were moving.

They didn't stop until Cab's calves bumped against the edge of the couch. Without breaking the kiss, they both began to undress. Her jacket, blouse, and slacks, his shirt and pants. They only broke apart for Cab to untie his work boots and pull them off. His pants followed and they pressed together, skin to skin.

Their hands explored each other, reading each other with their fingers. Rekindling their knowledge with a touch.

Cab's chest was hard and developed; dark hair grew in a diamond on his chest. His hips were lean. She pulled them closer. His erection was hot and hard against her stomach and she moved against him until he moaned and pulled her down onto the couch.

"I—I don't have anything," he said desperately as his legs tangled with hers. "I mean, I didn't think—there've been other women—"

Geena placed her fingers over his lips, cutting off his words. She didn't want to hear about other women. There had been other men, but none that made her forget her first love.

She raised herself on her elbows. "Don't go anywhere." She climbed off him, crossed the room to the supply cabinet, and rummaged in the top drawer for the box of condoms they kept there. She grabbed the box and took it back to the couch.

Cab's eyes widened. "Do this often?"

Geena smiled, delighted to see his sense of the ridiculous returning.

She climbed on top of him and straddled his thighs while she broke the seal on the box. "No. This was a gift from Nan's boyfriend. They're having monogamous sex, so he donated them to the cause. Never been opened." She took a foil packet from the box and let the box fall to the floor next to the couch. She tore the foil with her teeth and pulled out the condom.

She took his penis in one hand and Cab arched beneath her. His body wasn't the only thing that had matured in ten years. His cock was thick and long, the veins stood out like blue cords against the dusky pink of his skin.

"Hold still," she said. "I haven't done this in a while." She placed the condom over the head of his penis and slowly unrolled it down the length of him. Then her hands slipped lower until she held his balls in both hands.

"Genie. Magic Genie," Cab moaned and pulled her down.

She lifted her hips to let him slide his fingers between her legs. She was wet and slick and more than ready. His finger moved inside her, then out, sliding to the place that set her nerves on red alert. Then he lifted his penis to her and pushed inside, stretching against flesh unaccustomed to habitual sex. She felt splayed on top of him. He thrust all the way in and she caught her breath. He stilled, looked at her questioningly, but she just smiled, braced her hands against his shoulders, and began to ride him, slowly, her eyes open and intent on his.

She began to rock more quickly, until Cab groaned and closed his eyes. His hands tightened on her hips. He pulled her into his thrust and held her there as he moved inside her. Then he lifted her away, his eyes focused on the place where they were joined. He bit his bottom lip and slid his hands to where his thumbs could open her to his touch.

Geena stifled a groan of pure pleasure and began to roll her hips, moving against his thumbs until she began to shake. Then she steadied herself and he pulled out just enough to thrust into her again. She met his blow, grinding her hips against him. He released her and banged back inside her, faster and faster until thought was gone, rationality evaporated, and there were only two bodies, becoming one, racing mindlessly toward release.

It came unexpectedly—raw and overwhelming—grabbing Geena and propelling her over the edge. She bit back the ragged cry that erupted from deep inside her as waves of pleasure rolled over her. Her climax pushed him into his. He arched beneath her, nearly throwing her to the floor, his body rigid. For a timeless moment, they were caught, suspended in space. And then she collapsed on top of him, giddy and empty and full.

"Stars. I saw stars," mumbled Cab and closed his eyes.

Geena lay against him as she gradually succumbed to the afterglow of satisfying sex and to the realization that she hadn't been whole without him. Not because she needed him, but because he was a part of her.

"Cab?" she whispered.

Cab didn't answer, didn't move, except for the slow, steady rise and fall of his chest. She lifted herself away and braced her weight on her hands to look down at him. He was asleep.

She gently ran her forefinger across his brow and smoothed the frown that remained there even now. He was exhausted, whether from lack of sleep or years of being on the run, she didn't know. There were smudges under his eyes and lines of weariness creased his face.

The face of a stranger. It shocked her to realize that she didn't know this Cab at all. Too many years had passed, too much separation and too many life experiences had driven them apart. Made it impossible for them to find their way back.

At least she would have this. Full circle. Closure instead of a new beginning. She could feel it as surely as she felt his chest rise and fall with each breath.

She slipped off him, a deep sadness overwhelming her. "I love you," she whispered and kissed her fingers and pressed them to his bearded cheek.

Cab came awake with a start, then succumbed to the feeling of lassitude. He was lying naked on a sofa; someone had put a blanket over him. He turned his head and saw Geena sitting at her desk, her tortoise rim glasses sliding down her nose as she riffled through a stack of papers.

He smiled. This time it wasn't a dream. She was real and she was still magic. His smile tightened. And he'd taken advantage of her, just like he always did, even when they were kids. It had been a selfish thing to do, but he needed her so badly that he hadn't cared if she wanted him or not.

And it seemed that she did want him. Still, he shouldn't have. He was a wanted man. And nothing would change that. He'd realized that as soon as the freighter had docked and he'd made his way to Long Island with the vague intent of asking Geena to help him clear his name.

But he was here, and they had made love and he knew without doubt, she was still the girl for him. And that made everything even harder to accept. There was no future for them. He'd put her in jeopardy by coming back.

Such a bitter pill to swallow having tasted the sweetness of love again.

Cab pushed himself up to one elbow. "What are you doing?"

Geena jumped as if someone had goosed her. "Oh, you're awake."

"Sorry about that. I haven't slept since day before yesterday. How long was I out?"

"A couple of hours." She didn't look at him, but continued to study the papers spread out on the desk.

Cab became acutely aware that he was still naked and she was fully clothed. The mere thought was arousing. And embarrassing. When he was sure her attention was on her work, he eased the blanket aside and reached for his pants. He pulled them up his legs, realized he was still wearing the rubber, and rolled it off. He stood up and quickly pulled on his pants and zipped them up. He picked up his shirt and put it on while he crossed the room toward her.

Fortunately, there was a wastepaper basket next to the desk. He tossed the rubber into it and went to stand at Geena's shoulder.

He got the distinct impression that she was ignoring him. No reading could be that fascinating, and, besides, he could see the faint blush on her cheeks. She was uncomfortable, too. Probably regretting what they had done. Cab could have kicked himself for hurting her—again.

"Geena, I—"

"I've just been going over some of the old newspaper articles about your uncle's murder. I . . . kept them."

There were more than just a few newspaper clippings. There was a thick stack of paper. He reached for one and turned it toward him. "Where did you get this?"

Geena shrugged, her eyes never leaving the article she was reading. "When you left, I tried to find out what really happened. I compiled a sort of dossier. My first. I thought if I really tried, I could prove you innocent, and then you could come back—" Her voice broke and she took a minute to collect herself.

"You were always good at finding out stuff."

She shook her head in rapid little jerks. "Well, I didn't find out much. Nobody wanted to talk to a sixteen-year-old. And the detective in charge of the case gave me a pretty hard time."

"My poor Genie." Cab tentatively touched her shoulder.

Geena froze and Cab quickly removed his hand. He needed to remember that he didn't deserve that closeness now. He'd run away and left her to try to protect him, when he should have been protecting her. He was a coward and a fool, but he wouldn't make the same demands on her now.

"Geena . . ."

She swung her chair around so suddenly that he stepped back. "Look. Don't worry about what just happened." She made a vague motion toward the couch. "No big deal, okay? Just for old times sake. But since you're here, I think we should go over the files together and see if you can come up with something that I didn't see."

Cab just looked at her. She was treating him like he was just another client. Like they had never been best friends, like they hadn't just made love on her office couch. No. It was just sex; she'd made that painfully clear. And now she was going to help him, because she always helped him.

Despair burned through him as he made the fearful realization. Her loyalty had survived their separation, but not her love.

Chapter Three

Geena gathered up the papers and stood up. "Take these into the other room while I get your coffee. Do you still take cream and sugar?"

Cab shook his head. "Black."

"Fine." Geena shoved the papers at him and headed for the porch. Her throat felt raw. That one word "black" seemed to put the final period to their life together. Nothing was the same. Not Cab, not her, not anything.

Cab was a stranger. She had to remember that. When he started to tell her about his other women, she had cut him off. But maybe she shouldn't have. Maybe there was one special other woman and that's why he came back to clear his name. *But he just made love to you*, she argued. *For old time's sake*, she answered.

She would help him this one last time and then they could go their separate ways.

She gritted her teeth against the sense of loss that thought gave her and poured coffee into two large mugs.

When she entered the conference room, Cab had spread the papers across the table and was sitting in a chair, reading. He barely looked up when she placed the coffee on the table at his elbow.

"Thanks," he said distractedly. He reached for the cup,

while he continued to read. "I can't believe you compiled this."

"Well, I did," she said brusquely and sat down next to him, but not too close. "So let's see if we can ferret any leads out of what I have."

She took a handful of papers and started to read. Then she noticed that Cab had stopped and was looking at her. She glanced at him.

"You don't have to do this. I didn't mean to intrude into your life. God knows, I don't deserve it."

"Don't be ridiculous. This is my job." She knew she sounded cold, but being so close to him made her want to put her arms around him, lose herself in his body, and they needed to work, before he fell into the hands of the police.

Cab stood up abruptly. "Listen. That's not why I came."

"No? Then why did you come back?"

"I—" He broke off. "Just a minute." He left the room and returned a minute later with a wrinkled, dirty envelope. He thrust it onto the table in front of her. "Open it."

Geena frowned at the envelope, then at Cab. Slowly she opened the flap, caught her breath when she saw the green bills inside.

"It's what I owe you. It's taken a while but it's all there— with interest."

Geena bit her lip to keep her cry of outrage from exploding into the air. She dropped the envelope back onto the table and pushed it toward him. "You don't owe me anything. It wasn't a loan. I gave it to you. Freely and willingly. You've jeopardized yourself for nothing."

She picked up the clippings with hands she couldn't keep from trembling. Stared at the top paper through the blear of unshed tears. Everything he did or said tore her heart a little more. At this rate it would be in shreds by morning.

"There's another reason I had to come."

Geena gripped the papers, not daring to wonder what the other reason was.

"My uncle is going to have me declared dead."

Cab shifted uncomfortably as he watched the color drain from Geena's face.

"Ronald wouldn't do that. How do you know this?"

He couldn't meet her eyes. He already knew how she would feel when he told her that he had deserted her in favor of his relatives. Relatives that didn't even like him. "Jerrold wrote me."

"Jerrold? But how—"

She stopped there and turned on him, her expression one he knew so well from the past, the same face she gave him whenever he had disappointed her. And he remembered now that it had been often.

"Geena. You have to understand. I had to let my mother know I was all right. I was the only one she had after my father died. Before I left, we set up a post office box where I could reach her. We stayed in touch over the years, sending clandestine letters to different post offices. She kept me abreast of the news. Told me about you, how you had grown up." *And how beautiful you'd become.* "How you opened this detective agency."

"She never told me."

"I made her promise not to." He automatically reached for her hand, but pulled back. "I couldn't get you into more trouble than I already had. If they found out about the money you gave me—"

"They did."

Cab ran his hand over his eyes. "Oh, Jesus. What did they do?"

"Nothing. I got a big lecture on aiding and abetting suspected felons, then my parents shipped me off to Camp Wilderness to knock the defiance out of me."

"Camp Wilderness?"

"A place in the Adirondacks. It's where they sent society girls who didn't behave in an appropriate way. Three months of etiquette lessons and wilderness survival."

"I'm sorry. It sounds awful."

"It wasn't so bad. That's where I met Nan and Delia."

"Your partners."

Geena nodded. "And the camp was pretty exciting, once I got over my squeamishness of gutting game and sleeping without a tent. And I loved the mountain climbing. I go rappelling every weekend." She smiled. "But I still don't know which fork goes on the outside." She shrugged. "It didn't bring out my inner debutante, but it gave me a new attitude toward life."

Cab tried to imagine Geena slicing through a deer carcass with a bloodied knife. And strangely enough, he could see the new Geena doing just that. She had taken control of her life. She was strong and self-sufficient and she didn't need him anymore. Not that she'd ever *needed* him. He was the one who always had needed her. The realization hurt.

"Go on."

"What? Oh. A few months ago, the letters stopped. And I knew something was wrong. I almost came back then, but I waited—waited for another letter, that never came. She never told me she was dying, or that she was even sick. I should have been able to read between the lines, should have known something was wrong. But I didn't until it was too late. I went to the library in Paris every week to read the *Times*. That's where I saw her obituary."

"Oh, Cab."

He shook off the concern in her voice. He didn't deserve it. "And then last month a letter came from Jerrold. I guess my mother must have told him about me before she died. He said his father was starting the process of having me declared dead, so that Max's will could finally be probated and the next of kin could inherit."

Geena nodded. "I knew that they tried before and your mother would never allow it."

"It isn't that I care about the money. I don't. I just couldn't stomach the idea of letting Max down."

"So you came back."

Cab nodded. "I was homesick." *And I wanted to see you.*

Geena was frowning and the frown deepened as he told her the story of the letters.

"So why did Jerrold write to you? His father is next of kin, right?"

Cab nodded.

"So he's next in line to inherit a fortune. And in turn Jerrold would get it. Once you were declared dead they would be extremely rich."

"Yeah. I guess you're right."

"Then why contact you?"

"I wondered about that, too. But they're already extremely rich. Maybe he thought I should have a chance to salvage my life."

"Hmm," said Geena.

She gathered up several papers. "Let's start at the beginning. These are the newspaper clippings from the week of the murder and the weeks after you left." She pushed the pile to her right. "These are statements I collected from people over the following weeks." She laid them next to the clippings. "It's not much. I was inexperienced and mostly they were humoring me, poor little Geena playing detective."

She stopped suddenly, realizing she sounded like poor little Geena. To hell with that. "But I'm better now. These are the updates I've made over the years. The last one is almost two years old."

She swallowed. She had no reason to feel guilty for letting things slide since then. "There hasn't been anything new for a while. The case is still open, but no one seems to be doing much about it."

Cab hadn't responded or even moved since she began her explanation. She handed him the stack of interviews.

"Cab?" Geena sat with her legs crossed, her glasses sliding down her nose, and her pen poised over the paper. "I know we were both too horrified and grief stricken to think clearly in those last days, but you must have tried to put the pieces together since then."

Cab nodded. "A hundred—a thousand times. Sometimes, I lay in bed going over and over everything that happened that day, but—" He lowered his face to his hands. "If only I hadn't left that day. Max would still be alive."

"Cab." Geena's tone was sharp. He looked up at her. Her face was unforgiving. "Let's stop with the if onlys and tell me everything you remember."

Cab closed his eyes, reaching back into a past that had been his constant tormentor for the last ten years.

"Max called me into his office after lunch."

Geena nodded. Max only used his office if they were in deep trouble. "And?"

"And I remember wondering what I had done." He smiled reminiscently. "And wishing you were there to get me out of it." He caught the fleeting smile that passed over her lips before disappearing and was distracted until she brought him back to the point.

"But it wasn't something I'd done. It was something he wanted to tell me. That he had cut Ronald and Jerrold out of his will and left everything to me. I was to be his sole heir, the only stipulation was that I was never to let Ronald or his family have a dime. Ronald was to be the executor. I knew he hated Ronald, but I didn't and don't know why. Making him executor seemed unnecessarily cruel. Max could be a pain, but he was never cruel. I called him on it, but Max said that someday I would understand."

Geena remembered him pouring this out to her the day of the funeral, and she had been just as shocked as he had been.

"And I told him that wasn't fair. And he said he would be the judge. I told you all this before. You wrote it all down. It's in that stack of papers."

"Tell me again. Have you thought of anything else he said, since then?"

"No. Just that I was angry, because he was talking about when he died. And then I'd be alone, alone to face an irate family by myself." He shrugged. "Always thinking about myself, even when talking about Max dying."

"And?"

"And then he told me that Ronald had an appointment with him, and that I was to go upstairs and not come down again until I was called. Which pissed me off, of course, so I gave him major attitude and stormed off upstairs."

"Did you see Ronald arrive?"

"No, but I guess he saw me, because he told the police that he did."

Cab fell silent as he was dragged beneath the tide of unhappy memory.

"And I didn't see or hear him leave, because I crept out of the attic and went down to the Viceroy to shoot some pool. Only a pipe had burst and they were closed for clean up, so I just messed around for a while. When I came back home, Max was dead."

"And no one even knew you were gone."

Cab closed his eyes. "Only Elly. But no one believed her. Guess I was too good at sneaking out—and in."

Geena sighed. "Yeah."

It sounded like an accusation. And that was what it was. He could see the flint in her eyes, the distance she created by the way she sat.

The muffled sound of a door shutting interrupted the silence that fell between them.

Geena started from her chair. "Shit."

"Who is it?"

"I don't know. Stay here." She rushed across the room, turned out the light, and shut the door behind her.

Cab was left in total darkness.

Geena just managed to throw herself into her desk chair when the office door opened. Nan and Delia, wet from the rain and rosy from dinner and, Geena suspected, a bottle of wine, stepped through the door.

"Saw the light on," said Nan. "You can't still be working on the Hollander report. You got the bozo on film, and Delia completed all the credit reports this afternoon." She glanced at the empty desktop. "Can you?"

She sat down in the client chair that Cab had sat in. Geena strained to hear any sound of movement from the conference room, but could only hear the continuous pounding of the rain outside.

"No. I was just waiting for the rain to let up."

"For three hours?" asked Delia.

"Well . . ." Geena started to equivocate, but stopped when she saw Nan look at the floor. Her eyes barely registered a change, but Geena knew her well. What had she seen? Had Cab left something on the floor by the desk? His coat? Hat? No, she had put them in the closet when she returned the box of condoms to the cabinet.

Geena realized Delia had asked her a question, but she hadn't heard her. "I'm sorry?"

"So you want to go out barhopping? I haven't done that in years, so we decided to come back and get you. Sounds like fun, doesn't it?"

Nan was glancing surreptitiously around the room. Her eyes rested briefly on the conference room door, then moved back to Geena. "You know," she said, standing up. "I think it's a little late for barhopping. I'm for going home. I'll drop you back at the restaurant so you can pick up your car."

"Huh?" said Delia.

Nan nudged Delia toward the door. "See you Monday," she said before pushing her into the hallway. "Have a nice weekend."

And they were gone.

Slowly Geena got up from the chair. She peered over the desk but couldn't see anything on the floor. She walked around to the other side—and found it—the used condom in the trash can.

She was going to have a lot of explaining to do on Monday. At least she had two days to come up with a story that would keep them in the dark about Cab. She would jeopardize herself for him, but she couldn't jeopardize her friends.

Chapter Four

Geena watched from the porch window until she saw the headlights of Nan's car swing out of the parking lot and onto the street. She went back into the office. "You can come out now."

The conference room door opened a crack, then Cab's head poked out and he looked warily around the room. "Who was that?"

"Nan and Delia."

"You didn't tell them?"

"Of course not. I can't really involve them in this, can I? But Nan's suspicious." She shook her head, a gesture of exasperation he recognized from the old days. "She saw the condom. She thinks I'm having wild sex in the office and she couldn't wait to get Delia away."

"Which one is Nan? The blonde or the little black-haired one?"

Geena's eyebrows rose.

"You saw them?"

"This afternoon while I was waiting for the office to close."

"Oh. Nan's the strawberry blonde. Delia's the one with the spiked hair."

Cab ran his hand along the surface of the desk. Straightened the geode from a rock-climbing expedition that Geena used as a paperweight. "You'll all be in trouble if I'm caught."

"That's our middle name. Trouble. That's how we all ended up at Camp Wilderness. That's what keeps us in business."

He crossed the room in two lightning-quick strides and grabbed her shoulders. "Stop it. This is serious. I can't do this to you again. I'll leave. Just forget I was here. Just—"

"Cut it out, Cab. You're here and running won't change that." She knew he was hearing the "again" in her words and that was fine. Because suddenly she understood why he was so remote. It wasn't that he didn't want her. It was guilt.

It was time to start cutting through the crap. Their lives might have grown irreparably apart, but she needed to know. If they could love each other again, great. If not, well, she'd cope with that, too. But she wouldn't let him leave without finding out one way or the other.

"Now, let's get back in there and figure out what our next move will be. Then we'll both get some sleep and start out fresh in the morning."

His eyes flared with what she read as panic. He opened his mouth, but she turned him around and pushed him back toward the conference room. He went. Good. At least she still had the power to make him do what she wanted. And she wanted him.

It was close to two when Geena closed her notebook on pages of notes. Cab's stomach growled.

"When was the last time you ate?"

"I'm not that hungry. It was just that I was reading Elly's testimony. She made the best sugar cookies I ever tasted." He shrugged. "Where is she now? Did Max leave her any money?"

"Yes. A nice endowment. She's living in the Bronx with her daughter."

"It seems odd that of all the people you talked to, my relatives, my friends, Max's associates, that my mother and Max's cook were the only people who insisted that I didn't kill him."

And me, thought Geena. "You were always her favorite.

She cried in the kitchen the day I went to talk to her. Nobody would believe her because she was just a servant. That's what she said and it broke her heart."

"I don't guess she had any ideas about who did kill him?"

"She didn't say, or maybe I didn't ask. I can't remember. But I think I'll take a drive to the Bronx tomorrow." She stood up. "In the meantime, I know a pretty good all-night Thai place where we can get takeout. And then you can get some sleep."

Cab stood up, too, looking around like he might find a bed in the conference room. "I can find a room somewhere."

She went to the closet and tossed him his coat and hat. "Wait at the back door until I get the car. Then get in the back and stay out of sight."

"Jesus, Genie. Nobody knows I'm back."

"Maybe not," she said. "But we're not taking any chances."

The aroma of something wonderful wafted back to where Cab lay scrunched up on the floor of Geena's Honda. God, he was starving.

He had no idea where she was taking him. He'd started out by trying to guess their direction, but totally lost track as his senses gave in to the thought of food.

He must have drifted off and was dreaming about food, when the car came to a stop and seconds later pulled into a garage. The door rolled down behind them and Geena turned off the ignition. "You can get out now."

Cab pushed himself to the seat and peered out the window.

Geena opened the back door and pulled him out. He nearly fell onto her, his legs were so cramped from the ride.

"I'm sorry. Was it terribly uncomfortable?"

He shook his head. All thought left him when she thrust the bag of takeout into his hands and beeped in a code to a door off the garage.

"Where are we?" he asked as he followed behind her.

"My town house."

He stopped. "Genie. I can't. It's too dangerous for you."

"Listen to me, Cabot Vandermeer. You have no choice." She shoved him into a brilliantly lit hallway, painted in a stark shade of white. He blinked.

"Come on." She started up a stairway of equally brilliant white.

"You can be so bossy sometimes." He was too numb with hunger, fatigue, and surprise at how easily they had slipped into their childhood habits to do anything but follow her upstairs.

She opened another door and Cab stepped into a kitchen, all white and stainless steel. This place didn't seem like Genie at all. When had she become so hard? Had he been responsible for the change? Had that long-ago stint at the wilderness camp done it? Had life?

"Go make yourself comfortable in the living room. Fix yourself a drink—if you still drink. I'll bring the food out." She began pulling cartons out of the bag, obviously not wanting or expecting his help. And he wanted to help, but he was too tired to argue. He went through a swinging door and came to an abrupt halt.

The living room was painted a soft beige. A picture window covered the length of one wall, a leather couch and two armchairs were grouped around a fireplace. But what got his attention was the wall above the mantel. It was covered with weapons. Not rifles or pistols, but a primitive slingshot, a long bow with a clump of eagle feathers hanging from one end, a row of spears, some mere shafts of wood whittled to a pointed end, others with chipped flint arrowheads.

Jesus, this was a girl who was too squeamish to bait a hook or touch a fiddler crab.

He spun around when she came through the door, carrying a tray of food and plates. And he tried to reconcile the girl he knew with the woman who collected aboriginal weapons.

She placed the tray on a table by the window, pulled out a

chair, and motioned for him to sit in it. He shook his head, trying to clear it. There was a brief scuffle and he managed to push her into the chair instead. Not exactly a smooth move, and she looked a little startled. Then he pulled out another chair for himself and sat down. He stared out the window, trying to compose himself. There was no light except for a sliver of moon and a few stars and he realized they were overlooking water. The ocean or a bay. He started to ask her about it.

She was smiling at him and the thought fled from his mind.

"What?"

"I'm just glad to see you. You look so different, and yet it's still you."

She was glad to see him. Well, they'd just made love, hadn't they. It hadn't been love, thought Cab, ruefully. They'd banged away at each other and then he'd fallen asleep. How could he have done that, and with Genie, for God's sake. He wished he could tell her how good it felt, how much he had missed her, how the thought of her was sometimes the only thing that kept him from throwing himself into the nearest river.

"It's the beard," he croaked. Cleared his throat. "Part of the camouflage."

"Not just the beard." She helped herself to rice and handed him the carton. "I always thought you'd grow up to be one of those taut, lean executive types. But you're so . . . so . . . rugged."

God. She made him sound like a Neanderthal who'd wandered in off the tundra.

"So, what have you been doing these last ten years?"

He stopped chewing. "Whatever I could. I got passage to Marseilles. My French was pretty good, so I just bummed around France for a while. I worked on a farm, did some small construction jobs in the country, signed onto a few freighters going to places where they didn't care about your papers being in order." He thought about his life and tried to see it through Genie's eyes. He had had such promise. Bright student, promising future, all shot to shit in the blink of an eye.

"I liked it. Except the being a fugitive part." He preferred hard work to being a pencil-pushing golden boy, or one of the idle rich, which he would have been if he'd added Max's inheritance to his father's. "You probably can't understand that." He knew he sounded defensive. Well, he was.

Geena let out a bark of laughter. Cab looked up, shocked.

"I'm not the shallow, spoiled brat that I was when I was sixteen. I've witnessed things I never dreamed of. And I do understand the satisfaction of hard work. Those things on the wall. I didn't buy them in an antiques mall. I made them. Made them. With these ten little debutante fingers. And I can use them. So don't pull that high-handed shit with me, Goldy."

He'd made her angry and he'd only meant to apologize for his own failings. But he couldn't help but smile. She'd always called him Goldy when he'd pissed her off. Just to remind him what an effete little prick he was.

From somewhere deep inside him, a seed of laughter began to grow. He felt it rising and fought to suppress it. This was not the time to give in to feelings. He swallowed it back, choked on it, and sputtered into coughing.

Geena jumped up and patted him on the back. Her touch seared his skin. He wanted to pull her into his lap, part of which was already reaching up to meet her. He wanted to make real love to her, tell her he'd never stopped loving her. Even when he'd been with someone else, he'd always thought of her. But he couldn't. He had nothing to give her but trouble. Just like always.

"Thanks," he managed, then concentrated on eating while she went back to her side of the table.

Silence fell between them. At last she asked, "How did you get passage to Marseilles?"

Cab put down his fork. "You loaned—gave me the money."

"I know, but what gave you the idea to go to France? We were so frantic that night and when I asked you what you were going to do, you said you didn't know. How did you manage it? You couldn't have used your passport, there would be records and they would have extradited you."

"It was Jerrold's idea."

"Jerrold's?"

"I went to see Uncle Ronald. To ask him to help me. He wasn't in his office, but Jerrold was. He said that the police had been questioning his dad about me, and that they were going to arrest me. He said he wished he could help me, but that he didn't have any money. And somehow the idea of shipping out to Europe came up, and Jerrold said a lot of criminals did that to get away. And so I left, and went to find you . . . like I always did when I was in trouble.

"I shouldn't have asked you to help, but I was afraid to wait for Ronald and I didn't know where else to turn."

"Hey. You had every right to come to me. We were best friends, remember?"

And lovers, thought Cab.

"And they sent you to that terrible camp."

"That camp made me what I am today."

And what was that, wondered Cab. A strong, self-assured woman. Someone who knew what she wanted and knew how to get it. Someone who loved her work and was successful at it. Someone who didn't need him mucking up her life.

Geena pushed her chair away from the table and stood up. "Come on, no more questions, you look beat. I'll show you to the guest room."

Cab stood up. *Someone who didn't need him at all.*

Chapter Five

Geena stood at the picture window of her bedroom, look-ing out into the night. The rain had stopped, but drops clung to the glass. The glass was thick and she couldn't feel the chill of sea breeze or hear the underlying hum of the water, but she felt its pull.

Cab was asleep in the room next door. She'd had to stop herself from going to check on him several times already. Part of her was listening for the catch of her door opening. But the sound never came. She should just go to him, get under the covers and see what happened.

So he was a stranger. She had slept with men she knew less than this new Cab. It had never stopped her before. And she really was curious to see what it would be like. That first mindless, instinctual bout they'd had in the office was incred-ible. But that was before their guards had come up, before they realized what they were doing. Would it be as good now that they were fairly sane again?

She leaned her forehead against the window. She needed to stop thinking about him and start concentrating on how she was going to clear his name after all these years. She hadn't even looked at the case since she started Women-Tek. Had consciously tried to erase him from her mind and heart so she could get on with her life.

She blew out air in silent laughter. She had been the one who always took care of things when they were children, despite the fact that he was three years older. She was the one who got them out of trouble.

And then Max was killed, and Cab ran and decided to start protecting her by staying incommunicado. Honestly, she could smack him for such stupidity. If she had known he would someday return, she would have kept working to find the real murderer. Because not once had she ever even questioned his innocence.

Well, tomorrow she'd go to the Bronx and talk to Elly. She just hoped that the old cook was not too senile to remember what happened that day. And maybe by Monday she'd have enough new information that she could safely involve Detective Rogers, who had been the lead investigator on the case.

He hadn't retired. She occasionally saw his name in relation to some case he'd solved. He'd treated her like an irritating insect when she was younger, but she had her own reputation now, and he wouldn't dismiss her so easily.

She knew that this case had rankled him, and if he was anything like her, it would still rankle.

There hadn't been that many suspects. The police discounted burglary, though Max's office had been ransacked. Ronald seemed like the most likely suspect. He'd been at the house that day, might have been the last person to see Max alive. He'd just lost out on a large inheritance.

Max must have told him about the will and informed him that he'd named him executor. That might have made him angry enough to return later and kill him. And why did Max hate him? And what had happened to the money in the intervening years? Was it sitting in a bank somewhere waiting for probate to finish? They certainly hadn't been using it to keep up the old mansion.

It occurred to her that Ronald might be siphoning off funds. She needed access to Max's bank statements. And Delia was the only one she knew who could hack into files like that. During all those years as a lonely Fifth Avenue wife, she had filled her days learning everything about the finer operations of computers. And Nan could weasel information out of anybody.

But Geena shied away from enlisting her two partners. It was too much responsibility. If she failed to clear Cab, she would bring them all down.

It was too late to call them now; she'd sleep on it and decide in the morning.

She pulled back the covers, but didn't get into bed. Her desire to check on Cab was too strong. She'd just take one little peek to make sure he was all right. That he wouldn't panic and try to flee during the night.

She walked to the door, the plush carpet muffling her footsteps. Just one look. She wanted more, she knew that every time she looked at him, but not until he could cut through some of the barriers that he'd erected around himself. She didn't blame him; it couldn't have been easy living a lie all these years, wondering every moment if someone would recognize him and turn him in.

Cab was already living in a prison—one of his own making. Still self-absorbed, not as before when he was a self-centered, spoiled child, but because he was locked in his own nightmare, closed off from other people and his own feelings. She could tell he would break out if only he could; she had felt his attempts to open up to her during the evening and felt his failures with disappointment. Well, this was one thing she couldn't do for him. He'd have to find his own way out, and she would just have to wait until he did.

Quietly, she turned the doorknob, and stepped into the hall.

Cab stood naked at the window, fighting panic. It was a feeling that he had grown so used to that he didn't know what he would do if it ever went away. He couldn't sleep. He was beyond tired and all he could do was think of Geena lying in bed next door. Why hadn't he just asked to sleep with her. God, what would it feel like to wake up to someone in the morning.

No, not someone—Geena. Would things ever be the same again?

The same as what? asked a scoffing voice in his head. He'd learned to heed that voice over the years, as much as he hated it. Things would never be the same. They shouldn't be. He didn't want them to be. But hell, he wanted a future, one that didn't include being a fugitive or going to jail.

The night was dark, he was alone, and he was hard as hell. He'd spent many nights like this, so full of desire for some elusive thing, that he couldn't sleep until he had relieved his needs. And knowing Geena was so close and yet not within his grasp, made tonight worse than most.

He turned from the window and barked his shin on a chair that he hadn't noticed. He threw himself into it and looked down at the dim outline of his erection. Christ, he hated this.

He took himself in hand and slowly worked his way from base to tip. His hands were rough and callused. Not like Geena's, strong but soft, with a woman's touch. His dick throbbed, but there was nothing erotic about how he felt. It was painful.

He stood up and felt his way to the bathroom, turned on the light. It was pristinely clean. Not a jar or tube of makeup anywhere. Only the toothbrush she'd given him before she left him for the night.

He'd carefully squeezed out the toothpaste. Wiped off the top and screwed the cap on thoroughly. Then he'd put the tube in the medicine cabinet. He felt like a big, lumbering ox. Afraid to relax and risk breaking something or dirtying a towel. He should never have come back.

He opened the medicine cabinet. There was a bottle of hand lotion on the bottom shelf. That would make things go a little smoother. He took it out and saw the packets of condoms lined up behind it.

He snorted with disgust at himself. Of course, there would have been other men. Had they been more satisfying for her than his women had been for him? He hoped so. He wouldn't wish his feeling of alienation on anyone.

He resolutely closed the cabinet, turned off the light, and took the lotion back to the chair.

The lotion smelled like almonds. He squeezed a dab into his hand and put the bottle on the table next to the chair. He rubbed the lotion into his palms, then leaned back, closed his eyes, and started on the routine that would give him a little respite from his raging unhappiness.

The lotion made things better, a little easier to ignore the fact that he was alone. He squeezed harder, rubbed faster, felt the tingle begin as he forced himself toward climax. What a stupid word, climax. There was nothing climactic about doing it yourself.

Harder, faster, his hips began to move against the action of his hand. Come on, get it done. He should have gotten a towel. That's all he needed: to spew come all over Geena's immaculate upholstery. He covered the tip of his penis with his hand; it was too late to stop and find a towel or his socks.

"It's usually more fun when someone else does that for you."

Geena. He practically jumped out of the chair. Jesus. She'd caught him stark naked, masturbating. He sat up, pushed back against the seat hoping that it would hide him from view.

The hall light created a halo around her body. She was dressed in a simple shift and he could see the outline of her body through the fabric. He wondered how much she could see. Obviously enough to know he'd been jerking off. God, it was so humiliating.

She walked toward him, not hurrying. He pushed himself farther into the chair. A situation like this should be enough to deflate him completely. Only his cock wasn't responding normally; it was pulsing like a mad thing, practically reaching for her.

For an instant, he considered making a mad dash for the bathroom and locking himself inside. But he couldn't move.

Part of him was willing her to him, begging her to finish the job for him, wishing that she would take him to bed. But she had made it clear that things were ended between them. Even though she seemed to have liked it. If only he hadn't fallen asleep like that. She probably thought he was a barbaric oaf. He didn't blame her.

A hundred thoughts passed through his mind as she moved inexorably closer, then knelt in front of him.

"I used to be pretty good at this, remember?"

He could only grunt as her hand closed around him. He'd make it up to her later, if she'd let him, but he had no power to stop her now.

"Geena, I—" He never finished what he meant to say, because her hand scooped up his balls, as her other hand caressed the tip of him and he groaned and surrendered, the *I'm sorry* dead in his throat.

Her palm encircled him as she gently massaged his balls. Then she pushed down the length of him and pulled him upward and down again.

He gripped his toes, his hips, his jaw, caught between wanting to rush toward release or staying in this frantic, incredible tease forever.

Her fingers slid behind his scrotum to that sensitive skin, oh yes, that place. Nobody had ever come close to touching him like she did. She'd put her brand on him when she was just fifteen. It might be too late for them now, but he would never belong to anyone else.

"Genie."

"You like this, don't you, Cab? You still like the way my fingers make you feel. You especially like this, don't you?"

"Yes." The word was wrenched from him. He couldn't think, only feel, as he teetered on the brink of annihilation.

"You don't understand, Gen—oh, God. You should stop. No. Don't stop. Oh, God."

"Just enjoy it, Cab. No big deal. I like doing this. It makes us both feel good."

"But—"

"Don't talk. You've been gone a long time. You've grown up, but I still know what you're thinking, know what you're trying to say. Let me do this for you. Don't analyze it. Just enjoy it. And then you'll sleep."

He reached for her, a distant part of his mind on the condoms in the medicine cabinet. But it was too late, she was pushing him over the brink. He threw his head back and gave himself up to her ministrations, pressing himself into her hands. Rolling his hips as his fingers gripped the padded arms of the chair. He wanted to grip her but she was out of reach.

He couldn't see her face because she was bent over her task, her hair shielding her features. He wanted her to put her mouth on him, but had no ability to ask. She was in control of this. Controlled him. His whole body was pushing against her, raising him out of the chair as pure animal instinct took over.

He never had a chance against her magic. Not then, not now.

A cry erupted from him as his world shattered and he spewed himself into the air over and over again. Years of pent-up desire fell on his chest until he was too weak to even thank her.

She rose up on her knees until she could rest her arms on his thighs. She lifted one finger and traced a line through the tracks of his come. Up from his stomach to his chest, rubbing it into the chest hairs, then up toward his throat until she was close enough for him to capture her hand.

He brought it to his lips. "I always take and you always give," he murmured, contrite and satisfied at the same time.

Geena shook her head, but didn't pull her hand away. "It may seem like that. Guys don't get what women really need."

"I never did, did I?"

"No, but we were just kids, and the sex was great." She laughed softly.

"We're not kids now. I didn't have anything to give you then, and I don't have anything to give you now."

He felt her go still. "No?"

"I'm a fugitive. I survive by doing odd jobs, I don't even get a chance to bathe every day. I live hand-to-mouth, and sleep wherever I can find a place to crash. I'm not civilized."

She pulled her hand away and Cab lost all hope. Then she took his chin and pulled it down until they were eye to eye.

"I spy on scumbags for a living. I can eat raw meat, I can kill and skin a deer without batting a civilized eyebrow. I can drop a man with my fists or kick his gonads into the next century. I can go you one-on-one with uncivilized."

"It isn't the same."

"You know, hon. You were always a whiner. You could never live up to your own expectations of yourself, so you didn't try. I like the new, uncivilized you much better. We're both intelligent people. I never stopped loving you, but I never expected things to ever be the same. Who would want them to be?

"But you really need to eighty-six this 'I'm not worthy' thing. It was annoying when you were eighteen. It doesn't work at all at thirty. We might have no future as lovers. I'm willing to find out, but not until you've reconciled yourself to yourself."

She used his thighs to push to her feet.

"Now, get some sleep, we have a lot of work to do." She turned and walked across the room. She stopped at the door. "Good night."

He reached out to her. *Come back, please come back.* But

she couldn't hear words that weren't spoken and he didn't have the courage to speak them out loud.

She closed the door and he was alone again. His mind closed around one thing, held it tenderly so as not to crush it. She had said she still loved him.

Chapter Six

Geena cradled the phone between her shoulder and ear and stirred the eggs she was scrambling. "Great, I'll see you around one." She hung up and turned to Cab who sat at the kitchen table, nursing a mug of coffee.

"That was Elly's daughter. She said her mother was a little deaf and her sight was going because of cataracts, but that she's still as sharp as a tack. I'm going there this afternoon."

"I heard. I'm going with you."

"No, you're not. What if someone saw you and recognized you. What if Elly tells someone she saw you? She's old and may still have her wits, but she might let something slip."

"I'm going."

"No."

"Your car has tinted windows, and Elly's blind and deaf. I won't say a word, I'll just listen. So don't argue."

The toaster popped up. Gritting her teeth, Geena put the toast on a plate and began buttering it with slashes of the butter knife.

"Hey, don't take it out on my breakfast." Cab got up and took the knife out of her hand.

They were standing shoulder to shoulder, and when Cab smiled at her, their faces were so close she could feel his breath on her cheek.

His hair was wet from the shower. He'd combed it back

from his forehead and the ends curled at his neck. He was dressed in clean jeans and a T-shirt, wrinkled from weeks in his duffel bag. He smelled like soap and Cab and she wished she could see the face beneath the beard.

She stepped away. "You are so stubborn."

"And you are so . . . cute when you're mad."

Geena scowled at him, then her lips twitched. She struggled but couldn't help breaking into a smile. "Not fair. You always did that. And I'm not cute."

Cab's smile broadened. "You always said that."

"But now I mean it."

He stopped smiling. "I know you do, but I'm still going."

Geena turned onto Dysart Street and began looking for 143. The street was lined with brick semidetached houses fronted by small square plots of grass and rosebushes, and separated by narrow strips of macadam driveways.

The rain had swept leaves into soggy piles at the curb. Branches littered the street. Geena maneuvered the Honda around a ramp where a lone skateboarder had stopped, board under his arm, to watch them pass.

Cab was slumped down in the front seat, a baseball cap pulled over his eyes. "Are we almost there? I'm getting a stiff neck."

"Stop whining," said Geena, searching the house fronts for the number where Elly lived.

A block later, she pulled the car to the curb. "Here we are. I'll introduce you as my colleague. Don't talk, just nod and smile and look dense. But—*do not say a word.*"

Cab nodded and shuffled after her, his hands in his pockets.

Geena rounded on him. "This is not funny. You'd better not fall back into your old patterns or you might find yourself in jail."

"Sorry." He took his hands out of his pockets and gestured for her to continue. The door was opened by a pleasant-looking black woman in her sixties, who looked a lot like Elly had when she'd been Max Vandermeer's cook.

"Larissa?" Geena stuck out her hand. "I'm Geena Cole and this is my associate Roger Smith."

"Come on in. Mama's expecting you."

She led them into a softly lit living room, where a television was blaring out a game show. The room was crowded with overstuffed furniture and a profusion of crocheted doilies. Elly sat in an easy chair near the window, dressed in a floral house coat. Her hair was cropped close to her head and was pure white.

The television remote rested in her lap and one hand held a white handkerchief. Larissa took the remote and turned off the television. "Mama," she said loudly into Elly's right ear. "Miss Cole and her associate, Mr. Smith, are here to see you."

Elly looked up and Geena saw that her eyes were clouded by cataracts. Her first thought was that surely Max had left his cook enough money to afford the operation that would save her sight. She heard Cab's intake of breath behind her and turned to give him a warning frown.

Elly's mouth broke into a smile, her hand reached out in Geena's direction.

"She can see you as a shadow, can't you, Mama?" Larissa's voice modulated from loud to soft as she said, "It's her blood pressure. They can't operate until it's under control."

Geena came forward and took Elly's hand. Then she leaned in and gave her a hug and kiss.

"Hi, Elly."

"Miss Geena. I'm so glad you came to visit me. How you been? Larissa, pull up a chair for Miss Geena so I can hear her."

Larissa placed a dining chair next to Elly and Geena sat down. She was glad that Cab had the good sense to keep quiet and take a place on the couch several feet away.

Geena was trying to formulate the best way of asking Elly

about the murder without upsetting her, when Elly asked, "Have you heard from my boy?"

Geena was taken aback. Of course, Elly would think that was why she had come after all these years. Elly had been more than a cook. After Cab's father died, Cab had spent every summer and most holidays with Max. Elly made sure he had everything a growing boy needed—food, clothes, a home, and unconditional love. She always knew everything and had saved Cab and Geena's butts more than once.

Which was why her statement had not held much weight with the authorities.

The authorities thought that she was protecting Cab, that Geena was protecting Cab. Because that's what people who loved him did. Protected him.

Geena found it hard not to confess everything to Elly. She knew it was even harder for Cab. She shot him another warning look, but his gaze was focused on the old cook.

And Geena felt a pang of contrition. She should have visited Elly before now. They had been each other's sole source of comfort. Sitting in the kitchen, day after day, trying to figure out how to prove Cab innocent, an old cook and a sixteen-year-old girl. Both unheeded, condescended to and dismissed.

Then Ronald had closed up the house and pensioned Elly off. And Geena had been sent to Camp Wilderness and they hadn't seen each other again until now.

Geena took a breath and leaned close to Elly, talking into her good ear. "The reason I came is because Ronald Vandermeer is about to have Cab declared dead."

Elly gasped and began shaking her head. "That's a lie. My baby isn't dead. I'd know it if my boy was dead. And I don't know it. And I'll tell that Mr. Vandermeer to his face."

"Mama, don't you get upset," said Larissa, coming to stand by her chair. "That doesn't mean he's dead. Just that they can get on with settling the will."

Elly frowned, a stubborn set to her jaw. "Isn't going to be any settling of any will. Mr. Max, he left everything to Cab.

And it's going to stay right where it is until Cab comes back to claim it."

Larissa shared an understanding look with Geena. "She won't hear a bad word about that young Mr. Vandermeer. She still talks about him sometimes, when she's feeling low. You know, like old people do." She raised her voice. "That's right, Mama. There's nothing for you to worry about."

"I'm going to try to keep that from happening," said Geena. "That's why I came to see you. Do you remember that time, Elly?"

"Of course I do. It's burnt in right here." She pointed a gnarled finger to her head. "And here." Her hand moved to her heart.

Geena felt Cab stir and she willed him to stay put. She knew he was suffering. She was, too. But they couldn't reassure Elly. Not yet. "Tell me again."

So Elly started talking—going over the same things she had said ten years ago sitting in an empty kitchen, across the table from a frightened, inconsolable Geena. Max Vandermeer had called Cab into his office on the first floor. He was there for twenty minutes, long enough to cook two batches of the pecan tea cakes that Cab loved. When she heard the door open, she'd gone out to tell him the cookies were ready, but he ran past her and up the stairs.

"He and Mr. Max were all the time having a set to. Cab was sowing some wild oats, but it never lasted long. Mr. Max, he loved that boy and Cab loved him."

"I know," said Geena.

"I expected him to sneak out of the house that day. He always did that. Went down to the pool hall they had in those days. That's what he did. Lots of times. Then he'd come back and they'd have dinner like nothing ever happened between them."

"You saw Cab leave that day?"

"Sure I did. Like clockwork, that boy. He'd never make Mr. Max wait for his dinner." Elly smiled like she was seeing the scene in her head. "I was watching out the window of the kitchen, when he come shinnying down that old oak tree and took off through the woods." She shook her head. "Just like a little boy. He wouldn't never take the car, when they had a fight. Didn't think he deserved it, when Mr. Max and he were at odds. 'Cause you see, Mr. Max gave him that car."

They were the same facts Elly had told her before, the same one she had in her files. But today it had the ring of a story, a tale from the past, as if Elly thought Geena was hearing it for the first time. It also held the ring of truth.

"It was a Wednesday, the first week of November. I remember because we always polished the silver on the first Wednesday of the month. It took most of the afternoon. So I was in the dining room when Mr. Ronald Vandermeer came.

"They were shut up in the office, oh, not too long. It was unusual just him being at the house. Though there was no love lost between those two brothers. Mr. Ronald stole his sweetheart, way back when they were youngsters, and Mr. Max never forgave him. But after he left, Mr. Max asked Peters, the butler, to bring him ice. He always had a whiskey at five o'clock. So it wasn't Mr. Ronald who killed him, either."

Unless he returned later after everyone in the house could testify that Max had been alive when he left the house, thought Geena.

"I told the police it was a burglar, though I don't know how any burglar could get in without one of us knowing it. We never had any break-ins, but there's always a first time. And I told them so. But the police, they had already made up their minds."

"And no one else came that day?"

Again, Geena heard Cab stir and she darted him a warning look.

"Just Cab, later that evening, and he went right to Mr. Max like he always did to apologize."

Geena held her breath, wondering if the next part of her story would be the same.

"But Cab, he comes into the kitchen, looking white as a ghost, and he says, "Elly, somebody has killed my uncle. Old Peters was having a cup of tea and he runs into the office with me and Cab right behind, and that was true, Mr. Max was lying on the floor. And he wasn't breathing.""

Elly lapsed into silence, shaking her head slowly.

"And you knew he was murdered because . . ." Geena prompted.

Elly shivered. " 'Cause there was a nasty red mark around his neck and the buttons were tore off his shirt, like he'd been trying to get that thing off him."

The same as the police report. A piece of cord, never found.

"The wall safe was locked, but he had this box he kept papers in. It was still in his desk but it was empty. We didn't know that until the police came and started asking questions after the funeral. I told them it was a thief." Again, Elly shook her head.

Suddenly her hand stretched out and groped the air. Geena took it and Elly pulled her close. "I didn't tell anybody about the papers."

Geena stared at her, stunned. What papers? No one had mentioned anything about papers to her. She turned to look at Cab. His face was blank, then she saw dawning understanding and hope died a little. She turned back to Elly.

"What papers?"

"The ones Cab was carrying when he ran upstairs."

Geena's hope died a little more.

"But they won't ever find them, don't you worry. I put them where nobody would look. Nobody but Cab when he comes back."

"Can you tell me, Elly? I won't tell."

"Only Cab when he comes back."

Cab made a guttural sound and stood up.

Elly looked around, her head moving like a bird's until her clouded gaze stopped on what must be only a shadow.

Geena stared at him, anger clouding her senses. Why hadn't he told her about the papers?

He started to move toward Elly. Geena stood up, preparing to stop him bodily if she had to. Larissa stood guard over Elly's chair, the three of them posed like characters in an old melodrama.

"Who's here?" asked Elly. "What do you want?"

"It's only my assistant," said Geena, trying to sound soothing while yelling into Elly's ear and motioning to Cab to stay back.

"You tell them to keep quiet. I'll deny everything. They're not going to trap me into making my boy a killer. And they're not going to declare him dead. Because he isn't dead." Tears began to flow from her nearly sightless eyes.

Geena reached toward her, Larissa rushed around the chair. Cab got there first. He fell to his knees and took both of Elly's trembling hands into his larger, rough ones.

She tried to pull away, her expression changing to fear.

"It's me, Elly. It's Cab. You're right. I'm not dead. I came to see you."

"Cab? Let me see you." Her hands twisted in his and he let go. She groped in the air until they came to rest on Cab's head. She ran them over his hair, his forehead, nose and mouth. She let out a hysterical laugh when they touched his beard.

Then she wrapped both gnarled hands around his neck and pulled him toward her.

For a wild moment, Geena was afraid that Elly was trying to strangle him. But she pulled his face to hers and kissed his cheek.

Then she held him back and squinted at his face. "What you want to grow a beard and cover up that pretty face for, boy?"

Cab let out a bark of laughter, or maybe it was a cry. Then he leaned into his old friend and rested his head on her breast. And she patted him, saying, "It's gonna be all right, gonna be all right."

Larissa came to stand beside Geena. They both watched the reunion without speaking, while Geena wondered, *What papers?*

Chapter Seven

The attic. Geena swore as she swung the Honda into the street. Elly had hidden the papers in the attic. Papers that might acquit Cab of Max's murder—or prove him guilty.

"I can't believe you didn't tell me about the papers."

"I did." Cab paused. "Didn't I? I'm sure I did."

"I didn't understand half the things you said that night, but last night, when we went over everything you did that day, you didn't mention any damn papers." Geena kept her eyes on the street, not daring to look at Cab. She was angry and hurt and desperately trying not to think that he had kept that piece of information from her on purpose.

Cab rubbed a hand over his face. "I wasn't thinking that clearly, ten years ago . . . or last night. But I'm sure I told you about them when I came to ask you for help. Since you didn't mention them, I just didn't think about them."

Geena pulled up to a stop sign and cast him an exasperated look.

Cab shrugged and looked away. "Last night, I was thinking about you."

Geena's heart gave up the struggle. She reached for his hand and squeezed it before letting it go. "Tell me about them now."

With both hands back firmly on the steering wheel, Geena turned onto the main street, driving slowly, looking in the rearview mirror to make sure they weren't being followed. It was a habit ingrained in her since opening Women-Tek. And even though her mind was divided between solving the murder and desiring Cab, she couldn't fall down on the job now.

Cab continued to stare out the window. "They're the reason I ran. I mean, maybe I wasn't making much sense, but I meant to tell you about them."

"Cab, just tell me now, okay?"

"Max wanted to talk to me in his office. I figured I was in trouble, but I couldn't figure out what I'd done. But then he said he wanted me to know certain things about my future. So let's see, I sat down across that desk, which was strange because I was usually standing up getting a dressing down from him whenever we were there.

"He started talking about his will and how I was going to inherit and I told him I didn't want to hear anything about wills, because he wasn't going to die for a long time."

He broke off, and Geena knew he needed a moment to collect himself. How anyone could think Cab would kill his uncle was beyond her understanding. They loved each other as only a fatherless boy could love an uncle and a childless man could love him back.

"He said everybody died and I was a fool if I didn't plan for the future. That riled me, of course. He was always doing that, stinging me with something so off base. Just to get my attention.

"Over the last ten years, I've come to realize it was his way of preparing me for life, his way of showing his care—his love for me." He took a shuddering breath. "It just pissed me off in those days. I thought I wasn't living up to his expectations.

"So I did what I always did when he was lecturing. I tuned out. He talked for a while, then Peters came in and said Ronald was on his way over. Max seemed irritated. Ronald very rarely came to the house. I was so thankful to be let off the hook and not have to talk about dying anymore that I stood up and tried to leave.

"But Max stopped me. He said it was time I stopped acting like a spoiled brat and take some responsibility for my life. He had a sheaf of papers bound together with a rubber band. He told me to take them and put them somewhere I wouldn't lose them.

"And I think I said, I didn't want them. That he should keep them. Then he gave me one of his looks, so I took them and got the hell out."

Cab laughed bitterly. "I was mad. Because he was right. I was self-centered and selfish. And his words hurt. I was such an annoying shit, I don't know why he put up with me."

"Because he loved you."

"I knew that. But it took me a while before I could admit it. Then I went back to tell him, but it was . . . it was too late."

They were cruising down the FDR Drive and Geena couldn't look away from the road to see Cab's reaction, but she knew it would always haunt him, that he never got to tell Max that he understood.

"What was in the papers?"

"I don't know. I never looked at them."

"What did you do with them?"

Cab shrugged. "I'm pretty sure I put them on my dresser. Elly must have found them. Do you think they're important?"

"I don't know, but we're going to find out."

"They've had ten years to search that damn house."

"Yeah, and I'm sure they searched thoroughly. But if the police found them, I would have learned about it. They closed up the house several months later and as far as I know, it's still locked. I think Elly's right. No one would ever think to look in the attic."

They made the rest of the trip back to Long Island in silence. At the exit to Geena's town house, Cab said, "I'll need some clothes if I'm going to stay. You can drop me off at one of these malls and I can get the things I need."

"Yeah, so you can sneak back to Max's and find the papers yourself. Not a chance. You asked me to help you. Now let me."

"But if we're caught, you could be in a lot of trouble."

Geena grinned, the first time she'd felt like smiling since Cab walked into her office. She punched him on the arm. "Just like the old days."

Cab sighed. "But this time you may not be able to talk our way out of it."

"You came to me, remember?" Geena shoved a glass of wine at Cab and turned to the counter to pour another for herself. She heard him leave the kitchen, letting the door swing shut behind him. She snatched up her own glass and followed him into the living room. "So let me do my job."

Cab turned on her. "I wanted your help and I wanted to— hell, I wanted to see you. It was selfish and stupid. But I did it, anyway. I do want your help, your *help*, but I don't need you to protect me."

"For Christ sakes, Cab. This is what I do."

Cab growled in exasperation. "You'll never get it, will you? The guy's supposed to do the protecting."

Geena glared at him. "Well, I'm sorry. I don't usually have a guy around to protect me, so I do it myself."

Cab flinched, then lowered his eyes. "I'm sorry." His words were muffled but they pierced Geena to the core. He sounded so bereft, that she put down her wine and took a step toward him.

"That's not what I meant. It's just that I'm used to taking care of myself. I like it." This was not exactly what she meant, either. It would be nice to share the job with someone she loved and who loved her in turn. "And I protect my clients."

She looked at the man Cab had become, this stranger and

yet not-stranger, his features harsh, his body hard and capable. He had grown up in the last ten years and not just physically. And even though she hardly knew this man, he was still the one she would choose for mutual protection and mutual . . . everything.

Cab looked into his wineglass. "You always did the protecting. I know that. I think I always did." A hint of a smile passed over his face. "But you were so good at it, I just got comfortable letting you take care of me."

He shifted his weight, then looked at her, matching her penetrating look with one of his own. "But that was a long time ago. I can take care of myself now. I have for ten years. It took a while to get it right, but I'm pretty adept at it."

"And you don't need me butting in." *You don't need—or want—me at all, do you?*

"Of course I need—" He bit back whatever he was going to say and took a labored breath. "I want—" He stepped forward, the power of his energy drawing her toward him.

Geena swayed. Cab took another step. And another, until they were close enough to touch.

But they didn't. Just stood a foot apart. Their feet planted on the solid ground, their bodies leaning toward each other as if against their will. Closer. Closer, until his face was only inches from hers.

She had to fight the urge to close her eyes and yield to him completely.

His fingers closed around her shoulders and he pulled her into him. He lowered his head as she lifted her face to meet his. She could feel his breath on her skin, hot and seductive.

Geena closed her eyes as Cab's arms slipped around her, embracing her in warmth and strength.

His lips parted and she parted hers in response.

"No." Cab broke away, leaving Geena disoriented. Standing on the edge of a dark, empty chasm. Alone. More alone than she had been even before he returned. And despair welled up inside her and threatened to drown her.

When she opened her eyes, Cab was standing at the window, his back to her. Both hands gripped the sill and he leaned heavily on his arms, his shoulders hunched, his back expanding the material of his T-shirt as he attempted to control his breathing.

"I'm sorry," he said. "I had no right."

"Cab."

The air was rent with a sound that made them both jump. The telephone was ringing. Geena ignored it and after four rings, her voice mail picked up.

"Cab." She stepped toward him, touched his arm.

The intercom buzzed. Geena crashed back to reality. Who the hell was trying to get in and why? Surely, nobody—

The intercom continued to buzz, the phone rang again.

"Damn." Geena hurried to the console and looked at caller ID. Double damn. She picked up the phone.

"Hi, Nan."

"Is that Cabot Vandermeer the Third standing at your picture window? They don't call it a *picture* window for nothing."

Shit. Geena motioned Cab away from the window.

"Where are you?"

"Downstairs with Delia. Now, buzz us in."

"I can't let you get involved."

"Remember how mad you were when I went rogue on the Sims case? Well, that's like the smallest-grain-of-sand-in-the-desert mad, compared to how mad Delia and I will be if you don't let us in." A pause. The sound of Nan clearing her throat. "Unless we're interrupting something."

Geena could hear Delia's, "Come on, Geena," in the background. Of course, they would want to help.

"I'll buzz you in."

Chapter Eight

"You must be Cab," said Nan, bypassing Geena and making a beeline for Cab.

Delia stopped just inside the door and gave Geena an apologetic look. "I hope you don't mind. But we couldn't let you deal with this alone."

"Thanks." Geena closed the door and took her coat, a pastel version of the khaki trench coat she'd been wearing the night before.

Nan had already tossed her jacket on the back of the club chair and was studying Cab, who looked a little shell-shocked.

Geena made quick introductions, feeling absurd under the circumstances. But no one else seemed to notice, so she left them to bring out the bottle of wine and two more glasses.

When she returned a few minutes later, Delia's laptop was open on the coffee table. Papers from Cab's file lay spread across the surface.

Nan was reading, one jeans-clad leg swung over the arm of the chair.

Delia sat on the couch next to Cab, perched on the edge of her seat. Except for the leather pants and the new punk hair cut, she could be presiding over afternoon tea. Geena filled two more glasses, handed them to Delia and Nan and sat down in the chair opposite the one Nan was sitting in.

"Well," she said, not knowing where to begin.

Nan straightened up and grinned. "It was the condom that gave you away."

Cab had the decency to look contrite. Delia looked embarrassed. Geena couldn't begin to guess what she looked like.

"Knew it could only mean one thing." Nan turned her grin on Cab. "The boss would never do anybody at the office unless she was totally flummoxed. And there's only one person who could totally flummox her."

"And it's about time, too," said Delia, looking more comfortable now that the explanation was out. "I mean, it isn't really our business, but—"

"But it is our business," said Nan, overriding her. "And we knew you wouldn't come to us. So we came to you. Give us a minute to get up to speed, then you can give us our assignments."

"I don't know what to say," said Geena.

"That's a first," said Nan and sank back in her chair to peruse another newspaper article.

Cab stood up abruptly. "This is enough. I haven't been thinking clearly. I don't have a right to involve you with my problems. Not just you, Geena, which I didn't have a right to do, but your friends. I'll take care of things from here on out."

"Oh, no you don't." Delia grabbed his arm and pulled him back down on the couch.

Cab looked at her in surprise; so did Nan and Geena.

Delia smiled self-consciously. "It's the new me."

Geena stood up. "Okay. First let me say, that it isn't because I don't trust you guys. It's just . . ."

"You wanted to protect us," said Nan. "We've got your MO. And we aren't going to let you do this alone. We're a team."

Nan was right. She'd gone it alone on a case the past summer that had almost cost her life. Nan had learned her lesson and found someone to share her life with.

Geena looked at Cab, so strong, solid, rugged—and so lost. A ten-year chunk taken out of his life, cut off from everyone he could love or trust or ask for help.

If Geena hadn't realized how lucky she was to have Nan and Delia before today, she felt it now. In spades. They *were* a team and it wasn't fair of her to cut them out. "Okay."

Geena began to pace, suddenly clicking into what she did best. With the three of them on the case, things would begin to happen.

It took several hours to go through the file and fill in Delia and Nan on the background of the case.

When Geena opened the second bottle of wine, Nan threw her pen on the coffee table. "Dinner break. I'll call Rudolfo's."

Cab was banished to the bedroom while they paid the delivery boy. Then everyone filled their plates with pizza and salad and went back to work.

"If we assume for the moment," said Geena, picking up her slice and studying it. "That it wasn't a bungled burglary, which I thought unlikely even back then, we need to find out what's in those papers. They may give us a lead on who might have wanted to see Max dead."

"I'll get them," said Cab.

Geena looked at him long and hard. "We'll both get them." She turned her attention back to Nan and Delia. "I've begun compiling a preliminary suspect list. It's pretty slim."

Nan riffled through the mess of papers and picked up one. "Max's brother, Ronald. With Cab's father dead, Ronald would be next in line to inherit, right?"

"No wife?" asked Delia.

"Max never married," said Cab. "I don't even remember him seeing anyone the whole time I was growing up."

"Then there's Ronald's son, Jerrold," continued Nan. "Even if he weren't in the original will, he would inherit indirectly when his father died. Either one would have a great deal to lose. Did they know Max had changed his will in favor of Cab?"

They all looked at Cab.

He shrugged. "I don't know. I don't think so. Max just told me that day that he'd changed his will to make me sole heir." He grimaced. "Which is why everyone thought I murdered him."

Geena squeezed his shoulder. "Not everyone."

Cab looked up at her and gave her a tight smile.

"How much money are we talking about?" asked Nan.

Cab dragged his eyes from Geena. "I never saw the will and Max didn't say. Maybe millions, I don't know."

Nan nodded. "And Ronald was there that day. Do you think Max might have informed him then?"

"I guess. But Max was still alive after he left," said Cab.

"He could have come back later," suggested Delia. "Where was the household staff?"

"According to Elly, she and Peters, and the two day maids were polishing silver the whole afternoon," said Geena, pouring herself another glass of wine and feeling the burden of years lift from her shoulders.

"At least we know the butler didn't do it," said Cab.

The three women gave him a look.

"And they didn't hear anything?" asked Nan.

Geena sighed. "No. Everything is made of oak and chestnut. The doors are so thick you couldn't hear a freight train coming through the next room."

"Anyone else?" asked Delia, her fingers hovering above the keyboard.

Cab shook his head.

"Cab's mother sometimes stayed at the house," said Geena, "but she was out of town that week."

Cab exploded. "How could you think—"

"Chill, bulldog," said Nan in a friendly way that took the sting out of her words. "This is how the pros do it. Nothing personal. What about Ronald's wife or Jerrold's?"

"Jerrold was divorced when I left. Did he ever remarry?"

"I don't think so," said Geena. "I would have heard."

Nan and Delia nodded.

"Ronald has been married to Marie Phillips for . . . How long, Cab?"

Cab looked overwhelmed. "A long time. Forty-five years maybe. It can't be Aunt Marie. She's the sweetest, mousiest little creature you ever saw. And totally devoted to Max as well as Ronald."

"How devoted?" asked Delia, looking up from her laptop.

Cab frowned. "What do you mean?"

Geena knew what she meant. "Add her to the list." She turned back to Cab. "Anybody else?"

Cab shook his head. "Max was pretty reclusive. He'd sold out of his business and pretty much stuck to himself. He had a few friends, but none who would hurt him."

"I'll check them out," said Delia.

"And see what you can find out about the will," added Geena. "I want to know if the executor has been spending it."

"Who's the executor?"

"Ronald Vandermeer."

Nan frowned at Cab. "Your uncle cut him out of his will and then made him executor? That's bizarre."

"I don't understand that, either," said Cab. "For as long as I can remember, Max really hated Uncle Ronald."

"That's right," said Geena. "I remember a few of those stiff family Sunday lunches."

"Did Max ever let on why he hated him?"

"No. He never discussed it. I'm not even sure Ronald knew. Max was always frigidly polite to him."

"And did this dislike extend to your cousin, what's his name?" Nan scanned down the growing suspect list. "Jerrold."

"He seemed to like him okay. And I think he was genuinely fond of Aunt Marie."

"Did either of them come to the mansion that day?"

"No. Marie isn't capable of murder," protested Cab. "And Jerrold couldn't have done it. He helped me get away."

Nan raised an eyebrow at him. "Or made sure you were out of the way, so you couldn't defend yourself."

"Oh, God." Cab stood up, walked to the window, and stared out. "Maybe it's better not to reopen all of this. It's bad enough that my life has been shot to shit without taking anyone else down with me."

"Cab, move away from the window," said Geena. "And stop with the mea culpas or I'm going to smack you."

Cab came back to the couch and flopped down next to her. Nan grinned at him. "She's bossy, but she's usually right."

He scowled at Geena, but then his lips quivered as he wrestled with a smile. "See, everyone thinks you're bossy."

Geena made a face at him.

Nan closed the file she was holding. "What do you want us to do?"

"Delia, you get to work on the money trail. If there is one. And look into the finances of the rest of the Vandermeers."

Delia nodded and stood up.

"Nan, I'll need you to play backup."

"Will do. Got a plan?"

Geena shrugged. "A kind of plan. The longer Cab is here, the higher the risk that he'll be apprehended. Once Ronald finds out we're on the case, he'll rush that Declaration of Death through the system. And he has the clout to do it. We have to move on this."

She hoped she wasn't going too fast. Even if she found the papers Max had given Cab, they might not contain anything that would force the murderer into making a move. Might not contain enough evidence to implicate someone else in Max's murder. Might even be completely useless.

If things went south, Delia and Nan could be in trouble with the police. Cab could be sent to prison or worse. She looked around at the three most important people in her life.

She was responsible for them. She stifled a shudder and steeled her mind against doubt. She knew what she was doing. She wouldn't let them down.

She crossed the room and picked up the phone. "Tonight I'm going to search for those papers. Tomorrow I'm going to pay a visit to Ronald and Marie Vandermeer. Let Ronald know I'm upset that he's having Cab declared dead. I'll be properly weepy and hysterical." She shifted into a falsetto. "That I know in my heart he's still alive."

She cast an apologetic look toward Cab and dropped back into her normal voice. "Then I'll hint that I've found something that would prove his innocence. If I'm convincing enough, one of them might make a move."

Cab was staring at her in disbelief; Delia and Nan were nodding in anticipation.

"Excuse me," said Geena and took the phone into the kitchen to call Ronald Vandermeer.

"All set," she said when she returned to the living room a few minutes later. "Marie answered and said they would be delighted to see me. Four o'clock. For drinks."

Nan leaned back in her chair. "I hate to bring this up, but what if you don't find anything?"

"Oh, I will," said Geena. She'd look until she did.

"No," said Cab.

Geena turned on him. "I'm going to find those papers."

"No," said Cab. "*We're* going to find those papers."

Geena couldn't help it. She smiled at him. It was beginning to feel like the old days, before all the horror had destroyed their future. But she didn't dare let herself become too optimistic. There were too many things that could go wrong.

"No burglar alarm?" asked Nan.

They all looked at Cab.

"Not when I was there."

"Not likely now," said Geena. "It's completely boarded up, the last time I drove by."

Nan raised her eyebrows. "Then dare I ask how you're getting into the attic?"

Geena and Cab automatically looked at each other. Cab's eyes glinted with mischief, and Geena felt another surge of optimism.

"Like we always did. The old oak."

Chapter Nine

It was twilight when Geena and Cab set out for Max's old
Victorian mansion. Cab had insisted on coming with her
and she didn't have the heart to keep him away, though she
wondered at the wisdom of bringing him to the place where
he had spent most of his childhood after his father died. And
where he'd lost a second father to murder, and his future to
suspicion.

She drove several miles down one of the narrow, winding
roads that led to Long Island Sound. The roads were unlit
and at night it would be too dark to see the houses from the
road.

"I'd forgotten how deserted it is," said Cab, looking from
side to side as they drove deeper into the woods. "One
minute you're in bumper to bumper traffic and then nothing.
We haven't passed one car since we left the main road."

"Mmm," said Geena, concentrating on maneuvering the
Honda through twists and turns and dips.

Fifteen minutes later, she slowed down and began searching for the entrance to Max's house.

"There it is," said Cab, pointing to where two crumbling
stone columns peeked out from a blanket of choking vines.
"Jesus."

Geena slowed down to make the turn through the columns,
then drove up a paved drive that was eroded to the dirt in

several places. They bumped along in silence, Cab's anticipation palpable across the seat.

Fireflies were just showing themselves in the trees, casting an aura of magic around them. And suddenly memories rushed into her mind and heart.

Playing in the woods as children, hiding from Cab and scaring the daylights out of him when he ran past her unawares. Being chased and chasing in return. The summer they discovered a new and exciting dimension to their relationship. Their first kiss in the woods, awkward, and unsure, that ended in embarrassment then paroxysms of laughter. Walking back to the house, hand in hand, not children, not adults, just two best friends on the verge of discovery.

She glanced at Cab. His expression was far away and she wondered if he was remembering the same things.

They came upon the house without warning. One minute canopied by trees that blocked out the failing light, then back into a clearing where the old house sprang from the darkness and loomed above them in the deepening twilight.

Geena heard Cab's intake of breath and had to stop her own. The beautiful green and white clapboard Victorian was now a derelict shell. She had stopped here more times than she liked to remember and had witnessed the house's gradual decay. She could only guess what Cab must be feeling seeing his childhood home so neglected.

She drove slowly along the circular driveway, past the front door to the parking area behind an overgrown privet hedge. She turned to Cab, but he jumped out of the car and disappeared around the hedge.

Geena grabbed flashlights and a coil of rope from the trunk and followed after him.

Cab stared up at the front of Max's house, the place that held so many happy memories. Even the dim light couldn't soften what he was seeing and pain tugged at his heart.

Its paint had buckled and flaked. Two shutters hung by

their hinges. The wraparound porch sagged and several boards were missing. The windows were covered in plywood, except for one. The plywood lay on the ground; the window was smeared with mud and several of the panes were broken.

Anger surged through him. Not just for himself, how his life had changed, how all his hopes had been destroyed by Max's death. But for his uncle, too.

This had been Max's pride and joy, and they had left it to rot away. He'd make them pay. Even if he was never acquitted of that heinous act, he would make them pay for this. For Max.

He felt Geena come up beside him. Touch his arm.

"Vandals," he said between clenched teeth.

"And time," she said.

"And jealous relatives. They closed it up and let it rot to pieces."

"The will was tied up in probate."

Geena and her calm rationality. Cab snorted. "Ronald could have maintained it, made repairs. He's the executor. That's what executors do." His voice was tight, almost as tight as the pain in his gut.

"I know. Come on." She tugged at his sleeve as she might have done twenty years before or fifteen years ago, or . . .

He should have stayed away. But he had reached a point where he couldn't continue to live as a fugitive. And he was forgetting what Geena looked like, felt like, so he had risked his freedom to return. Now, he knew what she looked like, more beautiful than when he'd left, and how she felt, enclosed in his arms, the heated softness of her lips, her tongue mingled with his. Her breasts that made him die a little when he touched them. Her strong, capable hands sliding up and down his cock, her legs straddling him as he drove himself home.

Home. That was a joke. He had come back filled with hope. They would be together again. They'd live in the house where they had first discovered love, and that love would grow. There would be children and Max would somehow look down on them and smile.

It wouldn't happen now. None of it. There was nothing for him here. He felt another burst of hatred, this time mingled with despair, that someone had robbed him of his future, his dreams.

"Come on," Geena said gently.

Cab resisted for a moment then turned to look at her, a stranger in a strange land. She read the emotion on his face, anger, sadness, hopelessness, and she didn't know what to do about it.

She thrust one of the flashlights at him. They walked without speaking to the side of the house where the old oak tree grew three stories high. She fervently hoped that it was still there and that the garden shed, whose roof they'd used to boost themselves to the lowest branches was still intact. She was not optimistic.

The tree was there, more gnarled than before, its bare branches making a tracery of black against the gray sky. A ragged gash ran down its side where it had been struck by lightning. The shed leaned at a precarious angle. The glass had been knocked out of the windows and lay in jagged shards on the decaying leaves that clotted around the foundation. The roof had collapsed and the frame jutted naked in the air.

Cab pulled up short. "I hate this." The words were wrenched from him.

Geena sighed. "I know. I do too." She should have come alone. Anticipated what they would find and kept him from having to confront this.

"We might as well try the door," she said, giving a wistful glance at the oak tree.

"Might as well," said Cab. "No one but vandals have been here for years. One more broken pane of glass won't make a difference." His voice was bleak and she knew he was not only disappointed, but feeling guilty for having stayed away and let this happen.

They walked around the house to a back porch even more derelict than the one in front. The floorboards groaned as they made their way to the back door.

The door was flanked by two long windows, both covered with wood. Windows that had once let sunlight into the kitchen during the day and showcased eerie shadows as soon as the sun went down. Geena tried not to remember sitting at the kitchen table, sipping steaming hot chocolate while Elly told them tales that would set the back of their necks crawling.

Cab turned the knob. Nothing happened. He rattled it and tried again. The door didn't budge.

Before she guessed what he was doing, Cab reached up to the window on the right. He grabbed the edge of the wood in both hands and ripped it from the casing. Then he lifted his arm and shoved his elbow through the pane. Fortunately his pea coat saved his arm from painful lacerations, but she had no doubt that he would have broken that window, protection or not. Cab was in a dangerous mood.

He felt around until he found the window latch, then pushed the casement up. He climbed through, then reached out to help Geena over the sill.

The kitchen was shrouded in shadows. The air was dank and smelled of dry rot. The counters were cleared of all the canisters and jars that had been Elly's domain. One pot sat on the stove, tarnished and forgotten, forlorn in its solitude. And no amount of imagination could bring back the steamy warmth of cooking, or the bustle of Elly's dinner preparations, or the cool feel of linoleum as the ceiling fan kept a steady breeze on a hot summer's evening.

Geena pushed it all from her mind, stepped past Cab who was standing like a statue in the middle of the room, and opened the door into the hallway.

They climbed two sets of stairs without speaking; not looking into any of the rooms; not stopping until they came to the attic stairs at the back of the third floor. The door opened in a creak of rusted hinges.

As soon as they were on the first step of the stairs, Cab closed the door behind them and Geena clicked on her flashlight. They both hesitated before beginning the climb to the narrow door that opened onto their old hideout and trysting place.

Geena let Cab lead the way. She followed behind him, trying not to imagine what they would find in the attic. She had an overwhelming urge to turn out the flashlight so they wouldn't see.

But Cab took the flashlight from her and slowly panned it across the gabled room. Had he known what she was thinking? Had he been thinking it, too?

She watched the beam of light pick out discarded furniture they had arranged at the window, old trunks and crates that they'd spent many happy rainy days exploring. Then it came to rest on their corner and Geena caught her breath.

An amorphous gray mountain spread across the floor. Gradually it came into focus and Geena realized it was only a dustcover. And she knew what was under it, even before Cab pulled it away and dust rose in spreading clouds, the motes glimmering in the beam of the flashlight.

They stared down at the mattress covered with a madras bedspread, the pile of pillows, the books, stacked on each side.

She felt Cab's hand slip into hers. They had both lost their virginity on that mattress. Had experimented in the wonders of love and sex. Had explored each other's bodies in a growing sense of wonder and appreciation. Had spent season after season laughing and reading and dreaming about their future together.

They had been so young. So hopeful. But that was before Cab had to run away, and Geena was packed off to Camp

Wilderness to cure her of her defiance. She felt a tear roll down her cheek and she squeezed Cab's hand.

"She covered it up. So it wouldn't get dusty. So it would be ready—" Cab's laugh sounded more like a cry.

"What?"

"Elly. When she came to hide the papers." Cab shook his head. "If Elly knew about the hiding place, then she knew about this." He gestured vaguely at the mattress and pillows.

"And she knew what we were doing here," said Geena, suddenly embarrassed after all these years.

"That's why the place always stayed so dust-free. Elly was keeping it clean for us. And she never let on." Cab shook his head, a smile playing across his face. "If she were here now, I'd kiss her."

He dropped down and sat down on the coverlet, then smiled up at her, and his meaning went to her very depths.

"The papers," she croaked.

"Right." Cab swung his feet around to the side of the mattress and pushed against the floor. The mattress stuttered across the boards. Geena dropped down beside him and peered over his shoulder at the loose floorboard that had been their secret hiding place.

Cab shed his jacket, then rolled to one hip and pulled a pocketknife from his back pocket. He flipped it open and slid the blade into the crack between the boards. The board shifted, then fell away.

Cab closed the knife and shined the flashlight into the hole. And there it was: a bundle of papers, held together with a dried-out rubber band. He lifted the bundle out and handed it to Geena.

"Christ." He shined the flashlight back into the hole. An empty pint bottle of vodka lay at the bottom next to a small, dust-covered cardboard box. He rubbed his forefinger over the top, revealing the writing beneath. *Trojan Deluxe* stood out in red letters.

Geena looked away, caught between laughter and tears.

She pulled at the rubber band and it fell apart in her hand. She handed him the papers and they sat side by side, knees touching, as he began to riffle through them.

"Mortgage. Paid in full. Titles for land. Max must have bought up several parcels around here. Insurance. What's this?" At the bottom of the stack was another parcel of envelopes, not legal size, but almost square, like the ones that came in boxes of stationery.

They exchanged looks before Cab opened the first one.

My dearest Max . . .

There were eighteen in all, each declaring devotion and enduring love. Some almost Victorian in their gentleness. Some more risqué as Max's lover described her feelings about the time they spent together.

I never knew it could be like this. Your hands on my body make me wish the world away. That I could be with you forever, only you, naked to the touch of your strong, yet gentle, hands. How your special touch makes me shiver in your arms, the feel of you when I love you.

The letters covered a span of almost thirty years and they were all signed, *Yours forever, Marie.*

"Jesus," said Cab when he returned the last letter to its envelope. "Jesus."

"Marie and Max. It seems so unlikely." Geena took the letters from him and put them with the other papers that were spread on the floor beside the mattress.

"Elly said that Ronald had stolen Max's sweetheart, but I'd never have guessed it was Marie."

"Cab, the last letter is dated 1995. Ronald didn't exactly steal her. She was Max's lover before she married Ronald and was still his lover for years afterwards."

"Then why did she marry Ronald in the first place? Why not Max?" asked Cab. "It doesn't make any sense. And it doesn't do anything to help us figure out who murdered him."

He tossed the last letter on top of the others, then propped his elbows on his knees and rested his head in his hands.

Geena couldn't help herself. She reached out and touched his bowed head. There had been something extremely erotic in those letters, though not one specific sexual act had been described. She was flushed, a tugging warmth had settled in her gut, and she knew she had become more aroused with each letter they'd read.

She was annoyed with herself and she willed herself to be sane. But when Cab turned toward her, she knew that she was not the only one affected. His look was penetrating and his erection thrust against the fabric of his jeans. It was unmistakable and just as unmistakable to know where they were headed.

And even though she knew this could be their undoing, she didn't stop him when he leaned close enough for his hand to slide beneath her sweatshirt. When he pulled her toward him, she went willingly.

She fell across him and he pushed them both up the length of the mattress until their heads came to rest in the pile of pillows. He rolled into her, wrapped his arms and legs around her, while their bodies burned through the layers of clothing.

He nuzzled her neck, his beard tickling her chin. He licked and bit his way down to her collarbone, stretching back the neck of her sweatshirt. Ran his tongue along her flesh and up her neck. Bit her chin, her jaw. His tongue thrust into her ear, hot and rasping. Then out again, leaving her shivering in the chill air of the attic.

She could hardly move, could only lie back, her mouth open in an unsounding cry of happiness. Her fingers speared his hair, followed the outline of his ears, caressed the back of his neck, and pushed their way down the back of his flannel shirt.

He rolled on top of her, his body heavy, every bone, every button branding itself into her. He was consuming her, and her body broke into thrilling waves of desire.

He rubbed his beard against her cheek, scoring her skin in spite of its softness, then his tongue invaded her mouth. She was waiting for him and she sucked him in, as if she could swallow him whole.

They rolled from side to side, clinging to each other, wrapped and rewrapped arms and legs, trying to get closer, ever closer. His hands slipped beneath her shirt and his fingers went unerringly to the hook of her bra. He unclasped it as if he'd been doing it every day of their lives. Then in one movement, he ripped the shirt over her head. The bra went with it, and he buried his face between her breasts, massaging them and pressing them together as his tongue dampened the hollow between.

Geena was splayed on the mattress. She tried to reach the buttons of his shirt, but she couldn't get to them. Cab's mouth moved to one breast, nipped at the taut aureole of sensitive flesh. Kneaded the weight of each as he sucked and teased until she cried out. He was going to make her come before they even got their clothes off.

As if reading her thoughts, he rolled onto his back, taking her with him, and continued to knead her breasts as she straddled him and undid the buttons of his shirt. She yanked his belt open and peeled away the opening of his jeans.

His cock sprang toward her, dark with surging blood. He lifted his hips so that she could pull off his jeans. It brought his penis close to her mouth. She licked him, and when he groaned, she closed her lips around him. She sucked and pulled and caressed him with her tongue as she wrestled with his clothes.

Cab groaned. "Too fast."

She didn't stop. But she had to slow down, while she unzipped her own jeans and wriggled them off her hips.

Cab grasped her shoulders and pulled her upward. Her

lips tightened around his erection, wanting more. And they dragged him with her until she could hang on no longer. Cab cried out as he slipped out of her mouth and she slid up the length of his body. Hotter than anything she had ever felt.

Then he released her shoulders and moved his hands to her butt. His fingers lifted her into him and separated her. Then they slid down the crease of her butt into the slick valley that hovered just above his penis.

Geena tossed her head as his finger plunged into her and withdrew only to be joined by a second finger. She raised her butt so he could get farther inside her. And he plunged into her again, making her cry out, "Yes!"

They were like a writhing beast, fighting to the bitter end, not to death but to a fulfillment that had been denied them for too long.

His fingers penetrated her, withdrew, slid forward until they found the place that pushed her toward oblivion. She rested her forehead against his chest so that she could slide her hands between them and find his cock.

When his fingers plunged again, she lifted his penis and rubbed the tip between her legs. Bumping over that hard little nub again and again until his fingers gave a final thrust and she broke into a million pieces.

She was still rocketing on her orgasm when he flipped her over, grabbed her knees with both hands and pushed them up and apart. He rammed into her and she closed around him, massaging his cock with her contractions as his hands had massaged her breasts. He shuddered and pumped himself into her, driving them both into the pillows, and not stopping until she heard his head hit the wall.

His chest heaved and a sound broke from him that alarmed her.

"Cab? Are you all right."

He didn't answer, but squeezed her so tightly that she had to push him away so that she could take a breath.

He turned over and she straddled him, her crotch hot

against his stomach, and looked down at him. His head was buried beneath the pillows. She pulled them away, terrified that he had hurt himself.

She threw the last pillow away and his face appeared. And she realized that Cab was laughing. It was a sound she thought she would never hear again. A sound that was so Cab, and the past came back and flooded her present. And gave her hope that they might yet have a future together.

"Oh, Cab." She picked up a pillow and hit him with it. And he laughed louder and then she was laughing, too.

He stuck the pillow behind his head and drew her to him until she lay in the crook of his shoulder, her head nestled against his neck and her arm draped over his, holding him close.

"I've missed you," he said. She didn't answer because she couldn't form the words past the smile that held her lips in place.

The air began to chill their sweat-drenched skin, and Cab pulled the edge of the coverlet over them.

"I could stay like this forever," he said on a satisfied sigh.

She could, too. But not yet. Cab was still a fugitive. And as soon as she could get her bearings again, they would have to get back to making him safe. But for now, she just answered, "Hmhmm." And enjoyed the pulsing of his blood beneath her ear.

It was late when they finally roused themselves enough to dress and carry the papers and letters downstairs. Geena turned off the flashlight before they opened the door that led to the third floor. She wasn't about to start taking chances now.

They groped their way down the hallway and down two flights of stairs to the kitchen where moonlight lit the windows in an eerie white. They let themselves out the same way they had come in, Cab carefully and fruitlessly closing the window and locking it. Geena picked up the coil of rope she had left on the porch and they hugged the shadows of the house as they returned to the car.

She backed out of the parking spot and drove down the drive to the road without turning on the car lights. Her skin was suddenly pricking with awareness, her antennae out for any unusual sound or movement.

"You're kind of scary," whispered Cab, obviously affected by her change in mood.

"Learned it in the wilderness. Never let down your guard. Always be alert to anything and everything."

"This isn't the wilderness."

But it is, thought Geena. Where predators could be waiting anywhere to catch you unawares and rip your throat out.

When she was sure there were no cars approaching from either direction, she turned on the headlights and pulled onto the road.

They had gone a half mile when a car passed them traveling in the opposite direction. Geena barely had time to register that it was a large sedan, a Mercedes or BMW, before its headlights flashed in her eyes, temporarily blinding her. When she looked in the rearview mirror a second later, it was gone.

But that didn't mean it wouldn't be back.

She fought the urge to speed up, but the moonlight didn't reach through the overhanging branches and the curving road could be treacherous if taken at a high speed.

She was only mildly surprised when she saw headlights coming up behind them.

"Damn," said Cab. "Busy night."

"Yeah." Geena sped up, keeping a lookout in the rearview mirror. The car behind them sped up. "Get down. Now."

Cab's head jerked toward her.

"Now." She pushed his head down.

"This is nuts," he mumbled as he unbuckled his seat belt and slid to the floor.

"Maybe."

The car was gaining on them. She heard the squeal of its brakes as it took the last curve too fast. "Good, asshole. Knock yourself out, and turn yourself over."

It came back into view, fishtailing several times before the driver gained control. Geena pressed on the accelerator. To hell with safety. Somebody was out to get them, and she wouldn't let that happen.

The Honda swerved around another curve and Geena cut the headlights. Only the dashboard lights flickered out of the inky darkness. She was driving blind.

The other car began to fall back. Probably confused at their sudden disappearance and wondering what had happened to them. If she could just stay ahead of his beams, they had a chance. He wouldn't be able to distinguish their engine from his own.

She leaned over the steering wheel, her body taut, her eyes desperately picking out any detail that would keep them on the road. Once she veered too far to the right, and they bumped along the unpaved shoulder for several mind-numbing moments before she found the pavement again.

She could hear Cab breathing from the floor of the car. He must hate not knowing what was going on. But maybe it was better that way. He wouldn't like the idea that was forming in her mind.

When their pursuer's headlights disappeared behind another bend in the road, Geena sped up. Then seeing a black, blacker than the rest, she veered toward it. The Honda's wheels screamed, but made the turn. And they bumped and lurched down a rutted dirt road. At least she thought it was a road.

She put the Honda in neutral and cut the engine. They continued to rattle over bumps and gouges and finally came to a stop in a crunch of branches and pine needles.

Geena released her seat belt and turned around to look out the back window, just in time to see a car careen past and continue down the road. They were only a quarter mile from the first four-way intersection, and she prayed that he would choose one and keep going, instead of coming back to look for them.

Cab climbed onto the seat. She could barely see him, except for the teeth that shone between his beard and the night.

"Are we having fun yet?" he whispered.

Chapter Ten

It was noon before Geena opened her eyes the next day. She felt unusually optimistic. Possibly because of the man still asleep beside her. Funny how a combination of friendship and sex changed one's perspective of things.

She knew there were rough waters ahead, but now that she had her best friend back, she was determined not to let anything separate them again.

She planted a kiss on his forehead and went to shower before he distracted her again. There was a lot of work to be done today. And with any luck an end to the nightmare.

Of course, when theirs ended, someone else's would begin, but she would take that responsibility. She had no choice.

She wasn't too happy to find Cab awake and fully dressed when she came out of the bathroom, still wrapped in a towel. He must have showered in the guest bathroom while she was putting on makeup and drying her hair.

"Forget it," she said, reaching for the lavender cashmere twin set she kept in the back of her closet for just such an occasion. "You're not going."

She leaned over and squeezed her feet into a pair of two inch pumps that she hadn't worn in years, but that were a perfect complement to the twin set.

She turned around to find Cab grinning at her. "I know. I look like my mother circa 1980."

"I bet you can't remember 1980, and you're not going alone." He scooped his pea coat off the floor and shrugged into it.

Geena dropped him off a block away from the Vandermeers' Forest Hills Tudor, where Nan's Jeep Liberty was parked.

"Keep him stuck to your hip," she ordered and drove away before either could object.

A black Mercedes was already parked in front of the plaster and timber house. Geena pulled in behind it; a jolt of recognition zapped through her.

It could have been the car that followed them from Max's the night before. Big, dark—like thousands of other cars in Long Island. And like the rest of this case, she had no proof.

She picked up the little handbag that matched her shoes and opened the car door. The wind whipped at her knee-length skirt and she reached back into the car for her coat, another suitably demure costume.

All in all she felt . . . totally ridiculous. And totally determined.

She took a breath and started up the paving stone walk to the house. It was impressive, not grand, but solid, evoking stability and security. Even with the trees bare of leaves and the manicured lawn turning brown as fall moved into winter, there was a feeling of permanence.

And yet she was about to unravel their lives as hers and Cab's had been unraveled ten years before. One of them had killed Max Vandermeer and today they would begin to pay.

At the door she sniffed, practiced a trembling lip, and rang the bell. Fought the ridiculous urge to cry "Trick or Treat" when the door opened and Ronald Vandermeer smiled down at her.

As soon as he'd helped her to remove her coat, she turned frantically to face him. "You can't," she cried. "Cab isn't dead."

Ronald stepped back, flustered, his welcoming smile turning into a frown of confusion.

Geena fumbled in her handbag and pulled out a hankie, which she applied to her eyes while she worked up a few tears.

He awkwardly patted her back, saying, "There, there," as if she were a child and led her toward the living room.

At the door he stopped. "I know you're upset but try not to upset Marie, you know how delicate she is."

Geena flashed on one of the juicier paragraphs from Marie's letters to Max. *Not nearly as delicate as you believe, Ronald.* And felt an unexpected pang of contrition for what she was about to do.

Marie Vandermeer was sitting before a flickering fire. She smiled up at Geena as Ronald escorted her into the room. Her hands were folded quietly in the lap of her tweed skirt. A creamy silk blouse was tied in a soft bow at her neck. Her hair was cut short and flecked with gray. She was a petite woman, but today she seemed even smaller than Geena remembered.

She's like a timid little mouse, thought Geena and wondered how someone like this could have ever been the sensual vibrant woman of those letters. And Geena couldn't repress a shudder to think that if Cab hadn't returned, she might have ended up the same as Marie, caught by a love that she couldn't have.

"Please sit down. This is such an unexpected pleasure." Marie held out one small hand and gestured to a place on the sofa.

Hands too delicate to tighten a cord around a man's neck, thought Geena as she sat down. And why would she? She loved him.

"What would you like?" asked Ronald from a butler's table where an array of liquor bottles and glasses were displayed.

"Nothing, thank you," said Geena, looking properly weepy. It wasn't that hard. She felt terrible.

One of them is a murderer, she reminded herself. There were no other suspects. It had to be one of them.

Ronald handed his wife a cocktail and took his to sit next to Geena on the sofa. "My dear girl, tell us what this is about."

Marie pricked up her head like a little bird, and for a moment Geena's courage flagged.

She kept her eyes hidden behind her hankie, trying not to think what she was about to do to this family. "Cab isn't dead. And he didn't kill Max and I can prove it." She finished her sentence on a perfect little sob. Not bad for someone who had never even tried out for the school play.

"Ah," said Ronald. Marie didn't respond, but looked into her folded hands.

"Well, this is something new," said a voice from the hallway. Jerrold Vandermeer stepped into the room, a glass of amber liquor in his hand.

"Ah, Jerrold, there you are. You remember Geena Cole, don't you?"

"Of course I do." Jerrold crossed the room and leaned over the coffee table to shake hands. "How nice to see you again. And what a surprise."

Jerrold hadn't aged well. He was twelve years older than Cab, but he looked almost as old as his father. His nose bore the broken blood vessels of a man who drank too much. Geena glanced at the glass in his hand. Not his first of the day, she thought.

Geena smiled. "I thought that might be your Mercedes parked out front." Her eyes held his for a moment. Then his flicked away and she knew with certainty that it was Jerrold who had followed them. What would he have done if she hadn't managed to elude him? How far would he go to protect his father's inheritance? And had he gone on his own volition, or had Ronald sent him?

Ronald placed his glass on the side table and took Geena's hand, forcing her attention back to him. Geena let her hand tremble as he patted it.

"It's been ten years, my dear. And not one word. I don't want to think of Cabot as dead, any more than you do, but there are legal matters to attend to. These things can't just keep drawing out in the hopes of . . ." He wound down. Perhaps he couldn't think of something he hoped for.

"Well, as far as proving Cab innocent," said Jerrold, a slight edge to his voice. "The police made a thorough investigation at the time and they were pretty sure he was guilty." Jerrold didn't quite manage a sympathetic expression and Geena wondered why he had helped Cab to escape.

Marie was watching from her chair, but when Geena looked at her, she turned away to gaze at the fire.

Geena thought she saw the glint of tears. "Mrs. Vandermeer? Marie?"

Marie shook her head slightly. "It's all just so terrible."

"Marie, don't tax yourself," said Ronald, rising from the sofa to pat his wife's hand.

Geena stifled a surge of impatience. She needed more than serial hand patting from these people.

She lowered her hankie. "Did you even try to find him?"

"Of course we did," said Ronald. "But obviously Cab either didn't want to be found or he, er, met with an untimely accident."

Geena heard Marie's intake of breath, but Jerrold cleared his throat, overriding her reaction. "I know you and Cab were good friends. He was my friend, too. But it's better this way, really, if you think about it. If Cab returned, he would be arrested. Spend the rest of his life in prison. Surely, you wouldn't want that."

Now, was the time. "Cab didn't kill his uncle and I can prove it." Geena blurted out the words so abruptly that Marie jumped in her chair and Ronald took a step backward. "Max gave some papers to Cab before he left. Something that someone would kill for in order for it not to come to light." Her throat tightened and she was suddenly fighting back real tears. What a horrible thing to do to Marie, especially since the letters didn't prove a damn thing.

She saw Marie's eyes widen. Was it a flicker of fear or sadness she saw? Or guilt?

And suddenly Geena didn't know if she could destroy this woman. She looked away, straightened a magazine on the coffee table, picked up a heavy glass paperweight and replaced it, as she tried to think how to force the murderer's hand without giving away Marie's secret.

She couldn't. Marie's secret would have to come out.

"If Cab didn't kill Uncle Max, why did he run?" asked Jerrold, letting his exasperation come out in full force.

And why did you help him? she wondered.

"Especially if he had these papers that supposedly would clear him," added Ronald.

"I don't think Cab knew what he had, because he didn't take them with him. I have them."

She heard Marie's intake of breath.

There was a moment when nobody moved. The undercurrent of some painful emotion palpitated in the room. It seemed to arc between husband and wife and son.

Then Ronald shook his head. "Geena, dear. There are some things in life we just have to accept, no matter how painful they are."

Pain, thought Geena. Did Ronald know about Marie and Max? Had Max finally told him on the last day of his life. Had Ronald gone mad with rage and strangled him?

And to her horror, instead of hatred, Geena was moved to pity for him. A man who loved his wife and whose wife had loved someone else.

Geena pulled herself together. "I'm taking what I found to the police. I'm sure Detective Rogers would be interested in seeing them."

"Just what did you find?" Jerrold put his drink down on the coffee table and took a step toward her, his eyebrows furrowed as he stared at her handbag.

Geena clutched her purse as if her life depended on it.

Of course she wasn't carrying the papers on her. She wondered how long it would take before they realized they were talking to a nearly thirty-year-old detective and not the teenager they remembered.

"Leave it alone, Geena." Ronald stepped around Jerrold to take her elbow and gently lift her from the sofa. The visit was over, and he had accomplished it with real finesse.

But Jerrold barred the way. "Wait a minute, Dad. I think we should take a look at these papers. No telling what trouble a hysterical girl could stir up."

Marie rose from her chair. She didn't move closer, but watched the two men with a look of growing resignation on her face.

Geena tried to slip past Jerrold, but before she could, Jerrold grabbed her purse and headed for the door.

"No, Jerrold." Marie's voice was heartbreaking.

"Listen to your mother, Jerrold." Cab stepped through the archway. Jerrold skidded to a stop, rumpling the oriental carpet under his feet.

Marie cried out and swayed; Ronald scooped her into his arms.

In the momentary distraction, Jerrold shoved Cab away. He fell into the butler's table; glasses and liquor bottles crashed to the floor.

Geena kicked off her shoes, ready to pursue Jerrold. Then she saw the glass paperweight on the coffee table. She picked it up and let it fly.

It caught Jerrold between the shoulder blades. His arms flew out on impact and the purse fell from of his hands. He lunged for the handbag, but a kick from Geena's bare foot sent him sprawling.

Cab scrambled to his feet. He pushed Geena aside and pulled Jerrold off the floor. He pushed him into a chair, just as Nan sauntered through the doorway.

"All done?" she asked casually.

Actually, they weren't. No one had confessed. Trying to steal evidence wasn't a confession of murder. Shit, thought Geena. In for a penny, in for a pound.

"Call, the police, Nan. Ask for Detective Rogers."

"No," cried Marie. "You can't think Jerrold killed Max. You can't just barge in and—"

"Mrs. Vandermeer. You may not be aware of this, but I run a detective agency. This is one of my operatives." She mentally crossed her fingers and hoped that Nan didn't burst out laughing.

Marie stared at her in disbelief, then began to shake her head. Once she started, she couldn't stop. "No. I did it. I killed Max."

Oh, Christ, thought Geena. Nan rolled her eyes. Cab and Ronald stared at her. Jerrold shook his head.

"No you didn't. I did, but no one will ever prove it." He lunged for the purse and threw it into the fire.

Everyone stared in horror as the purse burst into flames.

"I never liked that bag anyway," said Nan under her breath. "We're up the crick; should I really call the police? Oops, never mind. It isn't over yet."

Marie slowly turned to face her son. She walked right up to him until she was standing close enough to hand him a weapon. Geena and Nan prepared themselves to act. But Marie hauled back and slapped him across the face.

The sound reverberated in the air. "You killed him?" she asked, no sympathy, no motherly love in her voice. "You viper. You changeling. You killed your own father."

Jerrold reeled. Ronald reached ineffectually toward his wife. Cab, Nan, and Geena stared openmouthed. Marie sank into a chair and wept. After a long moment, Ronald knelt by the chair and patted her back. "There, there," he said.

She looked at him through flowing tears. "I thought it was you," she cried. "All these years, I thought it was you."

"God," said Cab. "I can't stand this. Can we get out of here? Nan looks like she has everything under control."

Geena slowly shook her head, fighting off her own tears. "Not yet. We have to wait for the police." She sniffed. "This is always the hardest part."

"You do this often?"

"No. Thank God." And never when it was this close to home.

On Tuesday morning, Nan, Delia, and Geena finished up the paperwork on the Vandermeer case. Geena closed the manila file and tossed it on the conference table.

"Are you okay, boss?"

"Yeah, I guess."

"Well, I think you should be proud of yourself," said Delia. "Getting Jerrold to confess just like on television. I wish I had been there."

Geena snorted. "I didn't get him to confess. I still don't know *why* he confessed. He thought he had destroyed the letters. If he'd kept his head, he could have bluffed his way out of it." She sighed. "It was just pure dumb luck."

"Hey, don't knock it," said Nan, standing up and stretching. "We'll take whatever help we can get. And you did manage to sew up most of the case."

"But we still don't know why Marie married Ronald instead of Max," said Delia.

"No, and we probably never will," said Geena.

"So where's Cab? He's sticking around, isn't he?"

"I hope so, but we haven't really talked since they arrested Jerrold. There were reams of paperwork to go through down at the station. Stuff at City Hall, not to mention probating the will . . . and trying to decide what to do with his life."

"Just give him some time, boss," said Nan. "He'll figure it out sooner or later. Want to come out to dinner?"

"Not tonight." Geena followed Delia and Nan into the main office while they got on their coats. The outer door opened and a man stepped into the room.

"Can I help you?" Geena asked automatically, while Nan and Delia stood behind her and stared.

"I certainly hope so."

"Oh, my God," breathed Delia. Nan let out a whistle. Geena just kept staring. He was dressed in a charcoal gray overcoat, opened to reveal a dark blue suit, with a lighter blue shirt and pinstriped tie. His hair was several inches shorter and the beard was gone. He looked different, older, more civilized. He looked rich and in control.

Geena's gut twisted as she became aware of how different their lives really were. And would certainly be in the future. Cab would inherit millions. She had given hers up and now had to work to make ends meet.

She hadn't thought about how solving the case and proving him innocent would affect their life together. She knew she was about to find out.

"Could we talk?" He glanced toward Delia and Nan. "Outside?"

Geena nodded. Someone handed her her coat. She followed Cab out the back door. He sat down on the steps. She sat down next to him by the mere fact that her knees gave out from under her.

"Are you fabulously wealthy?" she asked, trying for a light tone.

"Not fabulously. Ronald helped himself to quite a bit of it over the years, in expectation of inheriting it. He promised to pay it back, but I won't take it. He and Marie have lost enough already."

Geena nodded as she watched a lone leaf roll across the parking lot. "What are you going to do now?"

"Depends." He leaned forward and tried to get a look at her face. "I can't go back to my old life, Geena, or the life that Max had planned for me. I'm too much of a free spirit to sit in an office all day."

She was going to lose him—again.

"I thought I might stick around, fix up the house myself. It's what I like doing. Then maybe we could . . . get to know each other again. If you want to." He took her hand, turned it over to look at her palm. "Life hasn't turned out like we planned." He shrugged, a shrug that said *c'est la vie*.

"No, it hasn't." Geena closed her fingers around his. "It's turned out much better."

LOVE BITES

Chapter One

"He murdered my sister and I want him to pay." Eileen Turner covered her face with her hands. The three partners of Women-Tek, detective agency to the harassed and beleaguered, watched sympathetically.

Geena Cole handed her the box of tissues that she kept on her desk for just such an occasion. "Ms. Turner," she said. "The police investigation is still open, and we don't really have the manpower to investigate murders."

Nan Scott nodded her agreement, but Delia Petrocelli just frowned. Geena had started the agency four years before to help women just like Eileen Turner. Most of their cases were divorce suits, but they had recently added murder investigation to their résumé. Both Nan and Geena had been personally involved in two of them. Delia had yet to go out on a dangerous case on her own.

She was the newest member of the firm and when she'd shown up at the door six months ago she had been fat, sloppy, with so little self-esteem that just getting to the door had taken every bit of her determination.

Just as it must have taken every ounce of Eileen Turner's nerve to come to them for help. She spoke in the soft twang of Oklahoma where she and her sister, Susannah, had grown up. Then Susannah had left the farm to try her acting skills in New York.

Eileen Turner was tall and angular, and her plain polyester shirtwaist did nothing to enhance her figure. Long legs stretched out from beneath the unflattering hemline and her shoes must have been bought at Kmart. The rusty red hair that hung lank to her shoulders would be lovely if given the right cut and style. And a little makeup would transform that pale, lusterless face into something that would probably rival her sister's beauty.

And her sister was a beauty. Her head shot lay on the table. So sophisticated and gorgeous that it was hard to believe the two women were sisters.

Delia glanced down at her own legs, encased in tailored navy slacks, and crossed at the knee. They were thin, well, thinner than they had been, and buff, thanks to constant exercise. She wore a lighter blue turtleneck and there wasn't a bulge in sight. She was always amazed to remember where she had started and how she had been transformed, thanks to two friends who believed in her.

Eileen Turner needed someone to believe in her. Women-Tek would be perfect for the case, if only Geena would agree to investigate.

Delia stole a look at her two colleagues to see which way the wind blew. Geena was going to turn her down. Delia could tell by the set of her mouth. And Geena was the boss.

Eileen Turner shook her head. "They won't arrest him. He's rich. Really rich. He can do anything he wants and nobody will stop him." Eileen burst into more tears.

Delia automatically handed her another tissue. Ben Michaelson was extremely rich, and an inveterate playboy, but he was also a philanthropist in a major way, helping fund the city's most pressing needs: community centers, satellite schools, health care facilities for the poor. Which didn't give him the right to murder anyone. But it would certainly give him an edge with the police.

Geena waited for the last onslaught of tears to subside, then said, "Ms. Turner. We're very sorry for your loss, but we really can't accept your case. I think you should put your trust in the police. They are trained for these things."

"I thought another woman would understand. Men get away with everything. My sister didn't stand a chance. He told her that he loved her, then he killed her. And you're just going to let him get away with it." Eileen stood up. "I thought you would be different."

"We do understand," said Delia, also standing up and putting a comforting hand on the woman's back. She knew about men who didn't have to pay for their sins. She had been married to one.

Not that she thought Vincent would ever stoop to murder to get rid of an unwanted female. After all, she had survived to tell the tale. Not that she'd ever told the real story of how her Cinderella marriage had turned into *Diary of a Mad Housewife*.

Delia's heart went out to Eileen Turner, desperate for justice, feeling ineffectual and useless. She caught Geena's eye and tried to telegraph that she thought they should take the case. Geena's eyes narrowed, but not before Delia saw them waver.

"Perhaps you'll excuse us for just one moment, while I consult with my colleagues." Geena flicked her head toward the conference room door. "We'll just be a moment."

Eileen Turner nodded. Her eyes were red and swollen, but she looked up at them with a spark of hope that touched the raw spot that Delia had yet to finally rub out. She gave the woman an optimistic smile as she walked past her.

As soon as the conference room door closed, Geena turned to Nan and Delia.

"I don't like this. We've never run an operation alongside a police investigation. It takes a kind of finesse I'm not sure we can pull off."

"Well, we aren't known for our finesse," agreed Nan, catching a wayward strand of her strawberry blonde ponytail and hooking it behind her ear.

"But we could string up the bastard and have him trussed and gutted before the NYPD planned a takedown," said Delia.

Geena and Nan looked startled.

"And this from a Camp Wilderness success story," said Geena.

"That's just the point."

"Lost me," said Nan.

Delia sighed. "The minute I left Camp Wilderness, I dropped my bow and arrows and hiking boots in the nearest dumpster and headed for Henri Bendel. Probably the same way Susannah Turner tossed her polyester dress and discount store shoes. I just got fat and frumpy and a philandering husband. You gave me a chance to get my life back. Susannah got murdered."

Delia shuddered and speared her fingers through her spiky black hair as the image of Susannah lying in a dark back alley with her auburn hair spread across the filthy pavement rose in her mind.

"You think we should take the case," said Geena.

"Yes. The police see hundreds of murders and . . ."

"And you think they'll look the other way because Ben Michaelson is a rich philanthropist and Susannah was a hooker."

"They will."

"Maybe you're right," said Geena.

"I am right."

Geena turned to Nan. "What do you think?"

"I think Delia's right, unfortunately. But I don't think we should jump into this without having a little more information. What if we tell Ms. Turner that we'll look into it and then decide if we can help her."

"Will that do?" asked Geena.

Delia nodded. She was sure that once they knew the specifics, they would have to help this poor woman out. "Let's go tell her."

* * *

Several hours later, they met in the conference room. Nan had downloaded weeks of articles from the *Times* and the *Post*. Geena had strong-armed a friend of hers in the NYPD into faxing over the public files of the murder case. Delia had made a big dent in background checks on Ben Michaelson and Susannah Turner.

They passed articles, police reports, and pictures around.

"Something is definitely rotten here," said Geena, tossing a color photocopy of Ben Michaelson onto the table.

They all looked at the two pictures that now lay side by side. Two beautiful people, thought Delia. One so evil, and one so dead.

"It's hard to believe that the man in this picture is a murderer," said Nan, picking up the shot of Michaelson handing a check to the director of the Bronx Community School.

The three of them peered at the copy. He was tall and thin, and good-looking in a Wall Street way: short brown hair, parted on the side and brushed back from a Fortune 500 forehead. Eyes that projected concern and compassion. A firm handshake as he presented the check.

But stranger things happened, thought Delia. The richer, the greedier, the more amoral. She knew that from experience. And as she looked at the picture, Ben Michaelson's image morphed into Vincent Dunmore, successful plastic surgeon, adulterer—her ex-husband.

She shook her head and the picture was once again Ben Michaelson.

Geena leaned forward on her elbows and steepled her fingers. "If we take this case, Eileen Turner might find out more than she wants to know."

"You mean about her sister being a high-class call girl instead of just a struggling actress," said Nan.

Geena nodded. "She already said she doesn't believe it. It will be doubly painful if she has to take that knowledge as well as the body back to Oklahoma with her."

"Their poor parents," said Nan. "At least I just left Anthony at the altar, though I did feel like killing him at the time."

"I still feel like killing Vincent sometimes," said Delia. "But I'm getting over it."

Geena slapped her hand down on the table. "There will be no vigilante behavior if we take this case. I don't want any of us to get close enough to Michaelson to test our theories. Understood?"

"Well, yeah, but how are we going to nail him if we don't get close to him?" asked Nan.

"Look, Michaelson may be a philanthropist, but he's also a playboy with a reputation, not to mention a murder suspect. Just collect evidence and if we uncover anything incriminating, we'll hand it over to the police."

"And this from a woman who survived a car chase and beaned the felon with a paperweight."

"Do as I say, not as I do." But Geena smiled. "Oh, hell. You're right. This is going to get up front and personal. It's the only way to flush Michaelson out if, and I repeat *if*, Michaelson is the murderer."

"Thanks," said Delia. She stood up and began gathering the files.

"I know I'm going to regret this, but I'll tell her we'll take the case, but you'll have to be the detective in charge on this one. I'm up to my ears on this Breakwater deal and Nan's covering her load plus mine."

Delia stopped and clutched the papers in her hand. "But I've never been the primary before."

"There's always a first time, though this wouldn't be my choice to start you out."

"Do you think I'm ready?"

"You know how to do a stakeout, how to tail a mark without being seen, and you've been working out, right?"

"Karate, the gym, the firing range. Barry, my instructor at the range, says he's never seen a steadier hand. And I broke

three boards with my forehead at the dojo this morning before work."

"God, we've created a monster."

"Nah," said Nan with a twinkle in her eye. "Delia has just
gotten in touch with her inner hellcat." She chuckled. "God,
you were ba-a-ad, when we met at Camp Wilderness."

Delia looked down at her figure. "I was, but what about
now?"

Nan laughed. "When it comes to the way you look, you're
ready. But we have to go shopping. You might win the best-
dressed detective award, but all your slut clothes are a size
sixteen."

"I didn't have any slut clothes when I was a size sixteen."

"All the more reason to hit the mall."

Chapter Two

Ben Michaelson pulled the collar of his dress coat up and pushed through the revolving doors of the Plaza Hotel. The frigid night air took his breath away. Wind whipped around the corner of the building and nearly sent his beret flying. He grabbed it just in time and pulled it down over his forehead.

Damn, it had been a long winter. Longer for him than he cared to think about. And there was no end in sight. And no respite from curious questions and knowing looks passed between acquaintances when they thought he couldn't see. The whispered comments when he entered a room full of people, or louder speculations when he left early, like he had just done.

Ben Michaelson, life of the party, lady killer. He shuddered as a chill that had nothing to do with the weather sliced through him. Once upon a time he'd gotten a kick out of being called a lady killer, but not anymore, not since Susannah was murdered. Now when people called him a lady killer, it wasn't a compliment.

But Susannah was no lady. Just a hooker, working for an elite agency that gave her entrée into the best parties. She had deceived him. How was that for the worldly man about town? It was hard to believe that her acting skills hadn't been able to land her a job on Broadway, because she was good, really good.

She was also young—too young for him. But charming and fresh. A girl from Oklahoma, hoping to become an actress, she said. And he was bored, a feeling that was becoming more and more of a problem lately.

So he thought what the hell. She'd entertain him for a little while, they'd go their separate ways. He'd even help her with her career. Yeah, the famous do-gooder had gotten duped but good.

Even when he came back to his penthouse early one day and found her riffling through his desk, he made excuses for her. She was naturally curious to find out more about him. He was known for his insistence on privacy.

He'd probably still be playing the dupe if it hadn't been for the anonymous letter. He got plenty of those. People in the limelight did. That's what he kept an office and secretaries for. But this one had been slipped under the door of his apartment.

Susannah Turner—prostitute. He hadn't believed it at first. And it wasn't something he could ask his in-house investigators to look into. So he had done the work himself.

Traced her back to the East Side Sports Club, a front for a high-class call girl operation that was subsequently shut down. Now its expensive hookers were spread all over Manhattan and working harder than ever.

But not Susannah. She wouldn't be getting her claws into any other man. Someone had knifed her in an alley, not six blocks from his apartment. And that's why he'd became the number one suspect.

And that's why he was leaving another party early. Nowhere to run, nowhere to hide. He couldn't stand being alone and he couldn't stand being with people who were always looking at him with a speculative eye, wondering, *Did he kill her?*

Ben waved off the doorman's attempt to put him in a cab. He didn't feel like going home. A walk would clear his head, chase the anxiety away, and leave him so cold that he'd be grateful for his empty apartment with its ghosts of unhappiness.

He struck off across the street, past the square and its fountain, shut down for the winter. Crossed the street again and headed down Fifty-sixth Street toward the East River.

He thought of the punch line to a joke about the river: Drop in and take a load off. It hadn't come to that, though it had crossed his mind more than once in the last few weeks.

He wasn't going there tonight, at any rate. He'd stop at The Shamrock before taking a cab downtown. It was only two blocks from the river and had probably saved a few other souls who were in similar straits as himself. At least there, they didn't beat around the bush. They kind of respected him for being in this mess. And they didn't think that he'd actually murdered Susannah, which was more then he could say for his rich friends upstairs in the ballroom of the Plaza.

Delia knew it would be hard to get to Ben Michaelson, but she had done her homework. She knew that even during the investigation he still went to parties, but he usually left early. That was why she was hanging out at the south end of Central Park, freezing her new size-eight-squeezed-into-a-size-six butt off for the last three hours.

She pulled at the short bunny fur jacket she'd bought that afternoon, trying to get it to cover more of her black leather pants. Her feet, cramped inside a pair of stiletto boots, had lost feeling an hour ago, and her butt was on its way.

The jacket was faux, not as warm as the real thing would be. But she didn't buy real fur. Not since Camp Wilderness. It was one thing to wear the pelt of an animal that you had tracked, killed, and slaughtered yourself, another thing entirely to buy it at Bergdorf's.

She had done a lot of shopping at Bergdorf's. The apartment she had lived in with Vincent was only two blocks north on Fifth Avenue. So close and yet so far. . . .

Nope. Not going there. Not ever again. She quickly pushed her insecure housewife aside and reached in for her inner hellcat. It had been buried deep for a long time, but it was still alive and kicking, she realized. And nothing or no one was going to take it away again.

By the time Michaelson finally made an appearance, at least three horny salesmen, a cab driver, and a street bum had tried to pick her up, so she was feeling a little more sure of herself.

She almost missed him. He was bundled up like it was February in Antarctica, not March in Manhattan. Long over-coat with the collar pulled up over his ears. Black beret pulled down over his eyes. But she knew it was him; she'd been studying him for days.

He stood on the sidewalk, looking up and down the street, and she prayed he wouldn't jump into a cab before she could get to him. She stepped off the curb and started in his direction, swinging her hips as much as she could while balancing on three-inch, pointed-toe ankle boots, and trying to keep the fur jacket out of her mouth.

Just as she reached the other side of the street, he started walking across the square. She did a little Wizard of Oz ball change and hurried after him.

He walked for blocks, past the elegant town houses, past the high-end shops and exclusive art galleries, and finally turned down a narrow, unmarked street that seemed to lead them under the Fifty-ninth Street bridge and into no-man's land. He occasionally glanced behind him, which made it necessary for Delia to human torpedo herself into a dark alley, drop behind a smelly row of trash cans, and slip between two cars, barely avoiding a pile of unscooped dog poop.

She did her own amount of backward glances as they traveled farther into don't-be-here-without-your-mace-canister country.

The man was as rich as—she couldn't remember the name

of the Greek god who he was as rich as. Surely he didn't *live* around here.

She was caught off guard when he suddenly turned into a door beneath a buzzing neon sign. Several letters had burned out and the ones that were left spelled out *The ham ock*.

But she was a detective and it only took a second or two for her to fill in the missing S and R. The Shamrock. Jeez. She *would* have to pick him up on a night he was out slumming. She could have outfitted herself in L.L. Bean and been comfortable and warm.

She waited exactly three minutes and went in after him.

Chapter Three

Inside The Shamrock was dark and hazy. "Louie, Louie" was blaring from an unseen jukebox. The dark shapes of patrons seemed to grow out of the uneven lighting.

It was a good thing there was a no-smoking law in the city or she wouldn't be able to see across the room to where Ben Michaelson sat at the bar, sans overcoat and beret, talking to a short, rotund bartender.

Delia gave herself a quick pep talk. She could do this. Once she had been the baddest of the bad. She could rise to the challenge. This was going to be fun.

She sidled over to the bar and plopped her butt on the torn bar stool next to Ben M.

He glanced over and gave her an incredulous look. Okay, so she was a little overdressed for the ambiance, but so was he. She didn't think he'd seen her hobbling after him. It would be so embarrassing to blow her first real assignment because she couldn't handle her shoes.

She gave Rotundo a come hither look. "Seltzer on the rocks with a twist."

He blinked but moved off to get her drink

She noticed that Michaelson was checking her out. Head to toe as it were.

She had her MO together: play uninterested, but not so

uninterested that he couldn't get her interested. *Okay, here goes.* She gave him a sardonic look. "Lose something?"

He answered with a half smile. One cheek dimpled in a way that made her understand why women loved him. Little boy in a sexy man's body. Yeah. She knew the type. Well, at least had known the type until six years ago, when she married the little boy with a so-so body and a huge Peter Pan complex.

"A little out of your element, babe?"

Delia lifted a newly plucked and penciled eyebrow. She'd *babe* him, before this was over.

"I suppose you want me to buy you a drink."

God. She'd never heard anyone sound so bored. Before she could think of an answer, a disembodied voice called out of the haze.

"Hey, Ben, how bout a game of darts?"

"Clancy wants to win back his twenty," said a second voice.

"But he's already ploshed," added a third. "So you could leave a richer man if you hurry before he passes out."

Surround Sound laughter. Delia squinted across the room. She could barely make out the shapes of men, much less tie a voice to a body. That's when she realized there weren't many women in the joint. Well, two others if she were counting. The waitress and a really fat mama who sat at a table with a couple of skinheads. Oh, boy.

"On my way." Ben M. picked up his drink, lifted it toward her, and left her high and dry.

Rotundo slid her glass of seltzer toward her.

"Give it up, babe."

What was with the *babe* shit? Men stepped through the door and became instant Neanderthals?

"Give up what?" she asked.

"If you followed Ben in here, don't plan to follow him out. You're not his type."

Yeah, well. She hadn't been anybody's type in a long time. She quickly plastered over the first crack in her new bad girl persona. *I am not a frumpy housewife*, she chanted to herself. *I am not a frumpy housewife.*

"Wouldn't think of it. Though I got to say, he kind of sticks out in this milieu."

Rotundo scrunched up the folds of his face. "If you mean he's too high class for the likes of us, you don't know him."

"I don't know him." She had to stop thinking of this guy as Rotundo. *You were fat just a few months ago*, she chastised herself. *And you'd hate it if someone called you Rotundo.* "What's your name?"

The bar tender blinked. "Hal."

"Well, thanks for the drink, Hal. And the advice." She slid off the bar stool and took her drink over to watch the dart game. Ben M. had deep-sixed his jacket and tie and the sleeves of his white shirt were rolled up to his biceps. Those she could see, in spite of the haze. The sinews stuck out like road maps to his wrists.

She sidled through a couple of bruisers and took a look at the board. Red darts plotted an extended tour over the cork. There was one lying on the floor beneath it. Four blue darts made a perfect circle around the center bull's eye.

A guy in a Con Edison shirt shrugged. "Damn, that one slipped out of my hand."

"So'd your twenty," said a short skinny man wearing a John Deere cap, and Delia got the Surround Sound laughter again.

Ben took his place behind a line that was marked out in grungy gaffer tape. He lifted the dart, aimed, and let it fire. For a second, Delia got a flash of hunting with bow and arrow. Then the dart hit its mark, and applause and back slapping destroyed the image.

Ben collected his money and started back to the bar.

Delia stepped in his path. "I'll play you for the next round of drinks."

A catcall, a whistle, a couple of hoots.

"Don't do it, Ben. She looks dangerous."

"Better watch your wallet."

"She's got the evil eye," slurred the man in the Con Ed shirt. Clancy, she guessed. He crossed himself, and held up his hands to ward her off before bursting into raucous laughter.

"Afraid?" She asked loud enough for everyone to hear.

Ben gave her the same look he'd given her when she sat down at the bar.

She gave him the same eyebrow lift.

He returned it with the one-dimpled smile. "You're on."

Clancy wove over to the wall and began pulling darts out of the board. Delia slipped off her bunny fur jacket and handed it over to the nearest beefy paw.

More hoots as the guy hugged it to his chest and rolled his eyes in ecstasy.

"Don't wrinkle it," said Delia, then had to control her face when the guy actually looked down at the faux fur and began to smooth it out.

Clancy returned with the darts, blue bundled in one hand, red in the other.

"Your choice," said Ben, looking bored again.

He'd just won with blue. She took the red.

Ben took the blue and made a slight bow. "Ladies first." His tone was so sarcastic that she wanted to rip his throat out. She took a breath. That's what she got for thinking about Camp Wilderness. Total cave woman behavior.

She stepped up to the tape.

Someone yelled, "Clear the deck!" A few people laughed, but after a look from Delia, the bar became quiet.

Delia hefted the darts into her left hand and fingered one to get the feel of it. Old, but fairly well-balanced.

She could feel everyone's attention directed at her. Shit. She shouldn't have been so eager. It had been a few years since she'd been the Camp Wilderness dart champion.

She lifted the dart, concentrating on the bull's-eye and

imagining the arc and speed that would send the dart home. She pulled back her arm and with a flick of the wrist let the dart go. It hit just outside the center circle. Not bad, but it wouldn't win her another seltzer.

A few "good goings," but mainly everyone just waited for Ben to take his place. She stepped back and made room for him at the line.

"Don't worry, Bennie. It was just a lucky shot."

Ben nodded, his eyes focused on the board.

Delia fingered her four remaining darts, while she waited for Ben to make his shot. Made a few mental calculations. A minor readjustment here and there.

Ben's dart hit the left edge of the bull's-eye. A murmur of approval ricocheted around the room. Ben stepped aside and gestured for her to take her place. It was a mocking, knight errant kind of gesture, but the glint in his eye told her he was taking her challenge seriously.

She smiled back at him to let him know she wasn't concerned. And she wondered how he could seem so at home here in this working-class pub and why the regulars accepted him.

She stepped up to the line, shaking her mind free of any thoughts but of winning the game. She took a breath, steadied her hand, and threw the dart.

Dead center.

The crowd was more vocal this time.

Ben narrowed his eyes as he took his place for the next throw. His dart landed a quarter inch to the right of hers.

Okay, she'd beat him on this round, but she still needed to make up for her first throw. On her next throw, the dart pricked the cork just above the two center darts.

Ben took his turn. He must be getting rattled, because his dart landed in the yellow circle. They were neck and neck, with Ben leading her by an eighth of an inch.

By the end of the game, the bull's-eye was a cluster of blue and red darts, except for the two lone darts in the yellow. It was too close to call and Ben was looking a bit grumpy. Sort of like a wily mountain lion—one that she wouldn't mind sharing a lair with.

One of the men pulled the two wayward darts off the board and handed them their respective colors. "Sudden death."

Delia shivered. That's why she was here. Not to play darts, or have randy animal fantasies, but to find out if Ben Michaelson was a murderer. Her eyes met Ben's, were held there as a black hole sucked her in. Then he blinked and released her.

Delia shivered. This guy was scary; he was also very hot.

The guy in the John Deere cap came up with a quarter and flipped it in the air. He caught it on the back of his hand and clapped his other hand on top.

"Your call," said Ben, his eyes fixated on her face.

"Heads."

"Heads it is."

Ben flashed teeth at her and stepped aside. The pub became totally quiet; even the jukebox was silent.

Delia took her place, trying to figure out the best way to play her final throw. Win and make him buy her a drink, or throw the game and hope he stuck around long enough for her to buy him one. There had been nothing about this kind of situation in the *Private Investigation for Dummies* she'd been studying. Should she win or lose?

Someone murmured, "She's getting nervous. You've got her now."

Delia lowered the dart and glowered at the man. "Do you mind?"

"Sorry," he said contritely.

Oh, hell. She aimed, slowly exhaled and let the dart go. It landed a half inch off center, but still in the bull's-eye.

A Surround Sound exhalation of breath.

Ben frowned at her as he stepped up to the tape. Stood looking at the board until the crowd stilled.

This would be interesting.

Ben took aim, threw.

The dart seemed to suspend in the air, sail slow motion, then *shhhp*ed into the board.

She squinted at the bull's-eye, before the men crowded around it and hid it from view.

"She beat you by a hair, Bennie. Looks like you're buying."

"Tough luck."

Murmured agreements. They were obviously disappointed.

Well, that was weird. She thought for sure she'd lost and that Michaelson would brush her off.

Men clapped Ben on the back. A few clapped Delia on the back.

Her coat was handed to her.

"I'll buy you that drink," said Ben as he led her back to the bar. He helped her none too gently onto the bar stool.

A sore loser. And she'd given him ample room to beat her.

Then she realized he hadn't sat down, but hovered over her, one hand braced on the bar stool so close to her butt that she could feel the heat of his hand all the way up her spine. His other hand rested on the bar. He leaned into her, near enough for her to feel his breath on her ear.

She forced back an involuntary shiver. How dangerous was this man?

He turned her bar stool around until she faced him. "You tried to throw the game. Why?"

"To let you save face." *Oops, never speak before thinking.* One of the first rules of investigation. She didn't quite have that part down yet. She had to concentrate, but the heat emanating from Ben Michaelson was making it difficult.

"I don't need to save face. Put it on my tab."

"What?" Then she saw the two glasses on the bar and

Hal's sardonic smile. He shook his head at her and moved away.

She took the glass and turned back to Ben. There was a gleam in his dark eyes that hadn't been there before, and her stomach did a little shake, rattle, and roll.

He sat down and stretched his long legs to either side of her bar stool, virtually trapping her. "Are you a reporter?"

"What?"

"A reporter. Are you a reporter?"

Delia's face went blank along with her mind. "Uh. No. I just shop a lot."

He unveiled that one-dimple smile and relaxed.

As long as he didn't ask her if she was a PI, she'd be okay. She'd once been a magnificent liar, but she hadn't used that skill in a really long time and she wasn't sure she was up to the mark.

Especially if he could really see into her soul, the way his eyes said he could. No wonder women fell over each other trying to get a piece of this man. And to her chagrin, Delia realized she wanted to be one of them. Damn. That was another rule. Don't get emotionally involved with the perp.

"So what do you do—besides shop?" Ben slid his drink to the edge of the bar and leaned closer. She leaned closer, careful to let one breast rest against the edge of the bar top.

That got his attention—for a nanosecond—before his eyes became opaque again. Had she misread that flicker of interest in his eyes, or had it merely been disgust?

A flash of insecurity stung her. *No*, she thought. *I don't do insecure anymore.*

She still had a few pounds to lose. She'd never be really thin like Nan and Geena, but some men liked voluptuous, and she was voluptuous. And she didn't even have to wear control tops anymore. That was a real boost to her morale.

He was nursing his drink and waiting for her to answer his question.

She shrugged, pressing her arms to the side of her breasts

and making them jut forward. Michaelson moved back from
them.

Be subtle, she reminded herself. He'll be gun-shy after
what he's been through. *Don't act like a hooker. Just hook
him.*

She ran her finger along a wet spot on the bar then wiped
it on her sweater right at her cleavage.

No response. Damn, the man was impervious. And she
didn't think it was just her. He was being cautious. Well, who
wouldn't be in his situation.

She took a sip of seltzer and just for fun sucked in a piece
of ice and rolled it around her tongue. Hell, she'd always
been good at this seduction business. She was still good at it
in spite of Vincent You've-let-yourself-go and I-don't-love-
you-anymore Dunmore. In fact, she was so good she was
turning herself on. Or maybe it was being so close to Ben
Michaelson that was making her hot in all the right places.

Cool it, she told herself. This guy is a murderer—probably—maybe.

Ben shifted on his stool. Getting just a little turned on? she
wondered. Then thought, *Why am I doing this? I'm supposed to investigate him, not seduce him.* And it occurred to
her that she'd like to do both.

She spit the ice back into the glass.

"What do you do?" she asked.

"Uh." He sat up. Hesitated. "You really don't know?"

"Besides playing darts."

"I play a lot of darts." He was talking darts, but his voice
suddenly grew husky, his eyes were sucking her in.

Shit. She still had it after all.

"Listen, would you be interested in a late dinner? I know a
little Italian place not far from here."

"Sounds nice," she said and slid off the stool.

"I'll just call ahead. Be right back."

He returned a few minutes later, wearing his overcoat. He
looked handsome, sophisticated, and sexy as hell.

"Ready?"

She nodded and let him help her into her faux fur.

"My name's Ben."

Delia smiled up at him and slipped her hand into the crook of his elbow. *Gotcha, asshole.*

Chapter Four

Domenico's was the Italian counterpart of the Shamrock Pub. The lighting was dim, Domenico was almost as fat as Hal, the room was packed with people sitting shoulder to shoulder around the Formica tables and standing in a line against the wall, waiting for a table. The air buzzed with laughter and conversation—until Ben and Delia stepped into the room and conversation faltered and died. Delia could feel the tension coiling around Ben.

Domenico's hearty greeting cut through the silence like a hot knife through butter. He waddled toward them and pumped Ben's hand. *"Buona sera."* He smiled at Delia. "Welcome. This way, please."

He led them through the closely set tables and conversation returned to its previous level. They followed him down a hallway, past the kitchen where a radio reported the evening news in Italian, and into a glass solarium, canopied by twinkling white lights, threaded through the bare trees of a courtyard.

The solarium was empty. Only one candlelit table was set for dinner.

Delia let Domenico seat her. Then he hurried off to fetch a bottle of Classico Reservo and their first course. Delia raised her eyebrows at Ben.

"I'm a regular."

More than just a regular, thought Delia. Maybe he owned the place. The fact that it was an Italian restaurant did nothing to assuage the niggling suspicion that she might be in over her head.

"I don't even know your name," said Ben, breaking into her thoughts.

"Delia," she said automatically. Damn, she'd done it again. Not that it mattered. She'd had plenty of time to deliberate about using an alias while she'd been standing out in the cold at the Plaza. As long as she didn't give him a last name, he wouldn't be able to trace her. She had a pretty good idea that if he hadn't checked out potential dates before Susannah Turner, he certainly would from now on.

"Delia," she repeated and looked thoughtful.

Domenico returned with the wine and a plate of bruschetti. Delia immediately did a calorie, point, and carb calculation and took the smallest piece. It was delicious and she savored the delicate interplay of garlic, tomatoes, and crusty warm bread.

Ben took a piece but didn't eat it, just watched Delia.

"Don't you like it?" she asked around her second bite.

"Huh? Oh, yeah." He took a bite, but didn't seem to enjoy it much.

Being investigated for murder probably had an adverse effect on your appetite, she mused. Which could account for the fact that he seemed too thin for his clothes.

Domenico returned with their second course, a veal milanese nestled in a brown sauce and covered with capers and confetti-size pieces of shallots. The aroma that wafted from the plate made Delia's mouth water. Actually, sitting solo with Ben Michaelson was making her mouth water, not to mention another place that was beginning to feel just a little damp.

Then she realized Domenico was waiting for her opinion. She cut into a paper-thin slice of veal and brought a forkful to her mouth.

"It's wonderful," she said when she stopped chewing.

Domenico nodded sagely. "I knew you would like it. You are a woman of excellent tastes." He smiled at Ben and said, "I'll leave you to your dinner," before waddling away.

Ben gave her a measuring look before he spoke. "Call girl?"

Delia's mouth opened. "What?"

Ben stared at his plate like it was liver and creamed spinach. "I'm sorry, but you're not a . . . you don't work for an escort service . . . do you?"

"What?"

Ben glanced up at her. "I wouldn't ask but—"

"No. I'm not a whore." Delia pushed her chair away from the table and stood up. "And I don't take insults even for veal milanese."

Ben stood up. "Sorry. I didn't mean to insult you. It's just that I—I needed to make sure."

So much for Mr. fall-over-your-feet-to-get-to-my-body-and-money playboy. This guy was a walking basket case.

Delia sat back down. "Go out with a lot of whores, do you?"

Ben flinched as is if she'd bitten him, which was definitely turning into an option. Who would have thought she could go for a guy who probably didn't weigh anymore than she did. Wait a sec, *did* was the operative word here. She had weighed in at a hundred thirty pounds just last week. She cut another piece of veal.

"Just once. It was a mistake."

Huh? Oh, right, they were talking about prostitutes.

"I mean. I made a mistake. I didn't know what she was. Uh. Not that I have anything against the profession."

"Took you for a lot, huh?"

"Yeah. More than I could afford."

"Well, you look like somebody who'd bounce back. You may hang out in dives and eat in neighborhood restaurants, but that suit must have cost a bundle."

"Money isn't everything. Married?"

"Divorced." This guy's mind was all over the place. And he was getting paler by the minute unless the candlelight was playing tricks. God, please don't let him be doing some Jekyll and Hyde transformation; she was beginning to like him. And she didn't think she'd ever like men again. Not after Vincent fuck-them-on-the-recovery-table Dunmore. She shivered as cold fingers of wariness skimmed across her shoulders.

"Why were you in The Shamrock? I've never seen you there before."

"Getting a drink. And I thought this was dinner, not the third degree."

"Sorry."

"And stop saying you're sorry." *It's creeping me out.*

"You're sure you don't know who I am?"

Delia rolled her eyes. It wasn't even hard to show exasperation. She was exasperated. She was supposed to be doing the grilling, and all she'd done so far tonight was beat him at darts and fend off questions that a politer man would never have asked.

"My name is Ben Michaelson."

"Mind if I call you Bennie? It has a certain *panache.*"

"I prefer Ben." His eyes bored into her again, exploring her soul.

"Then Ben it is."

"Ben Michaelson," Ben repeated, putting the emphasis on the last name. "I've been in the newspapers lately—in connection with a murder."

At last we cut to the chase, thought Delia and cocked her head thoughtfully. "I read about that. You're that rich philanthropist whose girlfriend was murdered? No wonder you were asking me all those questions." She reached across the table and squeezed his hand. "It must have been horrible for you."

"It was. It is." And for the next hour, through two more

courses, coffee and dessert, Ben Michaelson told her just how horrible it was.

Ben held Delia's coat for her to put on. He must be crazy. He had just told a total stranger his complete history of meeting Susannah Turner, dating her, dumping her, and being a prime suspect in her murder. All the fears he had had at the beginning of the evening rose up to paralyze him.

This woman could be anybody, anything. He might find himself on the front page of tomorrow's *Post*—again. Then she slid her arms into the coat, which made her body come almost into contact with his, and his suspicions evaporated and a warmth crept into a heart that had been cold way before the advent and demise of Susannah Turner.

He couldn't afford any more mistakes. His reputation couldn't take it, and neither could his heart. Not that he'd loved Susannah—not that he'd loved any of the women in his serially monogamous life. But it had been three months since Susannah had died and he longed for human contact with someone more alluring than Domenico or Hal and the guys at The Shamrock.

Susannah's death hadn't stopped the invitations from coming; hell, he was more popular than a trained bear at a kid's party. Women still came on to him, probably thrilled with the idea of sleeping with a possible murderer. It was sick. And it hurt. He might be rich as Croesus but he still had feelings. Didn't he?

"Uh, Ben? Are you going to let me have my coat?" Delia looked at him over her shoulder, the long bristles of fur softening her face. Tickling her lips in a way that made him want to kiss her. His body swayed toward hers.

"Sorry." He let go and his world seemed a darker and colder place.

She buttoned her coat and he buttoned his, thinking that it would be much more fun if they buttoned—or unbuttoned—each other's.

He shook the image away and ushered her out into a night so cold that it stopped his breath. It was hard enough to breathe as it was. Every time he looked at Delia, he alternated between the humiliation of spilling his guts like a neurotic mess and a desire so overpowering that it threatened to make him a blithering lunatic.

They stood at the curb looking at each other. He knew she was waiting for him to hail a cab for her. Which was what he was going to do as soon as he figured out a way to see her again.

And once he did, if she said yes, he would kiss her. He really wanted to kiss her, not just stand here with his hand on her back, his fingers afraid to move because they might keep going until he was sucked in and hooked. She was the most enigmatic woman he had ever met. Not a long-limbed beauty, but a compact dynamo. All hard façade, from her leather pants to her black spikes of hair, but with curves, all the softness on the inside, filling her sweater and—

"Ben?"

He was aware of her saying his name, but he was too gone to answer except with what he'd been waiting to do all night. He turned her into him and while her face was still lifted in question, he kissed her.

Not up to his usual finesse. Their teeth clunked together; she breathed into his mouth and he knew she was laughing. *Smooth move*, said his sarcastic, ever vigilant internal censor.

I'm the master of smooth moves, snapped Ben. Until tonight, anyway. He wrapped his arms around her—his hands got hung up on the coat. He deepened the kiss and felt her head snap back from the force of his mouth. He eased up while his hands tried to find a way under her coat and to her breasts.

Jesus, what a klutz. You're blowing this big time.

What was the matter with him? He could have any woman he wanted and he usually did. And where had they gotten him?

Farther than you're getting tonight.

Which was true. He was standing on a freezing sidewalk, wrestling with a woman he only wanted to make love to.

"Here." She moved away.

Shit.

But she just unbuttoned her coat and let it fall open. His groin tightened so fast and so hard, that he was afraid he might just shoot it right there. He disentangled his hands from the fur and slipped them inside her coat and under her sweater.

She yelped.

He jerked his hands out of her clothes. Of course. His fingers were freezing.

This was not following his tried and true scenario of seduction. But hell, it wasn't boring. Not like the others. They all paled after the first kiss, the first fuck, the first fight, and then he just went through the motions until they got bored or mad and he was free to try again.

Always dissatisfied. Always searching for something more.

This one would be no different in the end. Hell, what was the point.

He pulled away, an apology on his lips, but she captured his hands in hers. Then smiling up at him in an absolutely wicked way, she rubbed his hands and when his fingers were tingling with warmth, she guided them under the waistband of her sweater and placed them on her breasts.

His breath went out in a whoosh; his cock did a tap dance against his zipper. And he wondered if he suggested they share a cab, would she take him home with her.

"Uh, Ben. There's someone watching us."

Ben forgot about desire. He whirled around in time to see a hunched figure scuttle around the corner. "Just a bum," he said and went back to her sweater.

"I think I'd better go."

"Oh." He let go. Made some vague closing-her-coat motions and stretched his hand out to a deserted street. A vacant cab turned the corner and came to a stop at the curb beside them.

Perfect. The only time in his life he was glad not to find a cab, one shows up. He opened the door. She started to get in, but he had to kiss her once again before she left. He pulled her back. She tripped over his shoe and it took a few more gropes and fumbles before she was able to get her balance.

"Can I see you home?"

She shook her head, but her smile took the sting out of the refusal, almost.

"Can I see you again?"

"Sure."

"When?"

She bit her lower lip and he considered pushing her into the cab and fucking her brains out in the backseat.

Bad idea. No finesse. Oh, fuck finesse.

"Who's finesse?" she asked, laughter in her voice.

"Sorry. I'm really making a hash of this, aren't I? I'm usually not so forward on a first date, but you're different than the others."

She smiled. "Just an old-fashioned boy. Anyway, it isn't a date. You picked me up in a sleazy bar, remember?"

"Give me another chance. There's a gallery opening tomorrow night. Go with me."

"Okay."

"I'll pick you up."

"Are you gonna get in, lady? You're running up my gas bill."

"I'll meet you there." She reached up and kissed him on the mouth. Then she jumped in the cab and closed the door.

The cab pulled away and Ben snapped back to reality.

"Sands and Mariah." The cab was picking up speed. He ran after it. "Madison Avenue, between 79th and 80th." Delia was smiling at him from the window. "7:30."

He saw her nod and wave good-bye and the cab accelerated and left him alone and cold and feeling completely ridiculous.

Delia gave the cabbie the address of the parking garage where she'd left her Lexus and leaned back against the seat.

Ben Michaelson had to be shell-shocked. This was not the Mr. Love-'em-and-leave-'em Michaelson she'd expected. More like a lame-brained teenager than a richer-than-dirt playboy who might or might not kill his "dates" when he tired of them.

She probably shouldn't have let him kiss her, but she couldn't remember a chapter on cuddling with the perpetrator, and she couldn't very well have said, "Hold that thought," while she called Geena or Nan for advice.

Anyway, she didn't really want advice. She just wanted him to keep his hand in her sweater. She sighed, wondering if there was anything in her closet that was easier to get into that would still be appropriate for a gallery opening.

Chapter Five

Delia was wearing a smile along with a new pair of low-rise jeans and Scandinavian ski sweater when she walked into Women-Tek the next morning.

Geena took one look and said, "Conference room."

Delia brushed a flake of coconut off her sweater and followed Nan and Geena into the next room. She plunked her new Gucci briefcase down on the dark mahogany table with a flourish.

"You're awfully chipper this morning," said Nan, taking a seat across the table.

"I feel great." Delia stretched and started rummaging through the briefcase, pulling out files while she thought about Ben Michaelson. Suave, elegant, sophisticated he was not. But she had just done eight years of suave, elegant, and sophisticated and it was a dead bore.

She'd come closer to coming last night standing on a frigid street corner, dressed to the eyeballs, than she had in the last five years of her marriage with her philandering, I'm-doing-you-a-favor-fatso, husband.

Ben Michaelson was hot in his clumsy way. Hot enough to make her forget the brand of her vibrator.

Hell, she was ready. So what if he might have murdered his last girl friend? She flexed her bicep. She could take him—*after* he'd taken her.

"What are you doing?" asked Geena.

Delia lowered her arm.

"You didn't beat him up, did you?" asked Nan.

"Nope."

"You didn't fuck him, did you?" ask Geena.

"Nope."

Geena let out her breath. "Well, that puts you one ahead of Nan."

"Not fair," said Nan. "So what did you do with him?"

"Beat him at darts and let him buy me a drink." Delia didn't think they were ready to hear about dinner and confession. She was on thin ice as it was.

"You weren't even supposed to make contact," said Geena, giving her a stern look. "You were on a stakeout."

"We were in the same bar." *After I followed him halfway across town.* "I've done my homework, I know the rules, but it was too good of an opportunity to ignore. You're not mad, are you?" *Please don't take me off the case. I've got the perfect dress for tonight.*

"No. You did make a good call. Even though you shouldn't have. But god damn it, if you get hurt . . ."

"I'm not going to get hurt."

"Make sure you don't. Get any impressions of the man?"

Fingerprints on my push-up bra. "We talked a bit. He's not what I expected."

"Uh-oh," said Nan.

"You're out of there," said Geena.

"Wait a minute. I just mean that he wasn't creepy or anything. But he's also not your I'm-on-the-top-of-the-dunghill Donald Trump kind of guy. He's oversensitive, unhappy. This suspicion that he's a murderer is really getting him down. My guess is he's on the verge of a breakdown."

"Do you think he might snap?"

"It's possible," said Delia, kicking into professional mode. "But I don't get dangerous from him." *Except in a really in-*

appropriate do-me-now kind of way. "I think he finally figured out that money can't buy him love and he's having trouble coping."

"You think he was in love with Susannah Turner? Did he talk about it?"

"A little. He introduced himself as the guy in the news."

"Gloating?"

"No. He was afraid I was a reporter or another hooker." Delia grinned and did a little shimmy. "The nicest compliment I've had in years."

"Jesus Christ," moaned Geena and put her head down on the desk.

"Just kidding, boss. I played it sympathetic and straight." *And he trusted me enough to spill his guts.* But she wasn't ready to betray that trust until she had to . . . if she had to. "He said that he'd already broken up with her when she was killed." She pulled out several copies of news articles. "The headlines corroborate it."

"And if you read it in the *Times* . . ." said Nan.

"His statement to the police says the same, and witnesses also backed him up."

"Maybe she wasn't so easy to get rid of. Maybe she refused to let go."

"Ben Michaelson has a tighter security system than the president. Someone else opens his mail, he has an in-house investigation team."

"Who are probably doing everything they can to find their own evidence to clear him. Legal or not," said Geena. "Don't get mixed up with them or him."

Too late, thought Delia. *I'm going to prove him innocent or go down trying.* She swallowed. Where had that come from?

"What?" asked Nan.

"Oh. Nothing. It's just that I'm beginning to think he's innocent."

"Our client will not like to hear that."

"I'm sure she wants to learn the truth," said Delia, star-tled.

"Most people would rather blame anyone, even the inno-cent, if the alternative is not having anyone to blame but themselves."

"I hadn't thought about it that way. Well, maybe he did it, but there's no hard evidence that I could find—"

"That you could weasel out of the boys down at the donut shop, you mean."

"I only had two toasted coconuts and that was in the line of duty. And I walked there and back."

"You're an inspiration to us all," said Geena. "So what did you find out?"

"There were several strands of long blonde hair on her coat. Evidently her roommate had borrowed the coat the night before. But that was about it. Plenty of DNA samples, you can imagine with her profession, but none that matched Ben Michaelson. So he hadn't been doing anything with her lately."

"Doesn't mean he didn't kill her or have her killed."

"The second one is what the cops are after. But according to the boys, they're not having much luck. Of course they're just street cops and junior detectives, but word gets around."

"And we're just a three women detective agency. I don't expect you to find out more than they can. I told Eileen Turner that. She just needs to be reassured that every avenue is being explored. So don't get yourself in trouble over it. Do the drill, find out what you can, but don't jeopardize your own safety."

"I won't."

"What's next?"

"I thought I'd talk to a few of Susannah's associates. See what they have to say."

"Sounds like a fun afternoon. Are we ready to move on to Nan's report?"

*   *   *

There was something to be said for donuts, thought Delia as she looked up at the gray, five-story apartment building on East 93rd. If she hadn't been addicted to them, she would never have struck up a friendship with the detectives and patrolmen who frequented her neighborhood Dunkin' Donuts. And she wouldn't have the address of Susannah Turner's last residence.

The building was one of those experiments gone awry. Built in the sixties and already showing signs of wear, just like the woman who opened the front door and stepped outside.

Delia nodded to her as she passed by. The woman didn't acknowledge her, just whipped a fuzzy scarf across her mouth, ducked her head into the wind and hurried up the street.

Delia just caught a glimpse of platinum hair before she turned and loped up the steps to grab the door before it closed. The foyer was cold, dark, and a little dingy. The elevator was not much better. She rode it to the fifth floor which was just as cold as the foyer downstairs. She found Five-A and knocked on a red metallic door.

Appropriate color, she thought as she waited for someone to answer it.

Susannah had shared this apartment with four other women in the same trade. None of them had been too forthcoming to the police. Well, duh. Delia hoped they might be more willing to talk to "an old friend."

She rapped again, harder this time. There was a good chance that someone would still be home. Their work didn't begin until after dark.

"Who is it?"

Delia smiled tentatively at the peephole. "I'm—I was—a friend of Susannah's." She waited for a response. Nothing. "We went to school together. Can I come in?"

"Suse doesn't live here anymore. Go away."

"I know," said Delia. "I heard. I heard what happened to her. It's just awful. Poor . . . Suse." She stuck a trembling lip at the peephole and squeezed out a few tears.

She knew how to play the game. Surviving in the great outdoors wasn't the only thing she learned at Camp Wilderness. She had perfected her camouflaging skills: blend in with trees, society bitches, and, hopefully, with the call girls on the other side of the door.

Finally, the chain rattled, and the door opened a crack. A head surrounded by frowsy carrot-red hair appeared in the opening. Eyes, hard with mascara and life, checked her out.

Delia had planned for this. She was wearing tailored gray wool slacks and matching cable sweater, beneath a black wool coat with fur collar, that she'd bought at the thrift store on her way to work. She'd blow-dried her hair this morning, instead of gelling it into spikes. Clean cut as all get out.

The woman behind the door snorted, sending out a cloud of air into the chilly hallway.

"Please?" asked Delia.

"Let her in or get rid of her," said a smoke-raspy voice from inside. "It's cold as shitall out there and you're letting it in here."

The woman, who from the police description must be Cassandra Moulle, scanned Delia from her smooth bubble of hair to her Cole Haan loafers, then opened the door a grudging amount and stepped back.

Delia hurried in before she could change her mind. She stopped just inside and heard the door snick closed behind her. She had planned to be properly awed at being in her friend Susannah's New York apartment. But she didn't have to act.

The room was the silk purse to the building's sow's ear. Spacious and warm. It even managed to appear bright, though its windows opened onto an airshaft. The walls were stark white, and framed modern paintings hung above a leather couch where a svelte black Amazon lounged against a mountain of colorful pillows.

Sadetha, aka Shoshonna Rowena Williams.

A glass top coffee table held a bronze copy of *The Thinker* as well as a pack of cigarettes, a gold lighter, an overflowing ashtray, a jar of cotton balls, and several bottles of nail polish.

As Delia stood openmouthed at the unsuspected opulence of her surroundings, a model-thin woman walked through an archway that led to the kitchen. "Sadi, get the polish off—" She saw Delia and stopped, coffee mug extended toward the woman on the couch. "Who's this?" The mug swung toward Delia.

"A friend of Suse's."

"Don't be stupid, Cassy. Susannah didn't have any friends."

This new woman was Philomena; Delia could tell by the thick ebony hair that fell nearly to her waist. That only left Natalia unaccounted for. Three out of four was pretty damn good for a first try, thought Delia, then concentrated on her role as Midwest dimwit.

"I knew Suse in Oklahoma."

"Well, I hate to break it to you," said Philomena. "But you're too late to see her. Bit it big time."

"I know, that's why I came. They say this really rich guy killed her."

Cassy barked out a harsh laugh. "You got that right. Be careful what you wish for."

"What do you mean?" Delia turned toward the redhead. It was the first time she'd seen the whole woman and her eyes widened. She was barely five feet tall even in high-heeled mules. Two milky white globes of flesh tumbled out of a gold and black silk dressing gown. *Whoa, mama*, thought Delia. The guys weren't kidding.

"Look, honey. I don't know what Suse told you about her life here, but some things are best left unknown."

"You mean that she was a . . . a . . ."

"Yeah, one of those. So are we. And you are way out of your league."

"But I want to help."

"Help? You gotta be kidding." Sadetha sat up and propped both feet on the edge of the coffee table, legs spread, offering a view of more than Delia cared to see. "You better listen to Cassy and get yo little white ass back to where you came from. The big, bad city is no place for a sugar puss like you."

Trying to ignore the crotch staring at her from the couch, Delia said, "I'm going home just as soon as I find out what happened. So the sooner you tell me, the sooner I'll leave." *God, she did petulant so well.*

Sadi grinned up at her and shoved a cotton ball between her toes.

Delia turned back to Cassy. "She was my friend. She was a nice girl and—"

"Right, and we're the three graces." Philomena stepped toward Delia and raised her hand. Delia barely stopped herself in time before she blocked the woman's arm and brought her to the ground. She slowly let out her breath and unclenched her fists.

"Yo friend Suse bit off more than she could chew, suga. But I hear it sho was tasty." Sadi guffawed.

Cassy shot her a nasty look. "You'd better cut the ghetto crap or you'll be out on your black ass, shuga."

Sadi narrowed her eyes and went back to polishing her toenails.

"Some guy she was seeing killed her," said Cassy. "He didn't know she was accustomed to getting paid for her services. One little item she forgot to mention. Thought she could take him for more than an hourly gratuity. As it turned out, she couldn't."

"That's what you get for being a greedy, money grubbing

ho who doesn't know a good thing when you got it." Sadi curled her lip at Cassy and swept the brush over another nail.

"I guess you didn't like her much." Delia wondered if the police had gotten this much and if they were looking among her so-called friends for a viable suspect.

Philomena shook her head. "No one liked Susannah. She was a mercenary bitch. Women like her give the profession a bad rap. She tried to take that poor sucker for everything he was worth. And he's worth a lot. I don't blame him for snuffing her."

Cassandra and Sadetha murmured their agreement as Delia tried to assimilate what she was hearing. And what she was feeling. The disgust and hatred they felt toward the dead woman was electric in the air. Any one of them could have killed Susannah. Or all of them.

"Are you shocked?" asked Philomena, sliding a cigarette out of Sadetha's pack and lighting it. She exhaled, long and slow. It was a terribly erotic action. "It's a competitive business."

"Yeah, too bad you just missed Nat," said Sadetha. "If Suse's sugar cock didn't do her, then my money's on that bitch."

Delia shivered and it wasn't because of the role she was playing. It was an unsettling mixture of abhorrence at the idea of one of them as a murderer and desire at the thought of Ben Michaelson's sugar cock. She licked suddenly dry lips.

"Sadi, I'm warning you," snapped Cassandra.

Sadetha put up her hand. "I'm just saying."

"Well, don't," said Philomena. "And don't you get any ideas about asking Natalia. She doesn't know any more than we do. My advice to you is give it up. Susannah's dead. It's over." She leaned closer to Delia, until Delia could smell the coffee on her breath. "It's over."

Chapter Six

Delia spent the rest of the afternoon on the computer, accessing every search engine and invisible website that she knew and found little information about the three hookers she had met that day, and the one she hadn't: Natalia Bond.

A few newspaper articles in connection with Susannah's murder, an occasional hit in the gossip pages. They all worked in pretty exclusive circles, especially Natalia, whose name appeared more than once alongside a big-name movie star or foreign oil magnate. But for the most part, the world turned its back on the ladies of the night.

She got more hits for Susannah. There were several pictures of her on the arm of Ben Michaelson. She was beautiful and ethereal, tall and lithe, and Delia had to squelch a moment of envy, then jealousy. Christ, the poor woman was dead and she was alive, but Delia didn't think she had a chance in hell to compete for Ben's . . . what? Attention? Affection? Interest? Much less his body, which was the direction her imagination had been traveling since last night's dinner.

There was some background on Susannah after the murder and some scurrilous articles about Ben's involvement with a prostitute. Half of them made him sound like a profligate degenerate and the other half like a half-witted rube.

There were some specifics, where she was born, where she had gone to school, a few quotes from former associates who spoke on the condition of anonymity. But basically she had learned the same information from Susannah's sister, Eileen.

She successfully hacked into the bank accounts of the five women. They were all substantial but nothing that smacked of coercion. Susannah's account held enough funds to give Eileen a complete makeover if she inherited, but that was about it.

Farther back in time, she found Philomena listed in the 1997 graduating class of Radcliffe. Evidently there was more room for advancement in whoring than there was in English literature. Not surprising. A few notices of Natalia in off-Broadway plays that generally opened and closed without much fanfare, though Natalia herself received several glowing reviews. But no move up to Broadway, that Delia could find.

She gave up around six and began dressing for the art opening. She did a minimum spike look and meticulous just-finished-a-facial-at-Bliss makeup. She carefully unwrapped the new lace demi-bra and matching lace thong from the Victoria's Secret tissue paper. She slid the thong up her legs as she watched in the mirror. Not too shabby, she thought. And wondered if she would look as good to Ben, when he, hopefully, pulled them down again.

She shut down that thought. She was going on an investigation not a date, but she couldn't keep Sadetha's "sugar cock" from popping into her mind. Especially the sugar; everyone knew how much Delia liked sugar.

She smiled at herself in the mirror, pouted like she might have done when she was a hot sixteen year old. And was pleased to see that she still looked hot. She adjusted the thong until the thin strap of fabric nestled between her cheeks. There was hardly a ripple where the lace met her stomach. Even two weeks ago she wouldn't have been able to pull this off.

She slid her hands over her abdomen, stopping when they

came to rest beneath her breasts. She loved the weight of her breasts. They were more than a handful, even if you had big hands, like Ben Michaelson did. The black lace curved in an enticing line just above the nipples.

Delia ran her finger along the scalloped edge of Belgian lace to the front hook. She flipped it open and her breasts fell out of the fabric. Good. Easy to manage. Even Ben should be able to handle this.

She shook her head, a reminiscent smile playing across her mouth. For a playboy, he was certainly a fumble fingers. But she thought she knew why. Susannah Turner had knocked the sass out of him.

She hooked the matching garter belt around her hips, hesitated, then pulled the thong off and tossed it onto the dresser top. Smiled evilly to herself and sat down on the edge of her bed to pull up sheer silk stockings. Was she playing with fire? Sure. But that had always been her favorite pastime, even before Camp Wilderness. If things did go the way she was hoping, she'd be ready. And if Ben turned into Mr. Hyde, an open-palm strike to the groin would keep her from getting killed.

A tingle jumped from her stocking to the sweet spot between her legs as her thoughts of defensive punches turned to thoughts of sensual caresses. The rasp of his zipper, then slipping her hands past the opening. What would he look like, feel like? Thick and tight, or long and thin? Circumcised or not? Would he pulse beneath her fingers or jump at her touch?

Her hand went between her legs and she squeezed her thighs together. Her nipples hardened and she had to fight the urge to take care of that unsettling energy just so she wouldn't jump him before they got past the first painting.

Nope. She would mess up her hair and makeup, and besides, walking from showpiece to showpiece with that tingling between her legs would make her feel naughty—and nice. Nothing like the frumpy person she had let marriage turn her into. Delia Dunmore was history. Delia Petrocelli was back. Hellcat. Spitfire. The first girl to do it in an elevator, for which she'd received a special award, secretly of course, from the girls in her cotillion class.

You are on assignment, Mata Hari, not cruising for a quickie in a coat closet, she reminded herself. Though she didn't have anything against coat closets, and the one at the Sands and Mariah Gallery was fairly large.

Then it struck her so strongly that it snatched her breath away and made her forget all about sex. The gallery was an uptown East Side gallery. She and Vincent had been to several openings there. All of their friends went to openings there. What if she saw someone she knew? They could blow her cover. What if Vincent were there? Then she would be up the crick. He would find some way to ridicule her, make a scene. Ben hated scenes.

She stood up and pulled on her second stocking. It took two people to make a scene and she was above that now. She'd just stick to Ben's side all night. No one would dare risk offending him.

But her mood was destroyed, and when she slipped the shimmering dark wine sheath over her head, she didn't even notice that she could actually zip it up without sucking in her stomach.

She sat down at her dressing table and chose the diamond and sapphire drop earrings and matching solitaire diamond necklace. She loved this set, even though they were leftovers from her marriage. Some things were just too beautiful to ditch, even though they signified everything that had been wrong with her life.

Which made her think about Susannah Turner. Her beauty hadn't saved her.

She took off the earrings and necklace and replaced them with hand-tooled silver jewelry, slipped six etched, silver rings onto one hand, and picked up her clutch purse.

She looked into the mirror. This was her: the new her, the

old her, but not that thing she had become in the middle. And she knew in that instant that whatever happened, she was free of that life forever.

Ben sat in the leather club chair of his Greenwich Village apartment, a glass of Glenlivet in one hand, the keys to his Park Avenue penthouse in the other. He'd spent most of the day worrying that Delia would stand him up and he would never see her again. He wouldn't blame her if she got cold feet, not after the things he'd told her over dinner.

What had possessed him? He always made a point of keeping his business to himself. Hell, he was known for his discretion—in public, anyway. He liked his women gorgeous, smart, and sophisticated. Until he got them into bed. Then anything was a go.

Susannah Turner had seemed to fit the bill perfectly. Perfectly proper in public, and perfectly wicked in bed. And perfectly conniving. But why was he thinking about Susannah when he would soon be on his way uptown to meet Delia, who was as far from Susannah as a woman could get.

And maybe that was why he found her so alluring. A knee-jerk reaction to a perfect façade.

Delia. He smiled to himself, imagining what sex with Delia would be like.

He fingered the key ring. If things worked out at the gallery, he would take her to the penthouse afterwards. He didn't love the idea of making love to Delia in the same bed he'd shared with Susannah, but he never brought anyone here to the Village apartment. Not once in his long history of affairs. But he wanted to bring Delia here. And that frightened him.

This was his space. His alone. A place where he could retreat from his responsibilities. A haven from the cutthroat financial world, from the hundreds of organizations asking for support, from the unending stream of women who professed to love him.

That was a joke. None of them could see past his millions. Sometimes he'd just walk around Manhattan. Stop at construction sites to watch men in hard hats climb over the steel beams, yelling back and forth in a camaraderie that Ben had never known. He'd buy a frank with sauerkraut from a sidewalk vendor and wonder what it would be like to meet hundreds of people each day, whose only ulterior motive was lunch. The shoeshine men at Grand Central, the clerks in Bloomingdale's, policemen, sanitation workers. They all had work to do, comrades to shoot the breeze with, while Ben sat in an oversize office writing checks.

The only real friends he had were at The Shamrock. And he didn't even know most of their names.

Poor you, said his ever vigilant alter ego. So give up your millions. Go out and try to make a buck. See how you'd like getting up at five every morning. Get a job at the Fulton Fish Market. Gut fish all day, then come home to a wife who can't stand the way you smell.

Spend your two weeks' vacation at Wildwood with the kiddies and the *frau* instead of playing the field of beautiful women in every luxurious yacht, villa, hotel on several continents. *Yeah, yeah. Poor you.*

Derisive laughter rang in his head until he thought he was going insane. *Rich or poor, they just use you, use you, use you. . . .*

This time it might be different, he argued. Delia didn't even know who he was until he told her. He'd met her at The Shamrock. She was expensively dressed, but she fit right in. And she played a mean game of darts. She enjoyed eating, talking, playing, making out.

His fingers tingled at the memory of the moment when he'd finally touched her breasts—and she started because his fingers were cold as ice.

He'd really blown it last night. She unsettled him. Threw him off his usual suave agenda. He wanted to feel those breasts again, not the tiny little adolescent breasts of women whose idea of dinner was picking through a plate of lettuce. Not Delia. She relished the subtlety of Domenico's cooking.

He'd wanted her to relish him in the same way; to take her there on the table, spread her legs and feed her fingerfuls of zabaglione while he tasted her essence and drank his fill.

This was nuts; he abhorred public displays of affection. But the idea of public sex with Delia turned him on. Got him so hard and throbbing that it was painful. Delia would be different.

She's going to disappoint you. She'll use you, use you.

"No!" Ben stood up abruptly, almost knocking over his glass. He paced to the window and looked out at his partial view of the Empire State Building. She wasn't like the rest. He sensed it. Knew it. Needed to believe it. But . . .

To hell with it. He shoved the keys in his pocket and put on his coat. He'd take Delia to the penthouse tonight.

Chapter Seven

Sands and Mariah was brilliantly lit and filled with people, when Delia arrived fashionably late at eight o'clock. She'd purposely waited until she thought Ben would already be there. If she ran into anyone she knew, she would be on the arm of one of Manhattan's most eligible millionaires.

Delia deposited her velvet opera cape in the alcove at the end of the hall and looked around. It was just as she remembered it. Two rows of garment racks topped with mesh bins for hats, gloves, and umbrellas. And no attendant. Lovely.

Somehow Vincent had never inspired her with the kinds of thoughts she was having now. She had taken a six-year detour, but she was back on course and ready for love. Maybe not love, but wild, raunchy sex was definitely on the itinerary.

She returned to the gallery, snagged a glass of champagne from a waiter who was posted at the entrance and sipped while she scanned the clusters of bodies for Ben.

He was standing before a large abstract oil painting, flanked by two women. Both of them were decked out in slinky dresses, both were thin and blonde, and both were facing Ben instead of the painting. Delia ran her hand down the front of her sheath.

You're hot, she reminded herself. She might not be as thin, but she had more to offer.

Ben caught sight of her and extricated himself from his two admirers. As he threaded his way through the crowd, Delia heard her name called out, and she cringed. *Delia Dunmore.* It always made her think of some over-the-hill thirties film star. She turned around, smile plastered in place, to see which of her East Side friends had recognized her.

Elisabeth Wexford. Shit. Her husband was a gynecologist and played golf with Vincent. And with her was Janette fix-my-face-and-fuck-me Krups, one of Vincent's many my-wife-doesn't-understand-me excursions into adultery.

This meeting was bound to be a humiliating experience. Ben was half a room away and there was no place for Delia to run. She gritted her teeth and held her ground. She had been the brunt of social snubbing for more years than she could remember. Now that she was back, she had no intention of being their kicking girl again.

"I can't get over it," gushed Elisabeth, air-kissing Delia on both cheeks, while Delia tried to think of a way to get rid of her before Ben got close enough to hear.

"Hi, Elisabeth. Janette." Delia made a show of looking around the room. Smiled warmly at Ben, then changed it to a suck-on-this, bitch smile, when the women saw who she was making eye contact with.

They turned back to her with disbelief and Janette said sotto vocce: "You're with Ben Michaelson?"

"I will be, if you'll excuse me." *And I'm not wearing any underwear.* Delia stepped between the two women. They managed to attach themselves to her side.

"Excuse me?" said Delia.

"We're just so glad to see you. We were worried about you after Vincent left you. What have you been doing with yourself besides dieting? I said to Janette, that has to be Delia Dunmore, but you've lost so much weight, we hardly recognized you."

Delia blushed in anger and mortification, knowing that Ben was close enough to overhear them.

She managed a feral smile. "Well, that makes two of us. I hardly recognized *your* new face . . . and Janette's jawline and cleavage, too. It's remarkable what surgery can do, isn't it? Oh, there you are, Ben."

Ben was met not by three adoring females, but one hellcat with her claws out, and two struck-dumb hopefuls. So Delia used to be fat; her husband had left her. Normally, those two facts would have him running for the nearest exit, but tonight, he was almost glad to know these unflattering things about a woman he was about to sleep with. Delia was a divorcée, not a reporter or a hooker. Thank God.

"Hi, love." He leaned over and planted a kiss on her mouth while her two companions watched, speechless. "Excuse us," he said in their direction without really looking at them. The ultimate snub. *That will show them they'd better not mess with my girl.*

His girl? *Get a grip*, he thought. *Or you'll wind up groping her in the bathroom like a horny teenager. No repeats of last night, please.*

"Thanks," she said as he guided her away.

"Friends of yours?"

"One was, the other was one of my ex's many indiscretions." Delia stopped in front of a vertical collage, constructed from crushed aluminum cans and bird feathers. She frowned at it. If Ben mentioned fat, she'd take it off the wall and hit him over the head with it.

"Let's make the rounds." He slipped his arm around her waist and moved her to the next painting. While they were standing there, the gallery owner came up and began chatting.

"Gerard, I'd like you to meet, my friend, Delia . . ." He wondered if she still went by the name he'd overheard.

"So nice to meet you." Delia turned a megawatt smile on the gallery owner. Ben felt a jolt of surprise. She sounded like all the other jaded people there tonight.

Gerard made small talk for a minute and a half and moved away.

"Petrocelli," said Delia. "My name is Delia Petrocelli." Her tone implied that he could like it or lump it, but no longer held that bored note, just a wicked, delicious challenge.

He wondered if it was too soon to suggest they go back to his penthouse.

Delia stopped at the next painting and frowned at it, while she sipped champagne. Ben stood behind her wondering why there were pieces of rags stuck into the blobs of oil. Which gave him a rush when he easily transitioned into him being stuck in Delia. He moved closer until her firmly rounded ass nestled against his groin.

"I sense a feeling of growth here," Delia said, looking intently at the painting.

"Yes," said Ben. "The way two different media can join so effectively. It's astounding."

She moved against him, subtly, causing his dick to expand and a fire to streak outward to the rest of his body. The room became too small, and his trousers too snug, and he ditched the notion of having dinner before bed. Some kind of gentleman.

"Are you hungry?" he asked, hoping she'd say no.

"Famished." A little grind with her butt. He had to clench every muscle to keep from writhing. "Fine art is always such an arousing experience, that it leaves me hungry for more. Is it the same for you?"

"Yes." He could barely get the word out and he could feel her body shaking with silent laughter. He leaned over her shoulder, his mouth close to her ear, and pointed to the artwork. "You are a demon. And I want you now."

"*Ars long, vita brevis.*" She flashed an incredibly provocative smile at him "Long . . . and hard."

"Very." He leaned over farther as if pointing out a specific part of the painting. His arousal nested in the crack of her ass.

"Mmm." Delia nodded slightly, still intent on the painting. "I see what you mean."

Maybe there was a storage room that would be unlocked. He didn't think his reputation could survive taking her against the wall while a gallery full of people looked on. He knew his body wouldn't survive much more of this outrageous foreplay.

He'd never even had this kind of conversation while other people were around. Would certainly never stand this close to a woman he was with. He was as straitlaced as they came—publicly. He had a terrible suspicion that Delia Petrocelli was about to change all that.

"What about this?" She moved away from him, her hand managing to brush against his zipper as she turned to the next painting.

He felt hideously exposed. He hurried after her and came up by her side, this time so his erection rested above the soft curve of her hip.

"You're driving me crazy. I don't think I can hold on for much longer."

Delia tilted her head at the painting. "No, I don't think so, either." She turned and took his champagne glass and carried both of their glasses to the nearest waiter. Then she took his arm and guided him down the hall to the coat closet.

Ben resisted the urge to hurry her along. If they got a cab right away, they could be in his big four-poster in less than seven minutes.

"Which one is yours?" he asked as they passed between two mesh racks burgeoning with furs and designer outerwear. Delia didn't answer but continued to the very back, where she suddenly disappeared. Then a hand shot out and she pulled him behind the row of coats. She was standing up against the wall, grinning maniacally at him, and his blood surged with heat.

"What are you doing?" he whispered as she drew him to

her. He knew what she was doing, he wanted her to do it, just not here where anybody might discover them.

"There's a powder roo—" Her mouth covered his, cutting off his words; her tongue thrust into his mouth and he decided that moving would be way too much trouble.

Their tongues sparred while her hands roved over his sides and cupped his ass. Then she pushed him back just enough to unbuckle his belt and pull his zipper down.

"Delia."

"Shh. Silence is everything." She moved his boxers over his erection and pulled his trousers and underwear down to his thighs. She kissed him, while her hand slipped between his legs and cupped his balls so quickly and unexpectedly that he gasped.

"Shh." She smiled into his lips. "You don't want to get caught, do you?"

Ben shivered, whether with lust or horror at the thought of being on the front page of the *Post* with his pants around his knees, he wasn't sure. He just knew he didn't want her to stop.

She released her hold on his balls and her hand slid up his erection. He pushed into her and caught her hand between their bodies. Holding her there, he pushed up her dress, then ran his hands up the front of her thighs, and discovered the garters. He followed the straps upward, then stretched his fingers to find the elastic of her panties. He found a moist triangle of pubic hair instead.

He sighed, or moaned, or something. "You're not wearing underwear." He drew his middle finger through the folds of her slick skin until he reached that deep, heated place that he was about to explore with more than his fingers. With his free hand, he reached into his pocket, pulled out a foil wrapped condom. Thank God, he hadn't put it in his wallet.

He broke their kiss long enough to use his teeth to rip the packet open. Then he went back to probing her mouth with his tongue while he extracted the condom and fitted it to the tip of his penis. He rolled it down, his own hands nearly setting off his climax. He blew out air between his teeth and into her mouth. Then he grasped her butt and lifted her toward him, angling her so that he impaled her on the first try.

They groaned into each other's mouths, cutting off the sound except as it reverberated inside them.

"Delia." He thrust hard, driving her against the wall. Her nails dug into his ass. He withdrew partway—he had to slow down. Her grip tightened and she jerked him forward. His dick went right up to her throat, he was sure.

Her eyes were open and shining. She held his gaze as he pressed his body against her, holding her against the wall while he gripped her thighs and pulled them around his hips. She crossed her ankles behind him to anchor herself and he drove into her again.

"I know I saw them come this way."

Ben froze. Christ. This was a disaster. What had he been thinking? He hadn't been thinking and that was about to get him in a seriously embarrassing situation, not to mention scandalous.

He flashed Delia an SOS.

She grinned back at him. Shit. She was enjoying this.

He tried to pull out, but Delia held him in place by gripping his ass even tighter.

"You don't think they went into the powder room, do you?"

"I wouldn't put it past Delia. She was always a little slut."

Ben frowned at Delia, hoping she wasn't going to take this too hard. But she just kept grinning back at him and tightened her muscles around his erection. Ben gritted his teeth.

"Delia Dunmore? She was always quiet, and boring and . . . and fat. I don't believe it."

"Well, believe it. She had a reputation even when she was in junior high. I'm telling you, she was in demand."

"Not according to Vincent." Must be Janette, the indiscretion, thought Ben, trying to stave off an attack of panic.

"Vincent. No offense but he isn't exactly a turn-on. Who wouldn't be a cold fish if they had to sleep with that smarmy asshole night after night."

An indignant gasp from Janette. Delia opened her eyes so wide that Ben had to fight not to burst into laughter. She tightened her muscles around him again and held him there for an excruciating moment before releasing him.

"I went to school with her sister. Their parents had to send her off to some tough love camp in the Adirondacks to get her to behave."

"Doesn't look like it worked," said Janette sourly.

Delia's silent laughter tremored along Ben's chest and abdomen and around his erection.

He gritted his teeth *and* held his breath until he was back in control. If Delia was going to keep torturing him until those two bitches left, he'd join the game. Two could play at Russian roulette.

He slowly moved his arm, careful not to jostle the coats, and managed to work one hand between their bodies. His finger slid past the curls and into the groove of moist welcoming skin. He touched the button that should have made her squirm, but she just held his gaze and squeezed him back.

Christ, was it possible for a man to come without moving or making a sound? Ben was very much afraid he was about to find out.

There was a rustle of coats, the scrape of a coat hanger nearby. Ben stroked her again.

Delia returned with a double tightening that nearly brought him to his knees. God, the girl was a force in herself.

Another rustle of coat and hanger. The coats that covered them swayed. Then a coat was pulled away leaving a gap not two feet away.

Ben froze. He must have been out of his mind to have let this happen.

Delia slowly shook her head. Her eyes sympathetic, but unrelenting. She was in control of this situation now, those

eyes said. She kneaded his glutes and embarked on a rhyth-
mic series of squeezes that brought him close to shooting the
works.

"Well, I just hope he knows what he's getting himself
into."

He knew exactly what he'd gotten himself into. He was
stuck in Delia, paralyzed. There was nowhere to go but over
the top.

And he went. Another, more intense grip on his penis and
Ben tumbled into mindless ecstasy.

Delia held him into her, her arms like bands of steel, to
keep him from moving while his body vibrated uncontrollably. He buried his face in her neck, his mouth open, his
teeth digging into the smooth muscle of her shoulder, as the
coatroom and the world went black around him.

"Well, I'm for a drink and a Caesar salad. This opening
was a bore."

A murmur of agreement and Ben and Delia were alone
again.

Ben sank against her, his knees weak.

"I think it's time for us to go, too," Delia said matter-of-
factly.

"But you didn't—"

"You can make it up to me later." She eased him away and
smoothed down her dress, before parting the hanging gar-
ments and stepping back into the open.

He hurriedly put himself to rights and followed her out.
"Later is now. Which one is your coat?"

Chapter Eight

Delia and Ben stepped out of the gallery to a gust of March night wind that lifted the ends of her cape and whipped right up her silk dress to bare skin. Delia shivered.

Ben pulled her close. "You should have worn a longer coat. We wouldn't want anything getting cold." He smiled meaningfully. "I'll get a cab."

Delia waited in the shelter of the canopied entrance and watched a woman trying to light a cigarette against the wind. She looked vaguely familiar; obviously one of the gallery attendees. Delia must have seen her inside. Oh, yes, talking to Ben when Delia first arrived.

A cab pulled up to the curb.

"You're not waiting for a cab, are you?" asked Delia.

The woman shook her head and lifted her cigarette. "I'll take one when I finish this. Thanks." She smiled and Delia and Ben got into the cab.

Delia wasn't surprised when the cab stopped in front of a luxury complex that overlooked Central Park. Ben had several pieds-à-terres around Manhattan. She had learned that from the real estate records at the courthouse downtown. She also knew that he took women to all of them, except the brownstone in the Village. She had surmised that from reading several years of the tabloids and the *Post*.

She did remember to look suitably impressed when Ben

took out a plastic card to feed into the penthouse slot in the elevator.

To judge from the lighthearted smile Ben gave her when they stepped into an opulent spacious apartment, he was pleased to have surprised her. And she felt a pang of guilt at leading him on this way.

Guilt isn't your style, she reminded herself. Not anymore. And this was an investigation, not an affair.

She let him take her cape and pour her a brandy, though she was having trouble appearing to drink without really drinking enough to lose her edge. For a brief moment, she wished she could just enjoy her time with Ben and forget the real reason she was here.

But that didn't work. Men came and went. Even if they took six years to do it. This had no better chance of lasting than any of her former liaisons or her marriage. And proving Ben was a murderer would definitely put a damper on things.

She hardly had time to take in the heavy dark furnishings before she found herself on the couch, drink put aside, and Ben's arms around her. A more experienced detective would be able to case the joint while making passionate love with its owner, but Delia was more experienced in love—well at least sex—than she was at investigation. So when Ben's hand slid up her inside thigh and found its mark, she closed her eyes and gave herself up to the pleasure of the moment.

The way her libido was crescendoing beneath his touch, it would only take a minute or two before she zinged through space. Once she settled to earth again, she'd get back to work. But until then, oh, yes, there. . . .

Delia opened her knees a little wider as his finger circled her bull's-eye, each pass sending her closer and closer to the edge. She curved her pelvis to meet his finger as it glided into her, and she circled her hips against it and against his palm.

She opened her eyes when he slid off the couch to the floor, knelt between her legs and withdrew his fingers to push her skirt up to her waist. He caressed her thighs and pushed her knees apart.

He looked up at her then, his expression smoldering with more than desire—with need. She tried to pull him up to her, but he trapped her hands and, holding them to her sides, he leaned toward her, slowly, slowly, until Delia wanted to scream.

Just when she thought she'd have to break his grip and grab his head, his tongue slid through the wet curls of hair between her legs and she shuddered uncontrollably. Now he moved, circling, licking, sucking until she was bucking like a snared animal.

He paused long enough to look up at her, his mouth still attached to her skin, then with a final exhilarating sweep of his tongue, Delia soared.

Wave after wave drove her upward. She was free. And still his tongue didn't stop. It was almost painful, but when she would have pushed him away, another intense wave pushed her even higher. She gave in, as she spiraled into a place where there were no confinements, no rules, no soul-numbing propriety.

"Worth the wait?" Ben's voice sounded far away and Delia realized she had closed her eyes again.

She smiled. "Worth the wait. Take your clothes off."

He stood up and shrugged out of his jacket, pulled his sweater over his head, unbuttoned his shirt and let it drop onto the floor. Delia stretched her legs until her feet rested on the coffee table and he was penned between her knees. Then she leaned back to watch the rest of his striptease.

His hands moved to his belt, his gaze fastened on her open crotch. His fingers fumbled, then his belt opened. The zipper lowered.

Delia ran her tongue across her bottom lip and laughed to herself when Ben's cock jumped at her when he pushed underwear and trousers down his legs.

When he was standing before her totally nude, she hooked her ankles around the back of his knees and pulled him into her.

"You're—you're—" Ben sounded like he was choking or suffocating.

"I am, aren't I." She leaned forward to take his ass in her hands and his dick in her mouth.

Ben immediately fell forward until his knees were braced against the front of the cushions. He caressed her hair as she captured him with her tongue. She'd once been really good at giving head, and she got a thrill knowing that she hadn't lost her prowess. You had to really love dicks to give good head. And she loved dicks. Almost as much as she loved donuts.

Ben's hands tightened on her head. "God." Delia smiled to herself, but kept at him. His hands were kneading her scalp and he began to rock back and forth. She hung on, moving faster, sucking harder, clutching the taut muscles of his ass with her hands, her knees gripping his thighs.

The cry that was wrenched from him when he came bounced around the room. Delia drank him up as he shuddered and jerked against her, and it wasn't until he was collapsed against her, his head on her bare lap, that she realized that his cry was more than one of climax, but held a note of desperation. And she was hit by a feeling of compassion that sat uneasy on her heart.

She wanted freedom and wild, abandoned sex. She didn't want involvement. Especially with a possible murderer. But she stroked his hair until his breath evened out and she thought he must have fallen asleep.

Just like a man, she thought. She eased out from under him. She'd find a cab on the street and go home. Some things didn't change.

She managed to take one step before an arm caught her around the waist. Ben pulled her down on the couch and sprang on top of her.

"Round two," he said and wrestled her dress over her head.

Dawn was breaking when Delia let herself out of the building and hailed a cab. She resisted the urge to look up and find where Ben was watching her from the penthouse window.

She'd refused to let him accompany her downstairs. She knew that he valued his privacy and would have had her out of there earlier if they hadn't gotten so carried away. Already, there was a queue for the downtown bus. And several street people were waking to another bleak day.

By the time the cab let her off at the parking garage, she was aching in places she hadn't ached in years. It had been a long time since she'd had sex. A longer time since she'd had uninhibited, acrobatic sex. They'd gone at it like two starving animals and her mind was still reeling.

And she was already mentally kicking herself. She'd just spent twelve hours with the perp and hadn't stopped fucking long enough to ask a few questions. Served her right if she had to sit on a donut for a few days. Which reminded her that they hadn't eaten anything, at least not off a plate, all night and she was starving.

She drove straight to the donut shop. She was greeted by whistles and wolf calls when she opened the door and stopped at the counter. She gave the guys a brief salute, got coffee and two chocolate glazed and went over to the booth where five plainclothesmen and street cops were squeezed shoulder to shoulder.

"Hey, Gonzo, what are you doing in our neck of the woods?"

"Out slumming. Heard someone's been trespassing on my turf." Detective Rick Gonzales pulled a chair over and Delia sat down.

"I've got a client."

"Sure you do. You never could stay out trouble, half-pint."

"That's the nicest thing anybody's said to me in years," said Delia, taking a bite out of her donut.

"I oughta run you in just for old times' sake. How long's it been? Ten years? Fifteen?"

"Both," said Delia, chasing the donut with a swig of coffee. "Back when I was really a half-pint and you were a svelte beat cop."

Gonzales eyed her dress. "So. You just getting home or are you real early for a date?" He wiggled salt and pepper eyebrows at her.

"On a stakeout." Delia took another bite of donut. It was still warm from the oven. "I'm in heaven," she said.

"Yeah, but you should see the other guy," said Terry Nido, a street cop by choice rather than lack of advancement. The others laughed.

"You should really think about joining the force."

"Thanks, Terry, but I don't look good in blue." She shifted her attention from the sergeant to Gonzales. "Or gray pinstripes." She took another bite and let it melt in her mouth. "Plus the daily donuts would put my butt into competition with your waist."

Gonzales patted his stomach. "Adds character."

"Yeah," said his partner, who Delia knew only as Mac. "He stands around having character while I do the chasing, wrestling, cuffing and dragging them back to the car."

Everyone laughed. Nido punched Gonzales in the ribs, which wasn't hard since his arm was pinned in by the larger man's torso.

"All a matter of seniority," said Gonzales and turned to Delia. "So who are you staking out? Anything we shouldn't know about?"

"Yep. Something you shouldn't know about. But I did interview Susannah Turner's roommates yesterday."

"I knew that had to be you. Dammit. There's a killer out there."

"Oh, yeah? Wanna see my open palm strike?"

"Smart aleck kid. Give me the blow by."

She told them about the visit to the apartment. "Didn't learn much more than you reported. They didn't like Susannah much, and they didn't seem to like each other much better. The only one that I didn't see was Natalia Bond, though Sadetha did say something interesting."

Five cops leaned toward her. It was pretty funny so Delia finished her donut just to jack up the suspense. "She said if Be— if Michaelson didn't do it, she'd put her money on Natalia."

"That's the actress, right?" Gonzalez shook his head. "I wouldn't listen too much to Sadetha, she's one mean bi— lady. If I had to choose, I'd say it was the Ph.D. But it wasn't any of them."

"How do you know?"

Gonzales shrugged noncommittally. "Just know."

Delia dropped her second donut onto her napkin. "There was a witness, wasn't there. That's not in the report." Was that why they were still questioning Ben? Had someone seen him kill her? Jesus. It made her feel sick. She pushed the donut out of reach.

"I didn't say that."

"Well, why haven't they arrested someone?" She didn't need to ask. The witness couldn't be that reliable or they would have.

"Can't say. But you keep out of it." He wedged himself out of the booth. "I mean it. Ben Michaelson is a powerful man. And whether he killed her or someone else did, there's still a murderer out there." He motioned to Mac, who went to get their jackets, then he leaned over and tweaked Delia's nose before making a strategic retreat toward the door.

"One day, Gonzales. One day."

He saluted, grinned, and barreled out the door.

Delia frowned at his back while the three remaining cops tried to suppress their laughter. A sputter erupted from Terry Nido.

Delia gathered her trash and stood up. "Anyone who tries to tweak my nose gets taken down. Understood?"

The sputters erupted into chuckles. Delia turned on her heel and marched out. She wasn't offended; spending months in survival camp sure had a way of cutting down class barriers.

She toodled her fingers at them.

"Hey. Watch your back . . . half-pint."

The door closed as the three policemen gave in to guffaws of laughter.

Chapter 9

Delia was buzzing from coffee, chocolate, and good sex when she opened the door to Women-Tek a few minutes later. She hesitated, realizing she would have to edit her report not to include the night spent with the person she was supposed to be investigating. Clearly a conflict of interest and Geena would be furious.

Geena and Nan were waiting in the conference room.

"Sorry I'm late. I was doing an interview."

Geena's eyebrows lifted but she didn't ask.

Delia sat down and made a big show of riffling through papers, even though they were from the last case they'd worked on. She gave a detailed account of her visit to Susannah's apartment, what the three women had said, and what Gonzo had let slip, though she didn't mention him by name. When she was finished, Geena nodded.

"Good work."

Delia sighed with relief and turned the meeting over to Nan, who was doing a standard philandering-husband case, the bread and butter of the agency.

As soon as the meeting broke up, Delia gathered her files and headed for the door, thinking about grabbing a couple hours of sleep and congratulating herself on getting through her report without letting slip that she'd spent the night with Ben.

Nan followed her into the hall. "Dee, wait up."

Delia winced, put on a bland expression and turned to her friend and colleague.

"You *are* doing good work."

"Thanks."

"But I know that look. I've been there, myself. Be careful; and if you need backup, just yell." Nan turned and went back into the office, closing the door behind her.

Delia stared after her. Okay, so maybe she hadn't fooled them after all. She just hoped she was doing better with Ben Michaelson.

She backed her Lexus out of the lot and had to wait for a decrepit old woman to push a grocery cart across the entrance. She looked familiar; Delia must have seen her poking along the neighborhood before. She rubbed bleary eyes and stifled a yawn, before turning right and heading for home.

Delia lived ten minutes from the office on the tenth floor of a high-rise apartment building. She didn't miss her penthouse or the furniture. She'd been happy to cede it all to Vincent. It was his life, not hers. But growing up in Manhattan, she hadn't been ready to live in a place where the front door opened onto the street. She still needed the safety of a doorman and twenty-four-hour security.

She stopped by her mailbox and found several bills and a note that a package had been delivered and was at the front desk. She detoured to the doorman's station.

He rummaged through a stack of packages at his feet and handed her a large rectangular box tied with a gold ribbon. Delia frowned. She wasn't expecting any deliveries, not even from Ben, since she hadn't told him where she lived. And this box was too large for flowers.

"Thanks, Raul." She slid her mail on top of the box and took the elevator upstairs.

There was no card on the outside of the box. She pulled off the ribbon and opened it to find layers of tissue paper. She spread open the paper and jumped back in surprise.

Fur. Creamy, caramel-colored fur. Gingerly she touched it, half expecting it to leap out and attack her. But it was a coat. She lifted it out of the box. A full-length fur coat. And it was real. Way too expensive a gift for a second date, even if you were filthy rich. Too bad she hadn't told him she hated fur.

She laid it across the couch and rummaged in the tissue for a card. An envelope lay at the bottom.

Inside was a note and two keys.

> *Thought you might need something warmer than you were wearing last night. Meet me tonight. 6:00. I may be a little late, wait for me.*
>
> *Love, Ben*

There was an address, and Delia recognized it as the address to his Greenwich Village apartment. This was bizarre.

Why not the penthouse, since she'd already been there? He never took women to the Village apartment, not even Susannah, or so he'd told the police. But Susannah had been killed a mere two blocks away. It had to be a coincidence; there were hundreds of reasons Susannah might have for being there that didn't include Ben Michaelson.

Delia fingered the keys, trying to think. She couldn't accept a fur coat and let herself into the apartment of a man she'd only met two days ago. Shit, she sounded just like the proper daughter her mother wanted her to be, and the stifled wife that she'd become until Geena and Nan helped her extricate herself.

She tossed the keys in the air and caught them. Yes, she could. She picked up the fur coat and took it to her bedroom She had the perfect underwear for it.

Ben sat at his desk, staring out the window, and thinking about Delia. She said she'd call, but it was four o'clock and he was still waiting. He should have made her give him her number, but he was too afraid to mess up what could possibly be a different kind of relationship for him—one that might last.

He'd finally become so impatient that he'd put his investigative team on finding out about her. He hadn't wanted to do it. He wanted this one to be different, wanted to believe that she wasn't playing him, that she was exactly who she said she was. He smiled. Someone who shopped a lot. A divorcée. From one of the most successful plastic surgeons in New York. He'd found that out himself by piecing together the bits of conversation he'd overheard last night at the gallery and looking in the phone book.

Delia Petrocelli wasn't listed, but Vincent Dunmore was. He'd called his office, hoping they would give him a number for Delia, but they informed him they had no number for her.

So here he sat, waiting for a telephone call. It was stupid. But he didn't leave.

It was close to five when his secretary peeked into his office. "Delivery, marked personal. You want me to open it?" She raised a manila envelope in the air.

"No. I'll take care of it. Thanks." As soon as she was gone, he tore into the envelope. Maybe she had been too embarrassed to call.

He reached inside and pulled out, not a note, but a newspaper clipping. Before he even saw what it was, his world went cold. It was going to be something bad.

It was worse. Three women standing next to a young man in a business suit. And a caption that read: *Women-Tek Clears Missing Heir.* And their names. Geena Cole, Nan Scott, and Delia Petrocelli. He stared at the clipping. It was Delia, all right, looking a little heavier, but it was her.

Delia Petrocelli was a private investigator. His stomach tightened and for a moment he thought he was going to be sick. But he forced it back, as a rage he hadn't known in a long time rose up inside him.

Christ. What kind of fool was he? A hooker. An investigator. He crumpled the clipping into a tight ball and threw it against the window. God damn her. God damn her.

The intercom buzzed. "It's Mick Zabriskie from security. He says it's urgent."

Ben jabbed at the intercom button. "Tell him he's too late." He pushed out of his chair, grabbed his coat from the closet, and walked blindly out of his office.

"Mr. Michaelson?"

He didn't hear her. He was on the street before he realized he had left the building. The cold air brought him a moment of clearheadedness. It was gone an instant later.

He stood on the street, not knowing what to do, where to go, or how to get rid of the pain that was seizing his insides. The Shamrock. He'd met her there. Domenico's. Not there, either. The penthouse. He groaned out loud and someone stopped to ask if he was all right. He waved them away and started walking aimlessly down the sidewalk, downtown, toward the one place that was his alone.

Alone. The story of his miserable, wealthy life. He slammed his fist into his palm, making a passing pedestrian leap away. How could he have been so gullible? Just because she was a brazen, out-there kind of girl who beat him at darts. He'd taken that as a sign that she wasn't like all the rest.

Stupid shit. Of course she was. She was worse.

He'd walked fourteen blocks before another feeling stabbed through his miasma of pain and anger. His sense of betrayal. Delia was an investigator. She'd probably been waiting for him outside the Plaza that night because . . . she must be investigating him. She'd set him up so perfectly. A boy straight off the farm couldn't have been easier.

You're pitiful, he told himself. *Pitiful, and so lonely that you mistake hookers and worse for women you might be able to love. Why will you never learn? There's no one out there for you.*

*   *   *

It was a few minutes before six when Delia got out of the cab in front of Ben's Village brownstone apartment building. She was a little early, but that would give her some time to set the scene. She was wearing the fur coat over jeans and a sweater and running shoes, and carried an old Bloomie's shopping bag.

She took the keys to his apartment out of her coat pocket and headed for the door, keeping a wide berth around the bag lady who sat on the sidewalk, her back against the building, her head lolling on her chest. A faded cardboard sign was propped in her lap, and a paper cup holding several coins sat beside her. Delia fished in her purse for some change, and dropped it in, too.

Delia just hoped she was sleeping and not dead from exposure.

She let herself into the building. There didn't seem to be an elevator, so she walked up the three flights to Ben's apartment, glad that she'd had the foresight to wear comfortable shoes.

She knocked on the door to his apartment. No answer. She knocked again before unlocking the door and peeking inside. "Ben? Anybody home?"

No answer. She stepped inside and closed the door. She was standing in a small entry hall. To her left, an archway led into a cozy living room-study combination. A comfortable plaid sofa faced a fireplace of old brick. Two end tables were piled high with magazines and books. An open book lay facedown on the couch.

Delia let her eyes rove over the room trying to reconcile it with the man who owned the Fifth Avenue penthouse. She peeked into the kitchen whose appliances were at least ten years old. The bathroom was black and white tile and the bedroom—

Delia sucked in her breath. Not the high, four-poster bed and its sateen coverlet, the brocaded curtains draped over floor-length windows. But a double bed with a faded, dark green duvet, one small window, a tiny fireplace, and a . . .

rocking chair? Had she somehow gotten the wrong apartment?

Or was this some kind of a trap? Delia started at her own thought. What kind of trap could this possibly be, unless Ben was a schizophrenic killer who lured his victims here before he did them in.

She snorted. No way. It was more likely that this was the one place he could kick back without the responsibilities of his life following him. There was even a sweater draped over the back of the rocking chair. It was endearing, not frightening.

She felt totally out of place wearing an extravagant fur coat. She was the only jarring note in the whole apartment, and she couldn't figure out why he had chosen this of all gifts. She sighed. He probably only knew how to give expensive presents, and didn't realize how she would look wearing it here.

Like an expensive hooker.

Damn. She was beginning to see sinister signs where there weren't any. So maybe it wasn't the most tasteful rendezvous, but what the hell, she wasn't the most tasteful person on the planet. She tossed her coat on the bed and emptied the contents of the plastic bag she was carrying.

She pulled off running shoes, jeans, and sweater. Underneath, she was wearing a red thong and see-through bra. Definitely hooker clothes, but he seemed to like things a little raunchy and very hot, and she was more than happy to oblige. She smiled to herself as she put the coat back on and slipped her feet into her black slingbacks. She'd give him a greeting he wouldn't forget.

And in the meantime, she'd do a little snooping.

There was nothing of interest in his bedside table drawers, not even a box of condoms. The desk in the living room was covered in papers, but nothing that related in any way to Susannah Turner. She had just closed the bottom drawer when she heard the front door open. She leapt away from the desk and managed to be lounging against the back of the sofa, coat slightly open to reveal her lingerie when Ben stepped into the room—and stopped cold.

He stared at her, transfixed. Delia felt a rush of excitement. She let the coat slip off her shoulders to reveal more bare skin. He took a step toward her. He was obviously astounded. Maybe she was still more of a bombshell than she knew.

His mouth opened.

She ran her tongue over her lips. "Hi," she said in her sultriest voice.

"What are you doing here?"

Delia blinked. She hoped he wasn't going to be one of those role players. She hated that and she hadn't gotten any hint of it before.

"How did you get in here?"

His face was strained and a blotch of red had sprung to his cheeks. Delia felt a flutter of insecurity. He was serious.

"Aren't you glad to see me?" Her attempt at a sultry come-on rang false in her ears. Something was not right.

"What is this? What game are you playing?"

He was really angry. His face was a mask of hate.

She pulled up the fur coat and gripped the opening together. "Ben? What's this about?"

"Why don't you tell me?" He stepped toward her and grabbed her wrist. The coat fell open.

"Ben. Stop it. You're hurting me." Tears pricked behind her eyes. He'd set her up. He was a psychopath after all. She wrenched her hand free.

"Get out. I don't know how you got in, but don't ever, ever come here again."

"Why are you doing this? You sent me this coat and the keys."

"Liar. Ms. Delia Petrocelli. Of Women-Tek. Now get the fuck out."

He pushed her aside and she fell against the couch.

"I'll get my things." She stumbled toward the bedroom, dropped the coat to the floor, pulled on jeans and sweater and crammed her feet into her sneakers.

When she came out again, Ben was at the window, staring out into the street.

"I'm sorry," she said and let herself out.

She ran down three flights of stairs, hardly remembering to breathe, clutching her side and her stomach. She burst out onto the street and searched both ways for a cab. The street was empty. No cars, no pedestrians; even the bag lady was gone.

She turned right and headed for the avenue. She'd be able to get a cab there. She walked rapidly, the tears she'd kept at bay flooding her eyes, turning her surroundings to a blur.

He hated her. He'd found out that she was a detective and he'd set her up. No that didn't seem right. He hated her, but he hadn't expected to find her there. She'd never forget the look of bewilderment on his face, changing to anger, then rage. She sobbed out loud and covered her mouth with her hand.

She began to shiver as the night air pierced through her thin sweater. No matter. She'd be home soon. Home, alone. Like it would always be. *His fists clenched, the cords of his neck . . .* She had to get away. She began to run. Tripped on a piece of chipped concrete. Recovered her balance and kept going.

It came so fast that she didn't even realize what was happening. Grabbed from behind and dragged into a narrow alley, a glint of knife at her throat.

Susannah. Just like Susannah.

No, not like Susannah. She was Delia and she knew how to fight. Her head cleared, her pulse slowed and her mind focused on one thing—survival. She went limp, her dead weight dragging her and her assailant to the ground. He fell on top of her, his rough overcoat scratching against her, smothering her.

She drew in a deep breath and coughed, while hands clawed at her throat. Hands that—

Delia twisted to her left and the knife slashed across her sleeve, leaving a cold, searing tear across her arm.

Shit. Delia sucked in her breath and delivered a back fist to the thug's face. He wrenched away and it struck the side of his head. But he still went down. Delia rolled away and sprang to a crouch, ready to attack.

The man staggered to his feet. Delia sprang up and her foot connected to his rib cage. His breath went out in a falsetto shriek. He lunged toward her. She stepped to the side and he had to take several quick steps to keep his balance.

Delia turned on him. She was blocking his way to the street. He'd have to get past her to escape.

He looked up and their eyes met for a split second. And Delia got that same flash of recognition that she'd been getting for the last several days. It seemed like everyone she saw reminded her of someone, but who?

"Delia!"

Ben? Her turn toward his voice was pure reaction, but it gave the assailant just enough time to dart past her.

"Ben, watch out!" But she was too late. The attacker knocked Ben aside and disappeared around the corner of the building. Delia ran after him, but Ben grabbed her as she sped by.

"Are you all right?" He pulled her to him and she forgot the chase. Suddenly she was shaking, from adrenaline, fear, the cold.

"You're hurt."

"What?"

"Your arm is bleeding."

"Oh." The streetlight wavered. Ben's face blurred and she was falling. Her last memory was of being scooped off her feet. Then she floated away.

Chapter 10

"I'm taking you to the hospital."

Delia sat up and sighed for the fifth or sixth time since she'd awakened on Ben's sofa with Ben hovering over her. "It isn't that bad. And the police are coming."

Ben started to sit down, then thought better of it and walked to the window instead.

Delia wished they would hurry. She was uncomfortable as all hell. Not the knife wound. It was minor, and fortunately Ben's medicine cabinet included several butterfly bandages. But she was embarrassed and heartsick at what had happened. And she knew Ben must be anxious to get rid of her. And hating her for bringing the police down on his head again.

Why, oh, why hadn't she just behaved for once and not gone to his apartment wearing that hideous coat? And who had sent it? And why?

She wanted to ask Ben, but knew she'd better leave it to the police. Any trust she had earned from him was shot to shit because of that fur coat. And so were any hopes of—but that had never been a possibility.

Well, she'd learned her lesson. Never again would she let herself get interested in anyone having anything to do with a case.

She bit her lip to keep unexpected tears from falling. She'd managed not to drop a single one since they'd returned to the apartment. Not even when she realized Ben had carried her up three flights of stairs; not even when he poured antiseptic on her cut and bandaged it.

But she wanted to now. Seeing him standing at the window, lonely and bereft and betrayed. She hadn't meant to betray him.

The knock on the door made them both jump. Ben went to answer it and came back with two uniformed policemen.

They took down basic information and were beginning to ask about the "mugging" when a thunderous knock resounded from the entryway. One of the officers left to answer it and returned in the wake of a very large and very angry Detective Gonzales, followed by his partner, Mac, looking only a degree less savage.

The other uniformed officer stood up and wordlessly ceded his chair to Gonzales.

"Hi, Gonzo," Delia said meekly.

"What the hell happened?" His voice reverberated around the room.

Mac grimaced and said apologetically, "We heard it over the radio."

Delia nodded. But Gonzales was glaring at Ben, who had gone back to the window when Delia made it clear she didn't need him to hold her hand during the interview.

"Get over here where I can see you."

"Gonz—"

"And you be quiet. Damn if you're not more trouble than you're worth."

Delia hung her head like she had so many times when Gonzales had picked her up as a minor. He always called her parents instead of running her in, but not before giving her a blistering lecture. She braced herself for it now.

But Gonzales surprised her. "Start at the beginning. You know the drill."

Delia nodded. And carefully editing out the reason for her

being on the street alone, told him about the attack. "It wasn't a random mugging. I think I was targeted."

"Yeah," said Gonzales and frowned at Ben, until he sat down on the other end of the couch.

"It was him." Gonz lifted his chin toward Ben.

"Gonz, he interrupted the attack."

"And let the assailant get away."

Ben leaned forward. "I—oh, what's the point." He leaned back, resigned, and Delia had to fight the urge to take his hand.

"He called my name and, in the distraction, the assailant ran."

"If you came down and looked at some mug shots, think you could recognize the guy?"

"I don't think so. But it wasn't a guy. It was a woman."

"What?"

"Even though it pains me to have to admit that a woman caught me off guard, it was a woman."

"I saw him run away," said Ben. "It was a man." He turned to Gonzales. "And it wasn't me—I—or anyone I hired."

"I'll get to you," snapped Gonzales.

Ben opened his mouth but closed it again.

Gonzales returned his attention to Delia. "What makes you say it was a woman?"

"Her hands, for one thing. They had long nails."

"Maybe he needed a manicure."

"Nope. They *were* manicured. And the coat was padded, not just the shoulders but all over. When she grabbed me, I didn't feel the bulk of a body beneath the coat. And her balance was off, not just when we were fighting. There were lifts in her shoes; they kept throwing her forward. And then the hat. It covered her head, but . . ." Delia leaned over and lifted her tattered shirt from the floor. She pulled a long blonde hair from the pocket and handed it to Gonzales.

"Bums have long hair."

"But not dyed," said Delia.

"Well, I'll be damned." Gonzales handed the hair to Mac who put it in an envelope he took from his pocket.

Blonde hair had been found on the coat Susannah was wearing when she was killed. Gonzales and Mac exchanged looks and Delia could see they were thinking the same thing.

"Anything else?"

Delia shook her head.

"Then I'll take you home." Gonzales stood up.

"Thanks, but I need to talk to Ben."

"I have a few questions to ask him myself. And I'm not leaving you here with a suspect."

"Oh, Gonzo, he's not a killer. And I can take care of myself."

Gonzales eyed her bandaged arm and shifted his weight toward Ben. "The first thing I want to know is why she was walking alone at night outside your apartment."

"Gonz, it's the twenty-first century."

But Ben's quiet answer overrode Delia's outburst. "We had a misunderstanding. She walked out. She, uh, didn't want my company."

"Yeah, okay. She was always a hotheaded kid. So you followed her."

"Yes."

For the next few minutes, Delia and Mac watched silently while Gonzales grilled Ben. Ben faced him and gave him back stare for stare.

Gonzales finally hoisted his weight from the chair and stood up. "If anything happens to her, you're mincemeat. And yes, that's a threat." He gave Delia a long look, then motioned the others out of the apartment.

Delia let out a sigh. "Sorry about that."

Ben shook his head. "I deserved it. And he cares about you. How do you know him?"

"From my delinquent days. He kept picking me up and bailing me out. He was probably the closest friend I had as a teenager." She sighed. "I was not the debutante type."

"Thank God for that." Then he became serious. "Delia, I don't know what to say."

Delia shook her head, cutting him off. She felt ridiculously close to tears again. Not the persona she was trying to perfect. "I owe you an explanation, and if you'll just talk to me, I think maybe I can discover who really killed Susannah Turner."

Ben's eyes darted away.

"Ben, turn around and look at me. I owe you an apology and I want to make it to your face."

"Forget it. You were just doing your job."

Delia got up from the couch and went to stand before him. "I was doing my job. Susannah's sister hired Women-Tek to look into the situation."

"To find evidence to prove me guilty."

Delia made herself keep looking at him. "Yes. But by the end of that first night I believed you were innocent. And I liked you. I shouldn't have gotten involved with you. That wasn't fair. But it's been a long time since someone paid me compliments or looked at me the way you did. So I selfishly let you do it."

"It doesn't matter."

She couldn't stand the disappointment in his voice. She placed her hands on his shoulders. "It does matter. I'm leaving soon, but I want you to know that I really enjoyed our time together and I wasn't just using you to get information. I doubt if you believe that now. But I hope someday you'll be able to forgive me."

Okay, that was about as maudlin as she could be, but she couldn't help it. She wanted him to believe her; she wanted him to forgive her; and scariest of all, she just flat-out wanted him. She reached up and brushed her lips across his. "I'm sorry."

Then she turned away and hurried toward the door, before he could see the tears that were about to spill over.

So much for her inner hellcat. It had worked once, but

she'd obviously lost the knack. She was nuts to think things could turn out well for her like they had for Nan and Geena.

"Delia."

Her hand hesitated on the doorknob, but Ben fell silent. She turned the knob.

"Susannah never mentioned a sister." His words were rushed, almost pleading.

Delia turned slowly, steeling her expression. "Probably because she's an Okie. A real plain Jane." *Sort of like me*, thought Delia. Only without the edge.

She turned back to the door.

"Delia."

This time she only turned her head. "Yes?"

"Maybe you could keep working on the case—for me. I'll pay."

"I don't think so. The police are on top of things. I'm pulling out."

"Don't go."

Her fingers wrapped around the doorknob, whether to turn it or to keep from falling, Delia didn't know. She just knew that she wanted to stay. More than she had ever wanted anything in her life. But she knew it would just be prolonging the end. Better to make a clean break—if she could.

She couldn't. She could only stand and watch as he came toward her. Slowly, like in a movie, his expression stark, but not with anger—with desire and need.

She shivered and tried to still her heart, but she didn't try to leave.

He reached out one hand and she shook her head. His hand dropped to his side. Then he lowered his head and it took everything she had not to pull him to her. But this whole non-relationship had been doomed from the start. They might eke one more night out of it, but then it would be over.

"I can't stay. You might be able to love 'em and leave 'em, but I can't. I thought I could, but I was wrong."

"What are you talking about? I don't do that. I see a lot of women. It's kind of impossible not to. But I don't love them. If I loved someone, I wouldn't leave."

Delia raised an eyebrow, trying to look sardonic and not hopeful. "Really."

"Yes, damn it. Come here." His hands closed around her forearms and he pulled her into his chest. His arms went around her, gently, undemanding. Then he tightened his hold. "Stay with me tonight. We'll talk, we'll make love, you can interrogate me, anything you like. Just stay."

Delia didn't answer.

"You told Detective Gonzales you needed to ask me questions. Ask me. Anything."

He pulled her back into the living room and she didn't resist. She had forgotten all about the investigation the minute his arms went around her. She was thinking only of Ben, so jaded and worldly and now so vulnerable. This was not good.

"Okay," she said and let him lower her onto the couch.

Ben sat down beside her, his elbows resting on his knees while he stared fixedly at his clasped hands.

Delia focused her mind; it was hard with him so close. "Tell me about Susannah."

Ben looked chagrined, but he took a deep breath and began. "I met her at a party at Lincoln Center. She was flirty and fun and didn't come on too strong. We went for a drink afterwards, and . . ." He shrugged. "One thing led to another."

"I think I can guess the rest. Then what?"

"We went on a few dates. It seemed like a no-strings kind of thing. We both had a good time and I thought, well, I thought this could last a while. Then our picture starting appearing in the society pages. There was the usual speculation. She started getting more serious. And I started thinking about breaking it off."

Delia frowned.

"I know you think I'm shallow and mean-spirited. But you don't understand. Everybody I meet eventually tries to get their claws into me."

"Like me?" asked Delia before she could stop herself.

"Not like you. You've got claws, but the kind that make me want you to run them over my back. Shit." Ben shifted on the couch until he was facing her, his face intent. "God, what a dolt. It just occurred to me."

"What?"

"One day I came home and there was an envelope addressed to me, lying on the floor downstairs. Someone must have shoved it under the door. Inside was a letter, anonymous. It said that Susannah was a hooker."

"You didn't know?"

"Nope. I wasn't serious about her, so I didn't bother to have her checked out. I thought it was weird that someone would do that. Especially since not that many people know about this place. I never bring people here." He paused. "That's why I was so stunned when I saw you here."

"Someone sent me—"

"An anonymous letter. I know. And I got one at the office this afternoon, saying you were a detective." He took her hands. "I did have my people looking into your background. The letter just got to me before their report did."

Delia felt a frisson of pleasure. He must have cared for her a little to have her investigated. Not that it mattered now.

He shook her. "Don't you see?"

Delia pulled her thoughts back to Susannah. She did see. Suddenly a whole pattern fell into place. "Somebody is setting you up. Anonymous letter. A murder. Another anonymous letter and an attempt on me." She shuddered in spite of herself.

Ben slipped his arm around her and drew her close.

"Do you have any enemies?"

Ben laughed incredulously. "A lot of them. Wealth breeds

contempt. I just don't know of any who would actually want to frame me for murder."

Delia's mind was racing, putting pieces together, rearranging them. "Someone killed Susannah and set you up to take the fall, but the investigation was moving too slow for them. They got impatient. So they tried again. Two lovers, dead in the same violent way within months of each other would make you the obvious perpetrator."

"But who? It doesn't make sense."

"My assailant was a woman." Delia's eyebrows rose. "A former lover?"

"Oh, great, that really narrows down the suspects."

Delia snorted. "Maybe it's time for you to stop playing around and settle down—I mean—"

Ben ran his hand down her spine and Delia shivered. "I've been thinking that myself lately."

"Yeah, well. Uh." She pulled her mind back to the puzzle. "Someone so jealous they would rather see you in prison than with someone else. Someone who wanted to punish you but . . . but loved you too much to really hurt you? Ring any bells?"

Ben thought, then shook his head.

"Hmmm," said Delia.

"Hmmm?" said Ben. He leaned in and kissed her. Kissed her again. "Let's make love," he said against her cheek.

For old time's sake, Delia thought, and pulled him down on top of her.

They took it slow, trying to etch a lasting impression before it was over. Each kiss ratcheting up the heat while reminding them of what they were about to lose.

They took turns undressing each other, exploring and savoring, the ledge of Ben's collarbone, the valley between Delia's breasts. Slowly, holding the finish at bay, until they were completely naked and lying against the leather cushions.

She molded into his tight sinewed body and thought, *This is where I belong*, before she quickly erased the thought and replaced it with *One more for the road*.

Ben rolled away, reached for his pants, and fumbled in a pocket for a condom. He opened it and unrolled it down his erection, while Delia watched and thought, *this is more like a funeral ritual than an act of celebration.*

And she'd better stop thinking like that and just enjoy the ride. It might be the last one she would have for a long time. The thought hurt her. Just another woman who wanted to get her claws into Ben Michaelson.

She lay back as he knelt on the cushion and looked down at her. Then he leaned down and kissed her, exploring her mouth with the intensity of a blind man looking for a way in.

Delia closed her eyes, even as a tear rolled down her cheek. She would not be sad. She would not be sad. She would not—

Ben made a choking sound and stopped kissing her. She opened her eyes and he was looking back, his eyes stark and sad, then he moved back and licked her cheek.

"It's over, isn't it." He sounded so incredibly resigned that she didn't know how to react.

He rolled to the side and put his arm over her. His erection was hard against her thigh and she longed to take him and push him into her and let him fuck her until they were both mindless. It's what they both wanted, just get-down-blow-me-away sex. How had it suddenly gotten so complicated?

She didn't want commitment any more than he did. She had just stayed committed for six years, and for what?

He began moving against her leg, the condom sticking to her skin. His hand moved from her waist to her breast, and she grew heavy at his touch. Then his hand moved back to her waist, then to her abdomen, and hesitated. Delia took his hand and pushed it between her legs. His fingers tightened over her and a long sigh escaped him.

She opened her knees and lifted her pelvis against his fingers. They parted her and one slid into her, then another, and she rocked against them, trying to enjoy, trying not to think this would be the last time she'd feel his fingers there.

He pulled them away and rolled on top of her. But instead of entering her, he rubbed his cock through her slickness, up to her stomach, then back again until the condom was slick with her juice.

She rubbed her cheek against his and wrapped her fingers around his erection. "Inside," she ordered and guided it down between her legs. He finished the job, slipping into her so easily that she thought, *How could this not be for real?*

He held himself above her, looking down, not moving, except for the quiver of muscles held in check. Then without warning he rammed into her, crying "Sorry." She pounded back. And suddenly they were racing toward the cliff, mindless, driven, unstoppable. Faster, harder, faster, harder until they tumbled together into a place neither had been before and would probably never be again.

Ben's "Delia," echoed through the room and in Delia's mind as she flew through space, holding tight to Ben, flying up and up until they disappeared.

They lay panting side by side, looking at the ceiling.

"Jesus," said Ben.

"Yep," said Delia.

Sometime during the night, they moved to the bedroom and when Delia awoke, she was snuggled into Ben's side beneath the green duvet. She sat up with a jerk. How had she let that happen? She'd really meant to leave during the night, while he was sleeping. So they wouldn't have to say goodbye. She swung her legs over the side of the bed.

"Where are you going?"

Delia didn't look at him. "I have a murderer to catch, remember?" She started to stand up.

Ben pulled her back down and trailed fingertips down her spine. "Shouldn't you have breakfast first? There's a good diner on the next block. And I might think of something I forgot to tell you."

Delia hesitated, the image of a wounded deer springing to her mind. A quick kill was so much kinder than a lingering death. But she said, "Breakfast would be good."

A half hour later, they were walking down the stairs, showered and dressed and silent. Your basic couple on their way to work. Only they weren't on their way anywhere, thought Delia, except to breakfast.

The sun was shining but there was a brisk wind. Ben reached into his pocket for some change for the resident bag lady. She held out her hand, long fingers sticking out of half mittens. Ben dropped the coins into her open palm, and guided Delia away.

They had gone several steps before Delia exclaimed, "Hands!" and whirled around. "You," she said to the bag lady.

The woman jerked, then jumped to her feet, knocking over the paper cup of money. Coins rolled across the sidewalk as the woman fled in the opposite direction.

Delia took off after her.

"Delia, stop. What are you doing?"

Delia barely heard him and she didn't answer. Her whole mind, body, and energy were focused on her prey. Not a bag lady's hands—not a mugger's hands.

The woman reached the corner and skidded before she disappeared around the edge of a building. Delia was just behind her, but as she rounded the corner, there was a screech of tires, a bump. The bag lady bounced off the hood and fell against Delia, nearly knocking her over.

Delia grabbed a fistful of her coat. The woman flailed and kicked and finally tried to bring Delia down with a round-house swing of her arm.

Delia released her hold and found the woman's wrist. One twist brought the woman to her knees. Another twist and the woman was facedown on the pavement.

Delia could see Ben running toward them, followed by two other men in suits—plainclothesmen. Gonzo must have had them staked out on the street all night, poor things.

"Hey," yelled a man from the crowd that had gathered around the two women. "Get off her, what'd she do?"

Ben pushed him aside. "What the hell?"

"Care to explain, Ms. Petrocelli?" asked one of the policemen while the other cuffed the woman and dragged her to her feet.

"Sure," said Delia. She reached over and pulled off the woman's knit hat. A clump of gray matted hair came off with the hat and underneath was thick blonde hair pinned to the top of her head.

"Your assailant and murderer," said Delia, then she looked more closely at the woman's face. There was something familiar.

"Eileen," she exclaimed.

"Natalia," said Ben behind her.

Delia turned to him. "This is Eileen, Susannah's sister."

Ben stared at the woman, then shook his head. "She might be Susannah's sister, but I know her as Natalia. She was with Susannah the night I met her."

"Shit," said Delia.

"It was my plan," cried the woman. "I figured it all out and the bitch stole it." She lunged at Delia. The plainclothesman yanked her back and began reciting the Miranda as he led her back down the street to his car.

He was just pushing her into the backseat, when a black sedan pulled up beside them and screeched to a stop. Gonzales jumped out. "Damn it, half-pint."

"Got her," said Delia, grinning. "Though we're not really sure what's going on."

"Well, I do. I paid a little visit to the ladies last night when I left you. Ran into Sadetha just as she was leaving for work. She was in a talkative mood."

"Probably your inimitable charm."

Gonzales flashed teeth at her. "Something like that. Seems Natalia here had plans to move on Michaelson. But when she set herself and Susannah up at that Lincoln Center party, Susannah made the moves first. Your standard double-cross."

"But she came to Women-Tek as Eileen Turner. She wanted us to prove Ben murdered her sister."

"She wanted to set someone up for another kill. Guess she didn't like how the investigation was going, and she decided to help move things along." Gonzales shook his head. "Nothing more dangerous than a woman scorned. And you nearly obliged her, you little hellcat."

"Hey, I caught her for you, and I didn't even break a nail." Delia held up both hands.

Gonzales snorted. "Yeah, well, thanks, but don't make a habit of it." He looked past her shoulder and frowned. "Oh, shit. Come down to the precinct later and make a statement." He moved away and Ben stepped from behind Delia into the space he'd vacated.

"Well," said Delia, "I guess that's over."

"Yeah."

"They'll probably want a statement from you, too."

"Yeah."

"Well, it's been fun." She started to turn away, her heart jumping around like a caged animal. It was over. Next case coming up. Just walk away. You'll get over it.

"Can't we keep having fun?"

She slowed down.

"See what happens?"

She stopped.

"I'm not good at this."

"At what?"

"At committing myself."

He wanted to commit?

"But I'd like to give it a try, if you want to."

She peeked at him over her shoulder. "Really?"

"Really."

"Oh, shit," said a voice behind her.

"I say we go for it." Delia smiled and walked into Ben's embrace.

"Oh, shit," said Gonzales and left them to it.

Don't miss Amy J. Fetzer's ultrahot
and supersexy thriller,
NAKED TRUTH
coming in August 2005 from Brava . . .

Killian flinched, slapped his hand over his gun, instantly awake. The drapes leading to the deck blew inward and he slid to the floor, tracking shadows and moonlight. The remaining door was still locked, traps in place, and he rose slowly, moving to the open door, then relaxed when he saw her. She stood at the low rail, the east China breeze pushing her hair back along with the folds of the silk robe.

Hell of a sight, he thought, like a fantasy played out; hair flying, the thin fabric whipping and molding her body in the moonlight.

"Alexa." She didn't open her eyes but knew he was there.

"I didn't mean to wake you."

"Are you nuts to be out here?"

"Maybe."

He came to her, leaving the gun close. "How'd you get past the traps?"

She smiled softly. "I have my talents," she said, staring out at the port.

There was something different about her, her expression was more relaxed than before, almost serene.

"Isn't it beautiful out here?"

He glanced; the city and harbor lights sparkled on a sea of black. "I guess."

Alexa smiled. "Spoken like a true warrior," she said.

Killian was still, tempted to reach for her, but if he put a single finger on her, it was a mark he could never erase. Alexa could be programmed, a traitor, even if she didn't know it or had no control. That he hadn't updated his men said he was bending the wrong way in this battle, yet she'd proven to be his ultimate temptation. Everything he desired in a woman. He faced that somewhere around the witching hour, yet knew it long before, probably from that first kiss in the jungle. Halfway through his third shot of whiskey, he went macho, telling himself she was the best fuck on the planet and that's all it was. But he wasn't into lying, even to himself.

He didn't want just her body, he wanted her soul.

He took a step, crossing a line, and moved behind her, sliding his arms around her waist.

"Oh, I was hoping for that." She sighed back into him, closing her hand over his.

Just to feel her soft length against him was enough to make him rock-hard. The sleek curve of her throat beckoned him and he pressed his mouth there, feeling her pulse beneath his lips. It nurtured something in him, this need to close the distance between them, and when she twisted enough to kiss him, pushing his hands where she wanted, Killian wanted her more than ever. He pulled at the sash, exposed her warm flesh to the moonlight, circling her nipple with his thumb, his free hand sliding down to lay flat on her belly. She wiggled in his arms, pushing his hand, deepening his touch. He slid slower, his finger diving between her warm folds, becoming coated with her liquid. She moaned, a delicious purr as she pushed back into his erection. She turned, sliding her hand under his shirt and pushing it off over his head, Then her mouth was on his nipple, lips tugging.

"No clothes this time," she whispered.

"I thought you said there wouldn't be a next time."

"I lied." She slicked his nipple and Killian felt his world shudder, "Aren't you glad?" She opened his jeans.

"You have no idea."

Don't miss this super-sizzling
sneak peek at Diane Whiteside's
THE RIVER DEVIL
available now from Brava!

Hal Lindsay yanked her down across him and kissed her. Fast and hard, his tongue diving between her teeth.

She stiffened, affronted by the unexpected familiarity.

His mouth gentled. His tongue delicately caressed her lips as he rumbled something persuasive.

She sighed, captivated, and her jaw relaxed, admitting him. Then it was too late for objections as her sanity fled under his expert attentions.

He kissed her like a devil intent on sweeping a woman's soul away. His neat goatee caressed her cheeks and chin as his tongue claimed hers. He tasted of bourbon and sugar . . . and man. She moaned and her fingers caressed the whisker stubble on his cheeks. He was warm, and real, and infinitely better than any lonely dream.

Lindsay growled something and stood up, lifting her into his arms as if she were a petite demoiselle, not an overly tall Amazon. Fire flowed down her spine, from her throat to her core, at his easy mastery of her.

"What the devil do you think you're doing?" Rosalind gasped, stunned by how easily he carried her. Her breasts firmed, all too aware of the heat of his big body.

"What do you think?" Lindsay wasn't even slightly winded.

"Put me down!" she protested, trying to deny her own reaction to him.

"Not yet."

She considered shouting for help but decided against it: only his servants could hear her. Besides, the warmth building between her legs made it difficult to argue with him.

The terrier limped after them, his tail wagging jauntily. The undershirt was now just a distant lump on the carpet, an inconsequential oddity in the magnificent hallway.

Hal pushed open a door and dropped her on his big carved mahogany bed, taken by his grandfather from a British merchantman during the War of 1812. The crystal lamps and brocade coverlet had come from France by way of New Orleans during the last war; legally paid for, unlike the bed. Winds from an approaching thunderstorm set the Irish lace curtains to dancing at the windows. Lightning sparked the sky in nature's fireworks.

But his prize was more unique than anything captured by his ancestors. He'd beguiled her into his house as neatly as he'd grabbed that last pot at Taylor's house with an unexpected bluff. And now he could savor her to the fullest.

She fascinated him. He had a million questions for her, ranging from how she'd managed to disguise herself to her opinions on lower Mississippi riverboat traffic. But none of them came to his lips, not once he'd felt her lovely ass as he carried her. He needed more of the woman hidden inside that far-too-concealing frock coat.

His cock lengthened at the prospect.

Hal caressed her jaw lightly, surprised at how his fingers trembled. "Where did you get the name Frank Carstairs from?" he asked hoarsely.

She tilted her head slightly to consider him. Hal smiled inwardly; of course, his little poker shark would want to think first. He'd enjoy burning all that cool consideration out of her. Damn, he'd like to see her knocked off balance and into overwhelming lust, after watching her icy control at the poker table.

"My mother's maiden name was Carstairs," she answered

slowly. He continued to fondle her, wondering how he'd ever mistaken cheeks this smooth for a man's.

"And Frank?" His fingers trailed through the fine locks of hair at her temples.

"My second name is Frances." Her head turned slightly to follow his touch.

"Mine is Andronicus." Hal traced the outer curve of her ear and knew he deserved a medal for making conversation when his cock was this hard. But he needed to wait, needed to seduce her, his little poker shark who was all too comfortable with the guns at her waist. Damn, she was a better challenge then piloting the *Belle* through the great rapids before Fort Benton.

"Henry is your first name?"

Hal's mouth thinned briefly. No one, except his father, had ever addressed him as Henry and he'd never accepted that hated name from a lover.

Rosalind's breath caught as his fingers teased the pulse point under her jaw.

"Indeed. But you'll call me Hal tonight." He breathed the last syllables against her lips before he kissed her again.

And he'd wager a year's profits that this lady wouldn't bore him within the hour, unlike every other respectable woman he'd ever met.

Rosalind's willpower fled as soon as his lips met hers again. Her body had even less interest in maintaining sanity this time than it had exhibited on the stairs. Months of loneliness fled, banished by the hunger racing through her blood, fueled by his demanding mouth and hands.

His hands fondled her back and swept down over her ass, cupping it and pulling her close. She moaned and wiggled against him, driven half-wild by the first feel of his magnificent hard cock, outlined by his trousers' rough wool. The scent of lilacs spilled into the room from the garden beyond, like a call to sensual delights.

He growled something and slid his hand inside the back of her waistband.

Rosalind jerked and stared up at Hal, panting for breath. How had he known she loved to have her backside fondled? Her breasts ached for his touch, her pulse thundered through her veins, and heat pulsed and melted and pooled between her thighs. "Hal," she moaned.

He stared down at her, his chest rising and falling rapidly. His eyes blazed blue fire, like a pirate gazing at golden treasure. "Damn, I need to see you."

Fire seared her at the hunger in his blue eyes.